A small bag of dark cloth rested on the desk; tied to it were black feathers. It was rudely fashioned, as if by some small child. But instinctively I knew this was no plaything. I had always thought I was not a fanciful person, having always tried to curb my imagination, but there was something very odd—very dark and frightening about this. It riveted my attention as if it were a living creature snarling up in open menace.

"What is it, Tamaris?" Alain Sauvage said. "Did I startle you? Forgive me. But what is it that so holds your attention?"

"That." I pointed to the bag. "It—it looks so queer—and somehow I do not like it at all."

He rounded the desk and leaned forward. Then, with a muffled exclamation, he backed away, towards the fireplace, his eyes still on the bag. Groping behind him he caught at the fire tongs. Only with those in hand did he again approach the desk.

"You have not touched it, have you?"

I answered quickly that I had not.

"Good! Because one never knows—"

Fawcett Crest Books
by Andre Norton:

VELVET SHADOWS

THE WHITE JADE FOX

THE JARGOON PARD

VELVET SHADOWS

Andre Norton

A FAWCETT CREST BOOK

Fawcett Publications, Inc., Greenwich, Connecticut

VELVET SHADOWS

CHAPTER ONE

My hands were so tightly clasped that the lavender kid gloves covering my knuckles fitted as tight as another and thicker skin. It required strict self-control to keep from indulging in a fault I had been so often scolded for, pleating and creasing, in my nervousness, the overdrapery of my dull gray, corded silk, traveling dress.

Around me the walls of the ladies' parlor of the hotel appeared to stretch miles, aided in that illusion by numerous large mirrors. Red plush velvet drapery, which allowed little or no light through the long windows, was picked out with gilt fringe. And there were fat, button-studded chairs of little comfort, sofas all gilt and crimson, and a marble-topped table or two. All this was intended, I knew, to suggest the opulence expected in an establishment of the first rating, but to me it seemed vulgar.

Perched on a chair an arm's distance away from me, my escort held his watch in one hand, looked from the dial to the lobby door and back again at measured intervals. His impatience at being kept waiting was so very apparent that I felt guilty even though I had no part in this delay.

Twice I glanced at the mirror which fronted my present uncomfortable seat. My reflection should have given me confidence, but at this moment the knowledge that I was well dressed, coiffured in the best fashion, and in no way inferior to those others sitting here chatting and waiting was of little use in slowing the fast beating of my heart, the panic arising within me.

This invitation had come so unexpectedly that I still felt as if I had been whirled here on one of those windstorms they call cyclones. Out of my neat and staid life at Ashley Manor School into this—this—

I swallowed, though my mouth was dry. One does not

tear up a peaceful and somewhat monotonous life in a day without feeling the consequences. And it had been only a scant forty-eight hours since I had been summoned by Madam Ashley herself to meet this man now consulting his watch for the fifth time.

Mr. Thaddeus Hogle, man at law—for five years he had seen to the small estate my father had left when his ship and he had been sunk by a Confederate blockade runner during the late rebellion. When Mr. Hogle had made the trip out to Ashley Manor I had first believed that it was to tell me of a further loss of funds, or some such crisis which would make me more dependent than ever on my salary at the school. I was fortunate in being one of the teachers there, that I well knew. For Madam Ashley was unique in her treatment of her staff. She required that they be ladies of impeccable social standing (we numbered a De Lancy and a Carroll among us). And our students were also of a distinct type, the daughters of families newly rich who wanted the polish only those of higher society might give them.

Having been educated since I was twelve until I was sixteen in Brussels, my French and German were such as Madam considered excellent enough to equip young ladies who would make a grand tour of the Continent as part of their emerging into adulthood. And for that service I was well housed, adequately paid, and supposed to dress in good fashion—which I was and did.

But Mr. Hogle had not come with more gloomy news of finances; rather he had started his interview with a question which had surprised me:

"Miss Penfold, does the name Sauvage mean anything to you?"

But it had not and when I said so he had continued:

"It would have to your father. In 1848, when there was grave trouble in Paris, Captain Penfold was of great service to that family. They have a most unusual history. The founder of the line was a man of noble birth who was exiled to Louisiana about a hundred years ago. It is necessary to tell you all this that you may understand better the background of the request I bring you.

"The exile refused to use his name because of an injustice underlying that exile. He became a trader with the Indians and assumed the name "Sauvage" in consequence. In time he married, legally, a Princess of the House of the Wind, the royal line of the Creek Nation.

"When the first Napoleon offered amnesty to any of the old nobility who would back his own pretensions, the son of this Sauvage was sent to France. He became an official of the Court, but on the fall of Napoleon returned to New Orleans.

"As a family the Sauvages are unusually gifted with mercantile ability. In the early 1850s their interests spread into California, where mines, railroads, and large landholdings passed into their hands. However, they had never completely broken their ties with France and some of their wealth is also invested there.

"When the disorders of the February Revolution began in Paris, Madame Sauvage and her daughter were in danger. Chance brought your father to their aid. He gave the ladies his protection and support during a most trying time.

"Shortly after her ordeal Madame died. Her husband remarried—unfortunately." Here Mr. Hogle had paused, coughed dryly as if not quite sure how to phrase what else he would say. It was plain to me that he had no wish to go into what might lie behind that "unfortunately."

"There was a separation, the second Madame Sauvage remained in France. Her husband, his daughter and son by his first wife, returned to establish a home in California. Very recently, some years after his father's death, Mr. Alain Sauvage discovered that he had a young half-sister in France. Her situation there was bad and he arranged to bring her here to provide her with a secure and comfortable home.

"Traveling has proven to be difficult for her as she is not too strong. Nor is she accustomed to the manners and the language of this country. As I handle matters for him in the East, he consulted me concerning this problem. He desires a lady of good family, one who speaks French, is acquainted with some aspects of continental life, and who is young enough so his sister will not feel as if she is under the direction of a governess.

"A generous emolument, including a dress allowance (since this lady must accompany his sister into society), is offered. I chanced to mention your name, he immediately recognized it and connected it with your father, for whom all his family have had the greatest regard.

"He would be most pleased for you to consider this situation. I agreed to approach you. If you are interested a meeting will be arranged for you and the family at their hotel in New York."

At the time this seemed as if it might have been lifted from the pages of one of those light novels which we tried to discourage the young ladies of Ashley Manor from reading. But I could not imagine Mr. Hogle lending his prim person to any ill-founded romantic action.

I found myself asking for time to consider and he nodded, seeming to agree at once that this was only proper. It was later, that evening, that I had returned to Madam Ashley's study.

"You have come to a decision?" she asked with that remoteness I had long since come to accept as a part of her character.

"I have come to the decision that I need advice, Madam."

Then she had smiled faintly, but as if she were, like Mr. Hogle, pleased with my prudence.

"I have heard of the Sauvage family," she said slowly, "though not of this half-sister. They are well established, both financially and socially. The elder sister is now married to Lord Ellinboro and lives in England. In the business world Alain Sauvage has a name for shrewd but honest dealing. He is respected and his establishment in California is said to be of the first quality. He is unmarried and in his middle thirties. For a bachelor his reputation is acceptable."

At this point her gaze no longer met mine so squarely. Certain matters were never openly discussed. The eyes and ears of a respectable lady were carefully closed to those aspects of life. That these did exist were known, but they were not acknowledged.

"He is discreet"—she made a careful choice of words—"and bears a good name. Certainly what he offers you is worthy of consideration. You are now twenty-four, trained and fitted to move in the best society. Were you yourself of a less discreet temperament I would not speak to you this frankly. But the ability you have shown in handling the problems of some of our girls, without becoming emotionally involved, is noteworthy. Yes, I have every confidence in your being equal to this position."

Again she hesitated, and then spoke in a rush of words as if she must make me aware, almost against her will, of the importance of what she now said.

"I need not point out to you that marriage, except in very exceptional circumstances, is the only secure pattern of life for any lady. In California a female of good family and impeccable manners will have many excellent opportunities. Choices there are unlimited. You will be entering that society with the best of introductions and your want of a personal fortune will not matter.

"I am speaking plainly, but I think you will understand that I do so in your own interest. You may stay here and continue as a teacher, but this is a chance such as few are ever offered."

I did not have doubts, her cold estimate of marriage chances was that of society. This was logical and something the world in which I moved was well aware of. But I still had a personal aversion to such decisions made only for motives of a "secure establishment." Also what if I traveled a full continent away, only to discover the position uncongenial? Had I passed the age of youth when one was willing to take a chance on the unknown? And that thought aroused me to say, "I shall at least go to meet the Sauvages."

Which decision had brought me, this late afternoon in March, to sit waiting in a room of too many mirrors, too much red velvet, too—

A page approached Mr. Hogle. The lawyer rammed his watch back in his pocket and arose, offering me his arm. My hands were numb with the tightness of the grip I had on them. There was still time to turn and go. I was a little giddy as I got to my feet. This was all too fast, too unexpected. As if I were being whirled along without any will of my own. But I realized, too, that I had indeed made one decision, the results of which had to be faced. I must meet the Sauvages.

We were escorted upstairs into the sitting room of a suite. More red velvet, gold, marble, numerous bouquets of scented flowers surrounded the three people awaiting us. Three—no, four—for there was one who stood in the half-shadow behind a divan on which a girl half reclined, supported by a nest of small satin- and lace-covered cushions as if she found the effort to sit up beyond her capacity.

Though she was the central core of that group she did not dominate—one's eyes went first to the man who advanced from before the fireplace to bow. He was not as tall as Mr. Hogle, topping my own height by only a few inches. But he had an air about him which made him impressive in any company.

Not that he was handsome, his features were too harshly cut. But he carried himself with assurance, as if he had often faced situations in which his will had prevailed. Memory pricked me unhappily—so had my father been, ruler in his own ship world. But though I recognized that authority, in this man it made me uneasy for some reason I could not define.

His complexion was dark, his hair black. Contrary to custom he was clean-shaven, even his hair clipped a little shorter than eastern fashion dictated. He wore a dark suit, and there was only the spark of fire in a massive ring on his right hand to relieve the general somberness of the impression he made.

"Miss Penfold"—his voice was not as harsh as his face, rather gave a feeling of warmth; but that also I found disturbing in a new way—"this is indeed a pleasure." Neither his voice nor his words were familiar in a way I could resent, yet when he held out his hand, I had to make myself grasp it in turn. In defense against a stirring of emotion I could not give name to, I stiffened within, perhaps also without. I was aware of his touch as I had never been aware of any personal contact before, as he drew me forward to greet his companions.

"Mrs. Deaves, may I present Miss Penfold."

He made no explanation of his relationship to this woman. But I could guess it was a close one. She sat straight-backed, a piece of elaborate needlework lying across her lap, its colors in contrast to the garnet red of her dress. She must be, I speculated, some eight or nine years my senior and had used every art to preserve youth. Her fair hair had been puffed and built into a high coiffure in which was set a garnet-encrusted comb, and more of those sullenly red stones were at her plump wrists, her throat, and her ears.

"Miss Penfold." She inclined her head majestically as if setting between us from the first some barrier.

Being well schooled in the subtleties of a feminine world, I grasped easily enough that she resented me, for what reason I could not yet fathom. But already the master of this household had turned from her to the girl among the pillows.

"Miss Penfold, my sister, Victorine." His second introduction was as blunt as the first. The almost curt way of making me known to the others I found a little daunting. Was this his regular manner, or had it been assumed for me alone, to let me know from the beginning that I was on a different footing from his family and friends?

I shoved that suspicion to the back of my mind, intent now on the girl I was asked to companion. Her mass of loose hair, only token-confined by that latest fad, "flirtation ribbons" ending in tiny silver bells, was as dark as her brother's. But her skin was ivory fair, with very little trace of color, other than in the lips so fully curved and always moist, as if she had run tongue tip across them.

She was no pretty doll of a *jeune fille*. Rather there was a quality which made me, in a rare flight of the fancy I seldom allowed myself to unleash, think of those classic beauties of history who we have held up before us as the epitome of dangerous and sometimes fatal charm.

Yet her expression lacked animation, her eyelids

drooped, she presented the appearance of one whose inner strength was small, leaving only this perfect shell of what might have been.

She wore a pink wrapper, better suited to the boudoir than the parlor, and her feet were hidden by a silk shawl which had half slipped from across her knees, as if she were too wearied to draw it up again. She regarded me languidly, with no interest at all.

"Enchanté, mademoiselle." Her voice carried the echo of a childish lisp.

Then she held out her hand, but not to me. That fourth figure moved hastily out of the shadow to place in Victorine's fingers a crystal vinaigrette. She sniffed at the aromatic contents, sank back farther in her cushion nest, as if uttering those two words of dubious welcome had exhausted her. Her brother paid no attention, rather handed me to a chair so I was settled to face the ladies, subject to a sharp, if veiled, study from Mrs. Deaves, a lackluster stare from the girl.

She who had come out of the shadows was plainly a maid, a quadroon with the exotic, startling beauty of such a racial mixture. Across her arm lay a second shawl and she held a fan as if ready for her mistress's call.

Tea was served, we exchanged the stilted conversation of strangers. It was as if we were trying, on another level of understanding, to learn more about each other than each of us wished to reveal in turn. Victorine did not speak at all.

She accepted a cup languidly, drank perhaps two sips, refused, with an exaggerated shudder, any selection from a plate of small cakes and sandwiches. At length she closed her eyes. Neither Mrs. Deaves nor her brother apparently noted her rudeness. Had she been one of the girls lately under my supervision I would have spoken sharply. Only here I was no "lady instructoress." Though if this was a sample of Victorine Sauvage's usual conduct, I did not wonder that her brother wished her to have a companion.

Mr. Sauvage switched to French, perhaps so trying to awaken his sister to her duties as hostess. But he never glanced at her when she did not respond. At last he set down a cup, which I believed he had been holding merely as a matter of form, and launched directly into our business.

"Mr. Hogle"—he was abrupt, brusque—"has made known to you the nature of my offer." Awaiting no answer from me, he swept on, as if he found relief in direct speech rather than the polite platitudes of society. "I realize that such a radical change in your life will require reflection on your part. Unfortunately, I have only today received information which makes it necessary for us to depart to San Francisco earlier than I had anticipated. So I am afraid your choice must be made before this Friday.

"Yes"—he must have read dismay in my expression, for he continued—"I know that is asking much of you. However, our party will travel by private car, that belonging to the president of the railroad. If you choose to accept we can pick you up at Ashley Station."

"Alain"—having set a last deliberate stitch, Mrs. Deaves was folding her embroidery—"it would be better for you to discuss this business with Miss Penfold and her advisor privately. Victorine needs her rest, the poor child is quite exhausted today. I am afraid our expedition yesterday was too taxing. Miss Penfold, please excuse us."

Her voice added another thickness to the barrier she was erecting between us. Making very clear that my position, should I take it, would be that of an employee, not a friend.

With the aid of her maid Victorine was raised from her nest of cushions, and she leaned heavily on the girl's arm as they disappeared into another room. After the door was closed I asked Mr. Sauvage a direct question.

"Is your sister ill, sir? I have had no training in the care of an invalid, so my services might be of little use under those circumstances."

He was frowning, not in my direction, but at the door behind which Victorine had disappeared.

"Victorine is not in the least ill," he said with the force of a man holding back exasperation. "She has chosen to adopt this role because she is vexed. I shall be entirely open with you, Miss Penfold. I discovered my sister in France in a situation I did not like. She had impudently contracted an alliance with a person unsuitable in every respect. Now she bitterly resents my dismissal of that person, my forcing her to come to this country. But she is very young, and, I hope, in more natural surroundings, she can be weaned from both this entanglement and the unhealthy atmosphere in which she was unfortunately raised. Until a year ago I was unaware of her existence. When that was made known to me I had difficulty in tracing her. There were troubles—but it is unnecessary to go into those.

"What does matter is that Victorine needs to have about her people without any connection with that old life, who can urge her to take an interest in this country. Augusta—Mrs. Deaves—is an old friend of my elder sister's. I was most lucky to meet her in Paris, and she most graciously undertook to accompany us west.

"But in California she has responsibilities of her own. She will be at hand, but she cannot remain constantly with Victorine. I know of your own present duties, Miss Penfold. To a somewhat lesser extent my sister, coming from an alien background, needs the same guidance Ashley Manor has given its students. I am happy that I may so turn to the daughter of Captain Penfold. Your father saved my mother's life." He spoke very forcibly. "I believe if his daughter will accept this commission I will have someone upon whom I may depend. Mr. Hogle must have made it clear to you that in no way will you be considered a governess. You will be a guest in our house, accompanying Victorine into society as if you were—say—a cousin. A sum will be banked quarterly for you to draw on as you please."

"And how long"—I was glad my voice sounded businesslike, for my thoughts were troubled by the decision I must make in so short a time (and also because I found my employer a disturbing puzzle I did not understand; I was far too aware of him, of his strong personality)—"will this continue?"

"For at least a year." He surprised me with the surety of that prompt reply. "Perhaps even longer. At the end of your duties I shall see that you do not lose by coming to our aid. You may then return east or a suitable place can be found for you in California. Ladies of culture are not too common there."

At least he was not so blunt about my chances for an establishment as Madam Ashley had been. He was indeed a mixture of qualities—frank on some points to brusqueness, and fastidious on others. But I must have time to think.

"Be sure, sir"—I arose—"I shall give your offer a most serious consideration, and you will hear from me before Friday."

When I was no longer in Alain Sauvage's disturbing presence (for I readily admitted that he had troubled from the first my carefully cultivated serenity of mind) calm good sense returned. Of course I could not in three days prepare to tear up my life by the roots and go to live with total strangers for a year.

And I was thoroughly sure of that decision when I was once more closeted with Madam Ashley on my return.

"You have made up your mind?"

"Yes." I was unsure but I would not let anyone know that. "I do not believe I am the person best suited for Mr. Sauvage's purposes."

"Why?" Her question was so blunt I was astounded. She sounded disappointed.

I explained that a quick departure into the unknown was unreasonable, that the situation between Miss Sauvage and her brother was an unhappy one, into which one as young as I should not be drawn. An older and more mature companion would be better able to handle family discord. As I talked I noted she had a letter spread on the desk at her hand. Now and then she glanced from me to that closely written page.

"Prudent and reasonable to be sure," she commented. "However, after your departure, Miss Penfold, I received this letter from Mr. Sauvage. In it he stated that he might not be able to talk privately as he wished to any extent; therefore he asked me to be his intermediary. The situation is indeed a strange one, and I think he is right in believing he needs a young lady of proven discretion to handle it.

"First let me say that if you were not a seasoned traveler, having accompanied your father on his many voyages until the war broke out, I would agree that the short time of preparation would be a factor to consider. But the Sauvage party will be traveling in the greatest comfort and luxury. These private cars are like miniature fine hotels mounted on wheels. You will experience none of the fatigue and difficulties of an ordinary traveler, no need to change, no worry concerning tickets and the like, a full safety of luggage.

"Now as to your objection concerning the family situation. No one wants to act as a warden over another person. But in this case there is great need for an alert companion for Miss Sauvage. I must now enter into some distasteful facts necessary for you to know, which Mr. Sauvage could not reveal to a member of the opposite sex.

"Victorine, as you know, is not Mr. Sauvage's full sister. There is a disparity of nearly twelve years in their ages, and very little family feeling. The second Madame Sauvage"—she hesitated—"was, shall I say, indiscreet. She would not accompany her husband to this country. In bald fact she accepted the protection of another man, one highly placed in French society.

"Nor did she inform her husband of the birth of Victorine. After a number of years her relationship with her protector was severed, and she disappeared soon after. Victorine meanwhile was left in the care of a kinswoman from the West Indies, a woman about whom there was also scandalous talk.

"About a year ago this woman died, leaving Victorine without a home, and she appealed to the brother she had never seen. Unfortunately while her French guardian was living she met a connection of her foster mother, a most unsuitable man from the West Indies. That this man hoped to use Victorine to force money from the Sauvages was Mr. Sauvage's discovery.

"He went to France, took her from the vicinity of that fortune hunter, and from the very unhealthy atmosphere in which she had grown up. He hopes a complete change of scene will be beneficial since his sister is so young.

"But there is reason to think that the young man in question will not easily relinquish his proposed victim. Therefore Mr. Sauvage needs a companion to watch over his sister. To place a lady of mature years in this position would defeat his purpose. He hopes to win the confidence of his sister, rather than let her believe herself a prisoner in his house. A discreet young person near Victorine's age, a young lady who speaks her native tongue, yet one well aware of the dangers of unwise acquaintances, is what he needs. And in that I concur. You would not be set in authority over Miss Sauvage; rather you shall be there to supply wholesome companionship, to introduce her to another life."

She paused and I dared to voice my greatest objection: "And to report upon her to her brother!"

"Naturally you shrink from such an idea," Madam Ashley agreed. "But that is not what Mr. Sauvage wants. He wishes no report on his sister, but only knowledge of any stranger who attempts to meet her in a surreptitious manner. Your main duty would be to make life so pleasant and attractive as to persuade Victorine her brother wishes her well, with a bright and happy future before her. Does this allay the doubts raised by your natural scruples?"

"You advise me, then, to accept this position?"

"I believe it to be an opportunity such as one seldom is offered. But the decision must be entirely yours."

Perhaps I had meant to say "yes" all the time, retreating behind my common sense because of a timidity which was not natural to me. Perhaps the wanderer's blood bequeathed me by my father stirred now as I answered, reversing myself.

"I will say yes then—" It was excitement rising in me now, rather than fear, though it would have been far better had I allowed my first prudence full rein at that moment.

CHAPTER TWO

Friday morning Madam herself escorted me to the station. Now that there was no turning back I shivered, the palms of my hands damp within my gloves.

The Sauvage car was the last of the train, painted a dark green and with a brass-railed observation platform to the back. I could see passengers in the ordinary coaches ahead looking curiously for the passenger. Then Mr. Sauvage himself came to aid me.

I made my goodbyes in a flurry. The stares of the coach passengers were disconcerting. A lady, as had long been drilled into me, was never conspicuous. And my discomfort continued even as I went into the stateroom assigned me. But with the strangers' eyes now gone, I looked around with interest, to realize how unlike the usual train this car was.

My private quarters was one of four small rooms, with a divan to open out into a bed, a small table (fastened securely against the sway of the floor), a wardrobe, and, within a curtained cubby, a lavatory. I removed my hat and jacket, glanced into the mirror above the table to make sure I looked tidy, and then went in search of my fellow passengers.

Since the train was in motion now I felt unsteady walking the narrow carpeted corridor. It had been too many years since I had enjoyed the freedom of my father's ship, known how to adjust to unstable footing. As I went I passed a fifth stateroom, much larger, with a big desk at which Mr. Sauvage was seated, a pile of papers before him.

Beyond that was the parlor-salon with built-in desk, and bookcases, several large comfortable chairs which could be swung on their pedestals so that one could watch, beyond heavily draped windows, the rapidly changing

20

countryside. Mrs. Deaves was settled in one of these chairs, her back to the window as if she preferred to believe herself in an ordinary parlor. She had opened a large workbasket and skeins of silk were laid out on her knee as she matched color against color. She greeted me civilly but with no hint of any pleasure in my company. Of Victorine there was no sign so I ventured to ask where she might be.

"The poor child believes this motion makes her ill. She is lying down." There was a trace of indifference in her voice, and I wondered if she agreed with Mr. Sauvage that his sister was using the excuse of illness to avoid contact with us.

It was doubtless my duty, and also only civil, to go and inquire about my hostess. There were indeed those who were sensitive to such motion. As I returned down the corridor I again saw Mr. Sauvage, deeply absorbed in his papers. For a moment I paused, without being quite conscious that I was staring rudely at my employer. The formal clothing he had worn at our first meeting had given him a stiff appearance, adding to his harshness of feature to make him seem a formidable person. But now he had laid aside the fine broadcloth and wore light trousers and a loose brown velvet sack coat. His shirt was unstarched and he had a scarf of soft red material knotted to draw the collar together at the throat. It was a style I had never seen before, but it made him seem far less severe.

"You wish, mam'selle?"

To my annoyance I both started and flushed as if I had been caught out in some breach of good manners.

Victorine's maid held the next door open a little, eyeing me, I believed, with sly impudence.

"How is your mistress?" I asked in French. Perhaps my voice was a fraction tart, but I disliked the thought that the girl had been watching me before she spoke.

I had always believed that tales of one taking an instant dislike to another person at first meeting were exaggerated. But now I found this girl with her honey-golden skin, her dainty good looks, chilled me.

She wore a dark blue dress and a frilly apron (that more

the badge of her service than for any practical purpose)
and her hair was puffed and rolled up very modishly under
a cap as much a token as the apron.

"She is—" Whatever she might have said was interrupted by an imperious voice.

"If that is Miss Penfold, Amélie, bid her enter." The
words, if accented, were in excellent English. Did Victorine really need any coaching in the language of her
new home?

Amélie's face was shadowed by a faint sullenness, but
she squeezed to one side to let me by. As her hand dropped
from the door panel I sighted something on her wrist which
made me catch my breath, involuntarily throw out my own
hand to strike it away.

"Look—on your wrist!"

My answer was laughter. Amélie put out her arm nearly
at my eye level, to make very sure I would realize my
mistake. All my life I have had a horror of spiders. One of
my worst nightmares is to dream of such crawling on me.
But now it was plain that what perched on the maid's
wrist was not a living creature but a spider intricately
wrought in black enamel and gold, fixed to an arm-hugging
bracelet.

"*Z'araignée*, Miss Penfold. It is chic to wear such insects, never real, *naturellement*, but fine copies. See—
I, too, am in high fashion. I wear *la Couleuvre*."

Victorine pointed to her own throat where, above the
lacy collar of her chamber robe, coiled a snake with jew-
eled eyes, its tail caught in its mouth to make the circlet
complete. It was a strange, and to me, unpleasant, piece
of jewelry, certainly unsuitable for a young girl.

I thought I recognized a trace of slyness in her eyes. She
was like one of the Ashley Manor girls testing a new
teacher, trying to see how many freedoms might be taken.
And that realization banished much of my nervousness;
this attitude I had coped with before.

"That is indeed a fine piece of work, mademoiselle—"

"Not mademoiselle, I beg you. I am Victorine—and my
brother has said you are Tamaris." She stumbled a little
in pronouncing my name. "You see, we are to be friends.

Only in truth yours is a name I find hard to say. Is it common in this America?"

"No. But it is an old one in my mother's family, given to many generations of daughters."

"Tamaris," she repeated. "Now I begin to think it has a good sound. Come"—she reached out and caught my hand, drawing me down to sit beside her on the divan bed—"you must sit here while we talk and learn to be friends."

"Mrs. Deaves said you were not feeling well—"

Victorine laughed and made a mischievous face. "A headache, yes. There was such a bustle to get off this morning. But Amélie brewed me her special tisane, then she rubbed my poor head, and—now the pain is gone! Also, I will tell you a secret, Tamaris—I have been with dear Augusta now for many long days, and I find her tedious. She watches me so closely. I am sure she has a *tendresse* for my brother and wishes to impress him with her care of his poor little sister. She is less clever than she believes and I will not take part in her little play. Me, I have no wish to call Augusta sister."

She had herself been watching closely, watching me. Now she laughed again, louder.

"Do I startle you with the truth, Tamaris? Ah, but if everyone only spoke the truth many troubles could be avoided. Augusta thinks to use me to reach Alain and I—" Now she paused. "Poor Tamaris, you believe I have a tongue which wags too fast and free—even as my good *bonne* Sophie used to tell me when I was small. Let us hear of you."

She questioned me frankly, so frankly that I could not be offended. For her questions showed a deep interest in my past and this could well be the way to win that confidence we must have between us if were to live together as Mr. Sauvage wished. So I told of my wandering years on board my father's *India Queen*, of my time at the school in Brussels—and of my later life at Ashley Manor. That last establishment seemed to fascinate Victorine.

"A school for the making of young ladies! But can one make indeed a young lady from an aspiring female, Ta-

maris?" Her face was so comical when she demanded that
I had to laugh.

"Of course the will to learn must be very much a part
of it. Madam Ashley has had many successes, I assure
you."

"And now my dear brother wishes to make of me a
young lady of the proper pattern." The good humor vanished from her face. "Is that why you are with us,
Tamaris?"

I decided that blunt frankness such as she had displayed already was my best approach. "No. I am with you
because he believes you need a friend while you take
your rightful place in our society. There are differences of
many kinds between the customs of Europe and those of
this country."

"That I have already been told," she said with a kind
of smoldering emphasis.

There was a litter of small trifles strewn about, a lacy
handkerchief, a vinaigrette, a small hand mirror, a fan. She
picked up the mirror. The glass was framed in silver, the
back embossed with a design of a cupid amid roses. Now
she studied her reflection, not as might a vain person, but
searchingly, as if she hunted for something important.

"They tell me," she abruptly changed the subject, "that
in this country marriages are not arranged by the family,
that one can wed as one pleases."

"But one's family is still concerned for one's future and
happiness," I returned, wondering if I were now about to
hear the story of the unwelcome suitor against which I was
to form part of the barrier. "Those who love them strive
to keep girls from mistakes which could be costly."

"How correctly you answer!" Victorine yawned. "Amélie's tisane—it is apt to make me sleepy. Tamaris—you
will pardon me—"

My dismissal was rude enough to be irritating. But
patience and the need for outer serenity are early learned
in my profession. I said I was glad she could rest, and left.

As I emerged into the corridor I saw Amélie's blue skirt
whisk through the dining room door. She must be going to

the galley. Suddenly I was tired, too. And the idea of a rest in my stateroom was irresistible.

Once there I changed my dress for a loose wrapper, curled up on the divan with my mother's India shawl to draw over me. That had been my prized possession for so long. Unlike the Chinese ones, or the English ones we now use, it had been fashioned in the old way of many small strips of fine weaving embroidered together into a harmonious whole. I ran my hands over it lovingly, allowing memory to flood my mind.

But my roving fingers encountered a small hard lump I did not remember. Sitting up I examined the hem edge closely. There was a tiny bag, hardly thicker around than a stout cord, whipped in to lay as flat as possible at the base of the fringe. Had it not been for my stroking it might have gone unnoticed for a long time. With the scissors from my workbox I snipped with extreme care until I had it loose.

I found no opening but it was filled with something. Finally I used the points of my scissors to pull at some very tiny stitches at one end. Then I pinched the gap shut until I found in the small desk a sheet of paper onto which I could shake those contents.

A yellow dust finer than any sand sifted down. With it were three very tiny lumps. One—ivory white—the tooth of some small animal. Another was a seed. There was not more than a half-teaspoonful in all though I wrung and squeezed the cloth to make sure. From it arose a faint, sickly-sweet odor. I sniffed twice and then sat down quickly on the edge of the divan bed, shaking my head, sneezing involuntarily. There was something here—evil— or could it be only my imagination?

Quickly I twisted paper and bag together, took the packet into the lavatory and disposed of it. Then I hurried back to examine once more my shawl, inch by inch. That bag had been newly concealed there I was sure, for the shawl was my constant companion.

I shivered. Who had stitched that in the hem and for what purpose? So small a thing and yet—

Should I ask questions? But of whom?

I patted smooth my shawl and could not rid myself of the odd fancy that someone had besmirched it. As if before my eyes it had been wantonly draggled in some slimed pool. Though I determined not to dwell upon my find, or fancy such odd and disturbing reasons for it.

I had not been able to push away all those fancies when our party assembled that night in the elegant dining section of the car. I cheered a little in the brightness of the lamp-lit room. Now and then in a window one caught a glimpse of a light marking some farmhouse, for the thick brocade curtains had not been drawn against the dark.

Victorine sat across the table from me. Her languid airs were gone, lost in a vivaciousness I had not seen her show before. She seemed to be listening eagerly as Mr. Sauvage spoke of the sights of the West. He had a fund of exciting tales, showed an animation to match his sister's, his dark face losing that set expression which had made a mask of it at our first meeting. I wondered if the further we advanced toward his own chosen territory the more he would relax, to be the man he was underneath the veneer of the city.

As he spoke I could almost close my eyes and return through the years to another time, another table. Just so had my father opened new doors of knowledge for me. But that was all so long ago—

But at any rate I did forget the shawl, though when, at the end of the evening, I returned to my stateroom and found that looped across my newly opened bed, I felt again that prick of uneasiness, almost illness—so that I sat down and once more investigated the whole of the border. However, I found nothing.

During the next few days Victorine made no more excuses of ill health but apparently shared my delight in watching the unrolling country—sometimes from the observation platform, sometimes through the salon windows. We always spoke English at her request, she insisting that I correct any expressions she used that might sound odd or strange. In addition she had Amélie bring a number of fashion magazines, apparently brought from France, and

the three of us (for Mrs. Deaves displayed as much animation over these) made choices from their colored plates. It
was Mrs. Deaves who assured us that San Francisco was
no raw country town, but a city which possessed shops
easily comparable to those of Paris, in reality some staffed
by one-time Parisians.

A large section of that city was French in sympathy and
blood. Immigrants, some of noble families, had been
among the first gold seekers. She had laughingly said that
it was no secret today that counts had been among wharf
laborers when those golden dreams had been dashed, and
that others of the bluest blood had peddled oranges and
cigars in the streets. There existed a French newspaper
and a theatre.

As for shops—well, there was the Ville de Paris, named
for a ship from whose decks a fine cargo had been auc-
tioned off in 1850. There was also the silk shop of Belloc
Frères, Madame Oulif's bonnet-selling establishment. No
Frenchwoman, she assured Victorine, need believe herself an exile in San Francisco.

And Victorine listened, her eyes shining. It was plain
that such talk was fast reconciling her to her new home.
But it was that very night that my complacency was shattered.

Our car was dropped from the train which had brought
us thus far, left in a freight yard to await the second one
to which it would be attached for the rest of the trip. Mr.
Sauvage warned us—Mrs. Deaves reinforcing that warning with the strict tone of a chaperone—that while we were
so situated, we should retire early to our staterooms where
the windows would be completely curtained. There could
be the curious who would seek to peer in.

I was writing a journal letter which I had promised
Madam Ashley and had just reached out to dip my pen in
the inkwell of my traveling desk when I was startled by a
sound. It might have been caused by someone scratching
with a stick along the outside of my window. It came the
second time, impatiently, as if demanding my attention.
Remembering the warnings, I had no intention of looking

out, perhaps to face on the other side of the pane some befuddled drunk.

A third scratching—then a low whistle. I had set down my desk and now I strained to hear. For that tune I knew. Only this morning Victorine had amused us by whistling a series of birdlike notes she said had been taught her in France.

That man—Madam Ashley's warning, Alain Sauvage's letter—could the rejected suitor have followed the girl, be out there now in the night striving so to attract her attention? He might well have mistaken the position of her stateroom. I must find some vantage point from which I could see who was there.

The lamps in the corridor had been turned very low. I hurried through the half-gloom to the dining salon—to the door at its end. That was heavy but not locked and I pushed it open far enough to step on the small platform. From there I would look back along the side of the car.

I was right! A shadow by the shaded window. But the figure was moving—toward Victorine's stateroom. While from there came a sudden gleam of brighter light. The curtain within had been moved.

Gathering my skirts, I sped at a pace far from dignified back the length of the car to the door of the master stateroom where I rapped urgently. Mr. Sauvage answered so suddenly he might have been waiting such a signal. But during the few moments it had taken me to reach his door I had decided to edit my first alarm. After all I could not be sure Victorine welcomed this stranger in the night.

"Miss Penfold! What is the matter?"

"Someone made a noise outside my window, sir. I believe that there is a prowler—"

I did not have time to complete my sentence. He swung around to snatch up a pistol lying on his desk, and brushed past me through the salon and out the observation door. I heard his voice raised in challenge and then what could only be the crack of a shot.

"Miss Penfold!"

"Tamaris!"

Mrs. Deaves' door had been flung open. As she took a

step or two into the corridor I saw Victorine was behind her. So—I had been right to keep my first suspicion to myself. Victorine had not moved that curtain to welcome any lurker in the shadows. Then who—a sneak thief striving to discover if the stateroom was occupied? But for such a one to run such a brazen chance of discovery seemed hardly probable.

"What *is* the meaning of this?" Mrs. Deaves clutched the folds of her wrapper tighter across her ample bosom. Her hair cascaded loose over her plump shoulders, showing a metallic, almost artificial, gleam when so freed from its usual elaborate dressing.

"There was a prowler along the car. I went to see from the dining room who was causing such odd sounds. By that time he had reached Victorine's window—"

"A thief!" Victorine showed far more excitement than fear. "But what did he hope to find? My jewels are all in the safe. What could he have been looking for—this prowler?"

"Perhaps whatever he could find. Anything which could be pawned for money for spirits." Mrs. Deaves drew her wrapper closer, her voice was distilled disdain. It was plain that she found the adventure sordid and unpleasant. "But how careless of him to make enough noise to alert you, Miss Penfold. Doubtless he was drunk. Was he trying to force your window?"

She peered at me and it seemed that now there was a hint of excitement in both her full eyes and her voice. Did the thought of me as bait for such an intruder please her? It was hard *not* to make such assumptions concerning Mrs. Deaves after my enforced close companionship with one who made it very plain she did not approve of me, of my reason for being here—though she masked that all so well that only one very used to the nuances of feminine company could detect it.

And now I was certain myself that the shadow I had seen had had more than theft on his mind.

"I do not know what he wanted," I returned evenly. "I came to warn Mr. Sauvage."

"So you did." Mrs. Deaves gave a shiver. "Had you not

done so we might have all been strangled in our beds!"
Her tone, the exaggeration of that last, were meant far
differently, suggesting that I had created for some purpose
of my own, and doubtless a disreputable one, an unseemly
uproar.

Victorine had pushed past her and was crowded close
against one of the salon windows, her hands cupped about
her eyes to cut out the dim lamplight and see the better
what might lie outside. "There was a shot—did we not
hear a shot also?"

"Mr. Sauvage took a pistol with him—"

"A pistol! Perhaps then he has killed this bandit! He is
a good shot, my brother. I have heard this said of him.
Yes—there are lanterns—men coming with lanterns! They
are running—"

"Victorine!" Mrs. Deaves hurried forward, setting a
hand on the girl's shoulder to draw her away from the window. "My dear, if you can see out, it is even more certain
that they can see in. Come away at once! None of us are
dressed in a manner to face strangers, and we must not
present a disgraceful spectacle for the vulgarly curious!"

For the first time I became aware that one member of
our party was missing.

"Where is Amélie?"

Victorine whirled about. The rebellious pout which had
been her answer to Mrs. Deaves' warning faded.

"Amélie!" she repeated as if calling her maid. Then
she caught up the trailing skirt of her wrapper, ran down
the corridor. "But Amélie—she must have been in my
stateroom. Perhaps this—this thief has harmed her! *Ma
pauvre* Amélie!"

So—then there *had* been someone in Victorine's stateroom to answer that summons at the window. Had the
fellow come to meet Amélie? In spite of the careful prim-
ness of her clothing the girl was strikingly beautiful. It
could well be that she had caught the eye of someone of
the train crew; perhaps she was not adverse to such attentions.

Victorine tugged open the door of her stateroom with
another loud call of the maid's name:

"Amélie!"

Inside we could see the girl huddled down on the divan, her hands covering her face, her shoulders shaking. The small lace cap had slid from its anchorage on the coils of her hair and the hair itself straggled in elf-locks about her hidden face.

Victorine gave a little cry and sat down beside her, her arms around the shivering maid.

"Amélie—*ma pauvre petite*—what is it? What has happened?"

The torrent of French which broke in answer to Victorine's question was mainly unintelligible to me. It was plain in her fright the maid had reverted to a patois. But Victorine appeared to understand, uttered small murmurs of comfort, trying to soothe the overwrought girl. She looked up over Amélie's shoulder at us.

"This is indeed horrible. *Ma pauvre* Amélie has suffered such a fright. She looked to see what made a strange noise at the window and there was outside a face! A face of such horror that her senses nearly departed from her. She could not even cry out for help, so great was her fear!" Victorine shivered in sympathy. "Then the face—suddenly it was gone. She heard cries—a shot—it was terrible for her—

"Come, *ma petite*." Now she spoke more softly and a great deal more calmly to Amélie—it might have been that she had deliberately summoned emotion to make certain we understood the enormity of what happened. "You are altogether safe now—we are here. My brother, the men of the train, they shall make certain no more evil comes near you. And I have to thank you, Tamaris," she said directly now to me, "that so quickly you found help. Had you not done this—who knows what might have happened?"

Within moments, as Victorine continued to speak soothingly to the distraught girl, Mr. Sauvage returned. The intruder had vanished completely, the shot had been fired by him, but into the air as a warning.

However, noticing the set of his chin as he told us that, I believed that he wished he had aimed at his elusive target. From now on, he assured us tersely, there would be a guard set. And it would not be long before our car was picked up by the westward-bound train.

But when I returned to my stateroom I was unable to busy myself once more with my letter. Certain points of difference between the evidence of my own eyes and Amélie's story arranged a pattern as I pulled them out of memory. In the first place that first noise certainly had not been made by an intruder striving to force a window. No, certainly it had been a tapping to attract attention—and there was the whistling also.

Then when I had looked out and there had been that lifting of the curtain at Victorine's pane there had been no face pressed against the glass there—the shadow had been well away from the side of the car.

But these were small things, only enough to awaken suspicion, nothing to carry proof. I could not use them to impeach the maid's story. Amélie was lying, I was sure. I must watch her—

There was a sudden jar and then a jerk. We were once more ready to move on. Wearily I undressed and got into bed. There was a sense of relief at being free of the yard tracks and on the move. If Amélie had planned an amorous adventure it had failed and that was that.

CHAPTER THREE

Morning brought sunlight and disbelief. Now that we were well away from the dark and the would-be invader, I must not allow my imagination to build a shadow into frightening substance.

Mr. Sauvage spent more time with us in the salon, pointing out scenes of general interest. And Mrs. Deaves, now all smiles and soft words, appropriated all she might of his attention. He had shed much of that polished shell which had made him a forbidding person, he seemed less and less one of that fashionable world Mrs. Deaves seemed to consider her own. Yet apparently she welcomed this change in him.

Still I could see in him that which I had always admired in my father and the other ship's officers I had known as a child—competency and a sense of duty. His manners were never too brusque, yet his more negligent dress, the hearty note which crept into his speech, his enthusiasm, made me believe in New York he had been forced into a tight mold he disliked; now he showed the man he really was.

I think my first reaction was envy. It was so easy for a man to break with conventions, a relief denied to my sex. I looked back to those very hard months when I had been transferred from the freedom of my father's ship to the prison (for then so it seemed) of a school ashore. I had learned my lesson well, perhaps too well, for I had passed from student to teacher, only to discover that my new role required even more from me in the way of discipline.

When I watched Mr. Sauvage swing off the train at some station to visit a telegraph office (it seemed very necessary that he keep in constant touch with his affairs both east and west), I wished for the first time in years that I could claim only a few small liberties.

Several times he suggested that we also leave the car for a short stroll on the splintered wood of the platforms at such halts. Mrs. Deaves plainly disliked such visits to these stations where ragged Indians begged, small boys sold caged prairie dogs, and men in red or blue sweat-stained shirts, wearing high-crowned, wide-brimmed hats and great cruel-looking spurs on their boots, stood and stared at us, their jaws moving as they continually chewed tobacco.

But Victorine was eager to go whenever her brother asked. She rattled along in French, making rudely frank comments on what we saw, taking her brother's arm amiably as if she already held him in high affection.

Though there was much which was drab or unpleasing, there was a grandeur in the land itself. And there was a vigor in these rough men, akin to that of seamen. They were determined to bend the country, rugged and forbidding as much of it was, to their strong wills. Only, I thought, it was not a land which any woman could love with the same inarticulate passion.

Our silks and frills, laces and fringes, were as out of place as those red shirts, spurs, and neckerchiefs would be in the East. One had to learn to accept the stares and understand that we were the rarities here. And I came to understand that such stares were compliments and not a matter of rude discourtesy.

Other passengers from the forepart of the train also stretched seat-cramped limbs and we came in time to recognize faces among them. So I realized that there was one man who continued to position himself in order to watch our party as long as we remained outside the coach.

The stranger wore a wide-brimmed hat which well overshadowed his face, and also a full black beard. Thus between the shadow of the hat brim and that sweep of hair, he might as well have been masked. But I thought he was young. His body was slender, even though he wore one of the bulky dusters as a protection against the grime and cinders of travel. At the halts he opened that and tossed it back as one might a cloak, showing the broadcloth of a city man.

I had just become uneasy at this continual watch upon us when it ceased. When he did not appear again, I decided, with an odd feeling of relief for which I could not account, that he must have left the train. I must not let myself imagine things and hold in suspicion everything and everyone.

"What do you think of this country, Miss Penfold?" Mr. Sauvage's question started me out of that prudent resolution.

Outside there wandered a stream paralleling the tracks at this point. The tumbling water seemed to offer such cool refreshment that I wished for a moment I could walk beside it. Meanwhile my employer seated himself in the chair next to mine, adjusting it a little so his attention could be divided between the outer world and me.

I caught at words hastily.

"It is certainly very beautiful. But I do not think it will be easily tamed. I wonder how cool that water is—"

He smiled. "Yes, a stream in the heat of the day. Water in many places out here is more precious than gold. Men's lives depend upon it. While gold is wealth and not life itself."

"Though men believed otherwise in forty-nine," I ventured. "Did not many lose their lives in pursuit of riches then?"

"Too many. Gold fever is dangerous. But that is past; now we build, set our roots deep. We have railroads to tie us with the East, we open lands for crops, cattle—" He spoke quickly and then began to talk of life in California.

My father had never looked upon me as without intelligence simply because I had been born female. Until my twelfth year, when I was sent ashore to school, I, who had been born aboard ship, taught from an excellent library my father carried, I had always had my questions answered with respect for my mind. And I had not heard such stimulating conversation as this for years.

Most of the men I had met socially used an inane surface speech for ladies. To dip below that and display any understanding of or interest in important events was a social error. The enthusiasm for study my father had fostered in me had become a solitary act—near a vice. And at this moment I realized just how cut off from what I wanted I had been. I was the thirsty wayfarer chancing in a wilderness upon such a stream as that before us.

Mr. Sauvage encouraged the questions I asked, waited for me to make comments, which he accepted as natural. I began to mention things my father had drawn to my attention. For he had made it a point to see that I visited many unusual places in the lands to which the *India Queen* carried cargoes. That I had inherited his ability to pick up languages easily he had found a matter of pleasure.

"So you have then visited Canton and the Sandwich Islands?" Mr. Sauvage was really interested. "And what did you think of that part of China which you saw?"

He was not condescending and so I answered forthrightly what I had observed. I think I startled him when I explained that I had been entertained for two days in the women's quarters of one of the great merchants, seeing a part of native life which was open to no male travelers.

"You have had many advantages," he commented.

"One above all others, sir—that was having a father who trained in me an inquiring mind."

Perhaps my answer was a little too sharp, for then he asked, "You say that with such emphasis, Miss Penfold. Do you believe that your father's attitude was then out of the ordinary?"

"Judging, sir, by what I have learned since I lost his companionship, very much so. He fostered in me a wish to enlarge my horizons and then gave me every opportunity of doing so. Since such educational advantages are usually reserved for sons instead of daughters, I know now he was very much out of the ordinary."

I was skirting the edge of propriety in that answer. Was there the beginning of a frown to draw his dark brows together? He could well believe I was reflecting in some way on his own convictions.

"Alain! I did not know you were waiting." Mrs. Deaves swept down upon us from the corridor. "It is thoughtless of me to waste your time when you have so much to worry you. But I have all the papers here—"

She busied herself loosening the catch of the portfolio she carried.

"I am at your service, as always, Augusta." He arose and reached for the portfolio.

I realized this was a dismissal and was a little piqued that it was so abrupt. Not that I had any more claim on his attention than common courtesy dictated. Mrs. Deaves made no more acknowledgment of my presence than a slight nod of the head as I passed her on my way to my stateroom.

There was still my letter to Madam Ashley, but I was not in the mood to add the daily entry to that. Instead I gazed out the window at a land which now looked very forbidding. And I was still trying to sort out the puzzle of my own feelings when there came an imperative rap at my door and Mrs. Deaves entered before I could answer.

"Miss Penfold!" She used my name in the same tone I

had in the past employed to bring an inattentive scholar to order. Instant resentment was my inner reaction.

"Mrs. Deaves?" I returned inquiringly. "There is something I can do for you?"

"There is something you can do for yourself, Miss Penfold." Without invitation she seated herself.

Perhaps she expected a response from me, but I waited in silence for her to continue. This had always been an excellent device with which to counter such emotion as she displayed.

"I am referring, of course"—she fell to turning one of her many rings around on a plump finger—"to the fact that young ladies in good society do not seek to attract the attention of gentlemen—"

Did they not, I thought bitterly. Most of their time was spent in maneuvering to do just that, as subtly as possible, of course.

"Mr. Sauvage—Alain"—she used his given name as if she would so underline that fact that it was *her* privilege to do so—"is very good-natured. Though he is a man of affairs which need constant attention, he is well bred enough not to show impatience—"

I had continued to eye her with the perplexed look of one unable to understand. Perhaps my attitude puzzled her in turn for she paused, to begin again:

"You are quite young, Miss Penfold, and your circumstances have been such that you may be misled by some common civility. Mr. Sauvage found your recent conversation a little—shall we say, odd—in a lady selected to be a companion to his sister. Since this is a delicate matter she pressed me to speak to you about it."

"But, of course," I agreed blandly. "And it is most kind of you to do so, Mrs. Deaves. Though I am still somewhat at a loss as to the nature of my offense, since my most recent conversation with Mr. Sauvage was initiated by him. I thought he wished to know more of my background. That I believe to be quite natural under the circumstances."

She flushed. I think she had thought I could be easily cowed. And I was sure her dislike of me grew with each word. But I had spoken what could well be the truth and she knew it. Now having so temporarily silenced her, I attacked in turn—if one might think of our conversation as a skirmish.

"I assure you I have no wish to give any offense. And I believe, now that Mr. Sauvage has satisfied himself as to my background, he will have no need for any further conversations. You may tell him that I understand the message sent through you, and I will act with discretion in the future."

I was sure that she had never met my tactics in the past. By her standards I might seem insolent, yet she could not seize upon any words of mine to accuse me of that fault. Muttering something I could not hear, she left as abruptly as she had burst in upon me.

Now I had something else to consider. I must walk very warily indeed in the future, giving this woman nothing upon which she could build a plausible attack. If I had read Mr. Sauvage aright, I did not believe he had sent Mrs. Deaves here. He was the type not to move deviously, but rather express himself directly.

However, he could have made some casual comment to Mrs. Deaves which allowed her to believe she could so approach me. Perhaps I *had* been too carried away by his easy manner so that my own had verged on forwardness. I must watch my tongue and be on terms of strictly polite correctness when dealing with Mrs. Deaves' Alain. And that knowledge gave me a sense of loss and even a twinge of pain. It was as if I had been awakened out of a long time of boredom, given a glimpse of brightness, and been sternly forbidden to seek that out again.

It was with little pleasure that I answered the dinner gong. Mrs. Deaves dominated the conversation at the table, her purpose perfectly transparent to me. She sprinkled her sentences with names, taking as her subject the social round in San Francisco, the "season" to come, and the role Victorine would be expected to play. She was freezing me out of that charmed inner circle by all her implications. And if Mrs. Deaves achieved the goal Victorine had suggested, that of the mistress of the Sauvage household, I believed my term of employment would be far shorter than that which had been agreed upon.

When Mrs. Deaves at last suggested that we return to the salon Victorine yawned, saying that she was finding train travel very conducive to slumber and that she was about to retire. I said I had a letter to write and escaped so easily that I knew it was to the relief of Mrs. Deaves.

But I had no more than gotten into my wrapper and was giving my hair its nightly brushing when Victorine slipped into my room without any warning knock.

"What did that old henwife say to you earlier, Tamaris? She was hot with rage when she went past my stateroom. Was that because my brother had talked with you for a while?" She curled up on my divan without invitation.

"Bah—you are going to be discreet." Victorine made the last word sound as if it were a sin of sorts. "I see by your look you will not answer me. But I am not stupid, I can guess that is the truth. That one thinks to become Madame Sauvage—already in her ears she is called so. She is so afraid of not gaining her desire that she sees in every female a threat to her plan. Well, listen to me, Tamaris, she shall never get what she wishes!

"First—because she is really a fool, and, though I have only known my brother a short time, this much I have learned of him—he is not one to suffer a fool gladly. Also, she tries too hard. Sooner or later she will make plain what she wishes and that will give my brother a disgust of her. She is no fit mate for him!"

There was no hint of amusement in Victorine's eyes, rather they were brilliant with the same emotion which deepened her voice, low though that already was. It was plain that the girl did possess some feeling for her brother. And Mrs. Deaves might well be defeated before she realized she had this particular adversary.

Now Victorine laughed. "Do I frighten you a little, Tamaris, when I speak so? Do you think that I plan some dark way to rid my dear brother of Augusta? That I am, perhaps, even a witch?" She made a grotesque face.

"Good! Then I think I shall be a witch, and I shall lay

upon Augusta a curse, a strong curse. Shall I give her a
spotted skin so all will turn from her in disgust—or—? Do
I not frighten you now, Tamaris—just a little?"

I laughed. "Of course. Do you not see I am shuddering
in horror at your evil plans?"

She gave me an odd, searching look with no answering
amusement in it.

"Do not laugh at what you do not understand, Tamaris.
There are things—" She broke off abruptly. "But those are
of another time—another place—not of this safe little
world. Finish your letter, *chère* Tamaris, then sleep well."

As silently and swiftly as she had come she was gone.
My amusement of a moment before had ebbed. I glanced
about me sharply, seeking to know what had for a second
or two so disturbed me. But that feeling had been only a
flash, and if a warning, I was not wise enough to heed it.

During the course of the next morning Mr. Sauvage
received a telegram urging that he leave the train at
Sacramento to visit Virginia City where there was trouble
at one of the mines his company controlled. He assured us
that one of his men would be waiting in Oakland. This
gentleman would then escort us on to the suite at the
Lick House.

Fog was thick at the ferry. Such fog, I thought, as might
well furnish the horrifying background for some story laid
in the depths of London. Thus we stayed within the cabin
on board, depending on our waterproof capes to keep out
at least some of the damp chill. Victorine sniffed disdain-
fully.

"Me—I find this place abominable. Where are the
bright skies, the pleasant land of which my brother spoke
so much?"

The young man sent to assist us, Graham Cantrell,
stood as close to his employer's sister as decorum allowed.
It had been easy to see that from their first meeting he had
eyes for no one else. Even Victorine's present sullen pout,
I admitted to myself a little wistfully, detracted nothing
from her very real fragile beauty. Now he hastened to say
that these fogs did not always shroud the bay or menace
the city toward which our boat wallowed sluggishly.

But I knew the sea. And to me such a fog would always be a threat. To look out cabin windows blind-curtained by a thick mist was frightening. And I could hear the mournful sound of warning whistles, but so thick were the damp wisps that even those seemed muffled.

Moisture gathered in thick drops on the grimed panes. The smell of the cabin was foul—old dirt, stronger human odors, a stench of machine oil breathed out by the laboring engines.

Suddenly I could not stand this confinement any longer. Seasoned voyager though I thought myself, my stomach was queasy. I need only take a step or two outside the door to find cleaner air, mist-thickened though that might be. So I went, to draw that dankness gratefully into my lungs.

There were other passengers who apparently shared my desire for the open. Most of these were only vague shadows, but to the left of the cabin door two stood close together. And now and then I caught the murmur of voices.

The taller one must be a man. The other, muffled in a cloak twin to my own, was plainly a woman. Then a member of the crew stumped by, lantern in hand, and a flash from that illuminated both plainly. Amélie, who had promised to stay with our luggage, stood there.

However, the light had not risen as far as her companion's features. Only the fact that their situation suggested a degree of intimacy triggered my old suspicions. Was this another man attracted by chance to her pretty face? I knew so little about her—she might be very free with her favors when not under her mistress's eye. But it was also true that there was such a strong attachment between them that Victorine would defend rather than accuse her against any such vague suspicion as mine.

I must watch Amélie, make sure her conduct was not such as to embroil her young mistress in some disgraceful trouble. And worry gnawed at me as we disembarked and drove at a snail's pace through the nearly unseen streets to Lick House.

"*C'est magnifique!* See, even in this fog one may see the shop lights. What a pleasure to visit them—let us do so!"

Victorine turned away from the hotel window, letting fall the thick drapery she had raised to look down upon the life which was Montgomery Street even on such a bad evening. She was in one of her effervescent moods.

"Not at night, my dear." Mrs. Deaves was soberly disapproving at once. "A lady does not appear on the streets unless properly escorted—"

"But I *see* them!" protested Victorine. "There they are—there and there—" She stabbed a finger at the pane.

"Those are not *ladies*." Mrs. Deaves' verdict was meant to be final and quelling.

Victorine scowled, letting the red velvet drapes close out the lights and the bustle of life on the street. I was growing very weary of red velvet. Hotels seemed particularly fond of that as if it were a badge of respectability and luxury. And the Lick House certainly paraded the latter.

Its interior of carved woodwork, velvet, and plush marble floors made its tasteless opulence overpowering. Just as the meal which had been served in our private suite—six courses beginning with oysters and adding every imaginable delicacy in or out of season—had left me feeling there was far too much food in the world.

Champagne also seemed to be the rule, produced as a matter of course, just as a glass of iced water might be elsewhere. Also, and this had surprised me, both Victorine and I had been served it without question. I scarcely touched my glass. But Victorine and Mrs. Deaves did not follow my example.

"Your brother, my dear"—Mrs. Deaves held her ever-present embroidery bag on her lap but at this moment made no attempt to open it—"keeps his own carriage here in the city. And there is no reason why we cannot use that to visit some of the shops tomorrow. If there are any additions you wish to make to your wardrobe—"

Then she had glanced slyly in my direction. I caught her eye boldly. If she thought to daunt me with the implied disparagement of my wardrobe, she failed. I was secure in the knowledge that I made the proper fashionable appearance always expected of one of Madam Ashley's instructoresses.

However, a glance around the ladies' parlor, through which we had been ushered with no little ceremony upon our arrival, had made plain that what was considered correct taste in the East was very lacking compared to that worn in the flamboyant West. Such a wealth of overdresses —sometimes of two contrasting colors on a single gown— fringes, beadings, wreathing of flowers and laces, I had never seen displayed before.

It was the fashion here, Mrs. Deaves had informed us, during one of her instructive monologues on the uses of polite society, for families of wealth not to maintain a town house (though there were some of those, of palace size and design, on such likely sites as Nob Hill) but rather to retain a permanent suite in one of the major hotels, thus escaping the cares of homeowners.

This custom had begun in the early days of the gold seekers when the majority of arrivals were lone men and lived in boardinghouses. Many gentlemen banded together and established semiprivate places for boarding, presided over by competent and even highly talented cook-housekeepers. So attached had the gentlemen become to this state of affairs that, even after some of them had been provided with families and homes, they still kept up the "boarding" establishments and visited those in the evening to meet friends, talk business, and engage in activities one does not generally discuss openly.

During our dinner Mrs. Deaves had continued to talk, offering such a constant flow of information that I wondered how she found time to do justice to her food. But I listened closely, to learn we were indeed now faced by a world quite different from all I had known.

"Yes!" Victorine plumped herself down on one of the plush-covered love seats. "We must see all the shops! But—I forgot—we have no money. How, then, will we be able to buy—?"

Mrs. Deaves laughed. Her face was flushed. She had dined very well, though she must be tightly laced, so wrinkleless was her boned bodice. During the meal her voice had grown louder, her words a little slurred, her laughter more and more frequent.

"You need not worry. Alain's credit is very well established. Carrying money is tiresome. You see, they will not accept paper bills, such as one uses in the East. Here you can offer only gold or silver."

I was disturbed by that. My purse, safely pinned in my petticoat seam pocket, must then have its contents changed. Sould I seek out a bank to do that, or could I apply to Mr. Cantrell? I disliked being without ready funds. Not that I expected to shop for myself tomorrow, but if an emergency arose—

Mrs. Deaves got to her feet. Noticing the deepening flush of her face, I speculated as to whether she was beginning to regret the combination of an ample meal, those glasses of champagne, and her tight lacing. She made a slurred excuse and went to her room.

Victorine yawned. "Me—I am sleepy also. But in the morning"—she smiled as might a small child promised some treat—"we shall then explore this city. Shopping I love!" Her full lips (which sometimes with their ever-moistness seemed at variance with her girl's face in a way I found odd but could not explain why) curved into one of those smiles with which she could ever entrance. "We can dream tonight of what is to be seen tomorrow."

I entered my own room to discover someone there before me. Laying out my lawn nightgown was a maid I had not seen before. She was a Negro of middle years (though it is difficult to judge the age of those of another race), plain of face and thick of body under a dark blue cotton dress. Her apron was no froth of ruffled lawn such as Amélie wore, but plainly serviceable, and her cap hid all but a fringe of hair on her forehead.

She bobbed a curtsy. "I'se Hattie, Miss. I do for ladies does they want—" With her eyes cast down, she waited for orders. Something in her air of patient submission made me uncomfortable. It reminded me of those times before the war when my father, a man opposed to slavery and all it stood for (considering that it demeaned both master and slave), had engaged in secret actions I had not understood. The *India Queen* had several times carried dark-skinned passengers, not on any official listing, from such ports as New Orleans and Charleston.

CHAPTER FOUR

I was quick to assure Hattie I did not need her assistance but was careful to thank her for the offer. As she left with a soft-footed tread, I unhooked my bodice, my memory going back through the years to things my father and I had never discussed.

There had been a woman then, a very strange person with an air of authority, though she had worn the plain dress of an upper servant. She had dined with us twice on board the *India Queen* in the port of New Orleans, and afterward my father had sent me to my cabin while he talked with her in private. She had been introduced only as Mrs. Smith, a name which did not fit her, and her serene manner had been accented by the oddness of her eyes, one being blue, the other hazel. Her skin had been olive, her hair dark, and she was handsome, with soft and pleasing manners.

Afterward my father had cautioned me not to mention her visits, and I had always been sure that she had had something to do with the escape of slaves. Since those days I had never seen her, but now I recalled her as plainly as if she had been the maid I found in my room.

I firmly dismissed that particularly clear flash of memory as I picked up my hairbrush. The top of the dressing table was not littered as the one that served Victorine, which I had last seen in the greatest confusion. I had no set of scent bottles with blown-glass butterflies for stoppers, nor any other of the pretty clutter she gathered so easily. My possessions might be termed schoolmarm neat and so I could detect that they had been moved.

One of the first things I had unpacked was a curious box, my father's last gift to me. It had been made somewhere in the Far East of carved wood, parts of the design inlaid with mother-of-pearl. In it I always kept mementos of my family—the miniature of my mother which my father had given me, one of himself he had had painted at my urging, a few old letters, my mother's wedding lines, a letter to her from my long-dead grandmother. None of these had any value save for me.

The box had been moved. I set aside my brush to pick up the coffer. Its catch was a secret one, or so I had believed. For it was located in the carving where one must insert a fingertip to release it.

I needed only to glance within to know that the order in which my oddments had been left was changed. Someone had opened the box, made free with the contents. Anger flared in me. I could expect a thief to search for a jewel case, but mine was locked inside my trunk. Unless the thief thought this to be such, perhaps a natural assumption.

Who? Hattie? No, I had no right to make such a quick, damning judgment. The reputation of this hotel was such that they surely hired no employees of whom they were not certain. And I had no proof; nothing had been taken. But I did not want it to happen again.

As I continued to prepare for bed I realized that I could not entrap anyone unless I proposed to spend the day hiding in, say, the large wardrobe. And that made me smile in spite of my anger and uneasiness.

If not Hattie, or some other servant, then who? Amélie? I found in spite of my effort to be fair I could believe this of her. In my opinion she was sly and untrustworthy. But why she wished to rummage among my things—that I could not understand.

I held the box closer to the lamp to see if there was any sign it had been forced. When I did this, my face very close to its surface, I smelled a sickly sweet odor—a familiar one. Yes, that was similar to the scent from the contents of the tiny bag sewn into my shawl.

That absolved any servant here, but it pointed the finger more firmly at Amélie.

I must speak seriously to Victorine. The causes for my suspicions were thin, but taken together they should make her listen to me. Drawing on my wrapper I went back to the parlor.

The room was dark, but there was a faint reflection of light from the street below. At my tap there was no answer from Victorine's chamber. Surely she could not have fallen asleep so quickly? My second tap was delivered with more force and the door swung open as if inviting me to enter.

Emerging from the shadows was a massive bed possessing a pretentious tester. A subdued night light on a side table showed Victorine lying quietly on the bed, not in it. She had indeed removed her dress, but still wore a whirl of petticoats, her fine chemise slipping wantonly from one shoulder to show more of her breast than was modest.

Even her hair had not been unpinned, though some locks had shaken free. She seemed asleep, but so strange was this collapse (for so it seemed to me) that I caught up the night lamp and carried it to the bedside, holding it over her.

That her deep slumber was normal I doubted. I touched her shoulder. Her flesh was chill, yet there were tiny beads of moisture on her upper lip. She uttered a low moan and turned her head.

Now I hurried to light the larger lamp, then drew the covers up over her. I could not be sure, looking back, how much of the wine she had drunk. But where was Amélie and why had she left her mistress in such a strait?

As I came around the end of the bed, heading for the bell pull, I collided with a small table. A glass rolled onto the floor, the spoonful of liquid still in it dribbling onto the thick carpet. But something else fell and I stooped to pick up a fan.

The guard sticks were very thick, making it seem much heavier in consequence. And in one of these guard sticks a portion of the surface had slid to one side, to uncover a small compartment. There was a dust inside and I touched fingertip to that, raising it to my nose.

Again that sickly odor!

I shivered at what my imagination suggested. But surely
Victorine had not been drugged against her will, or such
evidence would not have been left in the open for the
first comer to discover.

I gave the bell pull a vigorous jerk. Since Amélie was
not here I had no idea where to find her. But Hattie or
some other servant answering my signal could locate the
maid.

As I paced nervously back and forth waiting, I twisted
the fan in my hands. Then realizing what I did, I pushed
the lid back over the compartment and laid it down just
as a tap sounded at the door.

At my call Hattie entered.

"Do you know where Miss Sauvage's maid is? Her mistress is ill."

" 'Deed no, miss." Her capped head swung from side to
side. "Mebbe I can do fo' the lady. There's Doctuh
Beech—he's right down the hall a ways. Though it's early
for genlemens to be comin' up yet—"

As she spoke she joined me by the bed, leaning forward
to stare at Victorine with what I thought was avid curiosity
but little compassion. Then I was sure it was not at the
face of the girl that Hattie was gazing so intently, but at the
ugly necklace Victorine so favored that she wore it almost
constantly—the gold and enameled snake.

Drugged, or under the influence of too much wine? In
either case I hesitated about calling an unknown doctor.
But I could summon Mrs. Deaves. As I opened my mouth
to order Hattie to do just that, someone brushed by me,
swung around to face us both, as if to protect her mistress.
Amélie, holding a small pot in both hands, eyed me
fiercely, her attitude one of outrage.

"What do you here?" she demanded in French. "My
lady—why do you come to disturb her?"

I refused to be intimidated. "She is ill. This is no normal
sleep." I replied in the same language.

"But, of course, she has taken one of her powders. Her
poor head, it was aching. I went to fetch her this tisane,

I know how to make her comfortable. Now you will wake her and the pain will return—" Amélie crowded us away from the bed, the pot still held before her as if that were a weapon she might use in Victorine's defense.

I heard a loud gasp from Hattie. The older woman was cowering away, her attention upon the girl's wrist, her eyes wide. She was staring at that gruesome spider bracelet which Amélie wore with the same devotion to the piece as her mistress showed in her preference for the snake necklace. With an inarticulate cry Hattie ran from the room.

Amélie smiled and said something in her patois. But the smile was gone in an instant as she looked once more to me.

"It is true what I say. My lady is asleep. Soon she will wake and want her tisane. Then her head will be better and all will be well with her."

I was sure that I was not reading concern for her mistress so much in her eyes now, as a cold and calculated dislike for me. However, her explanation had such logic I was forced to accept it. There were yet some days before Mr. Sauvage would join us, but I intended to report this scene to him when I could.

Amélie, her attitude near open impertinence, followed me to the door. That she closed firmly behind me, like one raising a drawbridge of a castle against the enemy. I still wondered if it was the wine or something else which had affected Victorine but I did not have the knowledge or the opportunity of proving any suspicion.

When I awoke in the morning memory flooded back. As I dressed I stared at the long wardrobe mirror, without being the least aware of my own reflection therein, but seeing in my mind the fan with its hidden compartment. How foolish had I been not to bring that with me when I left Victorine's room. I recalled now there had been initials inlaid over the compartment—but I somehow did not think those had been either a V or an S.

The room was chilly. Both Mrs. Deaves and Mr. Sauvage had warned that spring in San Francisco did not mean warmth and balmy air. Rather ladies here held to their furs long after those were laid aside elsewhere. So I chose a heavy dress, one of violet silk and worsted, its drapery and bodice trimmed with bands of deep purple velvet. And before I went into the parlor I took Mama's shawl, the cheerfulness of its color, as well as its warmth, heartening me.

Victorine was already posted at a window. The fog was gone this morning, but the day was gray and overcast. She, however, was in a sunny mood, her gaiety heightened by the bright blue of her dress.

"The shops—they are already open. Do you not long to visit them, Tamaris? See"—she gestured to a settee where rested a small hat of beplumed sapphire velvet, a loose gray jacket banded and collared with chinchilla—"I am prepared." She whirled around so the flounces and ribbons of her dress were a-flutter, a child excited by a promised treat.

But Mrs. Deaves did not share her enthusiasm. Victorine fidgeted during our breakfast when our chaperone did not appear, watching her bedroom door, which remained shut.

"How does your head feel this morning?" I asked one of the questions at the fore of my mind.

"My head?" Victorine repeated a little blankly. "Oh, you mean the aching. That is gone. Amélie always knows what to do for me. I think"—she was now prettily penitent—"that I drank too much champagne. For when I went to my room—poof!" She raised her fingers to her temples. "There was such a pain here, and the room—it was spinning around and around. So Amélie had me quickly lie down and gave me one of my powders before I had taken off more than my dress. She told me you were much alarmed for me, Tamaris."

"I was," I replied shortly. Her explanation was logical, yet something within me still questioned.

"I promise that never again shall this happen. I shall be most abstemious. Like you I shall say '*non*' and '*non*' to much wine, and then I shall not suffer. But this morning, thanks to Amélie, I am not in the least ill. Poor Augusta"—she looked again to the door—"do you think she now

has a head which aches? Perhaps I should offer to her
Amélie's remedy—"

Maybe the thought of shopping revived Mrs. Deaves.
When she did issue forth from her chamber shortly thereafter she was her usual self, showing no traces of a disturbed night. Also she was in excellent humor, smiling at
Victorine's excitement. When Mr. Cantrell sent up his
card with the message our carriage waited, she was as
quick as the girl to draw on her gloves, peer in the mirror
to assure herself that her hat was securely anchored well
to the fore of her remarkably puffed chignon.

Victorine took a small ivory-leafed tablet from her belt
purse, glanced over some notes as we went.

"Embroidered stockings," she murmured in French.
"Buff with violets, or pale green—Tamaris, was it the pale
green which had strawberries worked on them? I have a
sad memory and Augusta told us so much last night."

I laughed. "There were also pink ones mentioned—with
blackberries in floss work. Those seem a little startling, I
think."

Victorine made a face. "Me, I do not think black-
berries are in the least chic. But the poudre sachet of
Flowers of California—that I must certainly have. Oh,
Tamaris, is this not most exciting!"

I had to admit that visiting the notable shops of San
Francisco did attract me. But when Mr. Cantrell bowed us
through the damp chill air of the street into our carriage I
was not so sure. I could not guess whether dampness was
the last of the night's fog, or a promise of rain to come,
and the general drabness of the day was depressing.

Luckily our barouche was closed. The carriage was
smartly turned out and, if representative of Mr. Sauvage's
stables, I could see he chose always the best. Once we
were seated Victorine leaned forward to study the luxurious appointments of the yellow satin upholstered interior,
uttering exclamations of surprise at each new discovery.
Though Mr. Sauvage had, since the marriage of his sister,
kept a bachelor establishment, the barouche suggested
that he was not unmindful of female needs. In various
small pockets and compartments Victorine discovered,

and displayed to us, a card case of tortoise shell, a vinaigrette containing smelling salts, a mirror, a box of hairpins, and a pincushion.

"We are so well provided for every eventuality," I commented.

"Perfectly ordinary and in good taste," Mrs. Deaves returned coldly.

Victorine laughed. "How very clever of my brother! Though it may be that he does not care at all, and it is the duty of some servant to see this is kept in order. Now here, Augusta, where do you conduct us?"

"First I think the Chinese Bazaar. You shall find that most unusual, my dear."

We threaded through traffic as thick as any choking a busy New York street. Here, in addition to the horse cars for public transportation, were those peculiar to this city, traveling on a cable of chain, which was in turn controlled by steam engines at either end of the line. Victorine, enchanted, wanted to take a ride. But our chaperone appeared so shocked at such a departure from ladylike behavior that even the impetuous Miss Sauvage was subdued.

We drew up to one of the sidewalk posts intended to aid the descent of carriage passengers and she was smiling again. A Negro footman handed us down and we stepped almost immediately into what was indeed a very different shop. There was a huge banner across the front above the entrance, on it a prancing, fiery dragon, a vast scarlet tongue lolling from its jaws. And from the open door issued a heavy scent of incense. From here, too, came the chirping of birds as a number of canaries swung in fanciful cages from the ceiling.

A Chinese wearing a blue merchant's robe ushered us within and I, too, was lost in viewing rare and unusual wares. Nor did Victorine leave empty-handed. About one wrist was a bracelet of cool jade. And carried behind us, wrapped in the red paper of good omen, was a shawl of ivory white silk patterned with branches of flowering plum embroidered in thread only a shade or two darker than the background.

From the Bazaar we went to the Ville de Paris where one feasted eyes on velvets, French brocades, airy-light pineapple gauze from the Sandwich Islands. Then to Wakeless's so Victorine could indulge her fancy for the Flowers of California sachet, as well as a bottle of frangipani—which I found too cloying for my taste.

There was lace to be viewed at Samuel's, and so on, but before noon we came to a smaller shop—that of Madame Fanny Perier. Though she dealt in small fripperies, laces, and trimmings only, her shop was artfully designed to soothe clients wearied from such activity elsewhere.

The turkey red carpet was in cheerful contrast to the drabness of the outer day. And many stateroom-sized lamps were screwed to the walls, artfully intermingled with mirrors framed in gilt which reflected and magnified the room. We were seated by a small table on three gilt-legged chairs. Madame herself brought in a tray of elegant gold and white chocolate cups, together with small plates on which lay thin slices of Droste to melt on the tongue.

She talked eagerly to Mrs. Deaves, with whom she appeared to be on familiar terms. And then she produced, not as if displaying such for sale, but merely as if she wished us to see the latest amusing trifles, some of her stock.

Victorine was much taken with a crystal vial fastened to a hairpin which, as Madame demonstrated, might be skillfully inserted into one's coiffure, to be a life-prolonging holder for small fresh flowers. And she promptly added that to her other purchases of the morning.

It was while Madame was showing her just how to adjust this that I saw the woman standing in the doorway leading to the back quarters from which Madame had brought the chocolate.

The stranger was tall and, by the mirror and lamp reflections, fully revealed to me. Instantly years were wiped away. I had been thinking of her only last night. This was that "Mrs. Smith" my father had known.

From my right I heard a gasp and I glanced at Mrs. Deaves. Her high color had faded. She closed her eyes as if she were suddenly faint. I put out my hand impulsively, and, as if she did not know, or care, who offered support, she caught my wrist in a bruising grasp.

"No!" I heard her whisper in desperate denial.

Was Augusta Deaves reacting so to the sight of Mrs. Smith? From her stricken face I looked quickly to the doorway. The other woman still stood there, watching. But, to my surprise, I found her eyes on me, not my agitated companion, and there was an odd feeling in my mind that she surveyed me not as a person, but rather as a problem it was necessary for her to solve. Then, her lips curved in a slight smile, she stepped back into the shadows, vanishing as abruptly as if she had indeed been a part of some dark dream.

I blinked before I spoke. "Mrs. Deaves, are you ill? Can I help you?"

For her face was near the color of clay, and her breath came in shallow gasps.

"Yes, yes—" Even her voice had shriveled into this hoarse mutter. "Go—let us go!"

Madame now hurried to us in a flurry of concern. Only when we were again in the carriage did Mrs. Deaves exert a visible effort to regain self-control.

"Augusta, what is the matter? Are you ill?" Victorine exhibited more feeling for her brother's friend than she had ever shown before.

"That—that woman! That was Mammy Pleasant— no!" Mrs. Deaves sat up straighter, regained a measure of self-confidence again. "Do not ask me any more. Just pray God you will never know that wicked, wicked woman!"

I did not try to press her, but Victorine did. Though her voice was soft and carried still a note of concern, it was almost as if she took some pleasure in continuing the inquisition in spite of Mrs. Deaves' manifest discomfort. However, as the moments passed and we left behind the scene of her momentary fright (for fear I was sure had been the base of Augusta Deaves' flight), the older woman regained her old serenity and refused to satisfy Victorine's curiosity. By the time we had reached our hotel her armor was again complete.

However, I believed that she was bitterly unhappy about

her self-betrayal. And once we were within the suite again she left us hurriedly for her own room. Victorine was not yet ready to let the matter drop.

"Who is this Mammy Pleasant, then, to upset Augusta so? Who *did* you see in the shop, Tamaris? I saw no one at all."

"There was a woman standing in the doorway of the inner room—that was all."

"Just a woman? But what kind of woman would make Augusta's hands shake, turn her face so white? Augusta was afraid, Tamaris, truly afraid."

"I do not know anything more than we saw the woman," I answered carefully. That it was Mrs. Smith I had no doubt, her personality was such that having once seen her, one was not likely to forget her easily. But I had no idea of telling Victorine what little I knew. And the reason for Mrs. Deaves' display of fear even my imagination could not supply.

There was a tap at the suite door and Victorine, who was nearest, answered. She returned with a sealed note.

"A message for Augusta. From this Mammy Pleasant, do you think?" She weighed the envelope across her palm as if so she could guess the contents.

"That would be none of our business." I summoned my small authority, if I *did* have any authority. Truly it *was* none of our business and I did not like this avid curiosity on Victorine's part.

"Ah, but here is a mystery. And mysteries are delightful." Victorine now held the note between fingertips. "What a pity we cannot read this—"

I nearly feared at that moment, so mischievous was the glance she sent me, that she might indeed open it. But it seemed that even her curiosity did not lead that far. She went to Mrs. Deaves' room, tapped, and called, "A note for you, Augusta. There is an answer expected, a man is waiting for it."

So long a pause followed that I first thought Mrs. Deaves did not intend to answer. Then the door opened only wide enough for Victorine to slip the note within. But a few moments later Mrs. Deaves threw wide that door and sailed out, looking far from the hunted and haunted woman who had earlier taken refuge from us.

"Dear James! I might have known James Knight would do something like this." Her speech bubbled. "Teresa is here! James heard of my return, immediately hunted her up. Oh—to have Teresa with me again!"

She brushed past Victorine to fling open the outer door also. A man in groom's livery stood waiting.

"Please tell your master that of course Teresa must come to me. As soon as possible—no, let me write a note!"

Leaving the door open, she bustled to the desk by the window and seized upon a sheet of paper. Her pen scratched swiftly and she thrust the result into an envelope, went to hand it to the groom. When the door closed she rubbed her hands together.

"Things always work for the best after all—" I think she spoke her thought aloud. Then, as if remembering us, she added hurriedly, "An old friend is staying here. He chanced to see my name registered and has done me a great service. I had a maid before I left two years ago, one I greatly trusted. Unfortunately I was going abroad for an extended stay and she could not accompany me as her mother was ill and she did not want to leave her.

"But Mr. Knight met her by chance a week ago and she asked concerning me, since her mother is now dead and she wishes very much to return to my service. Oh, to have Teresa back again—with her I shall feel so safe!"

I think she realized that revelation the instant she uttered it for her expression was momentarily confused and she added hurriedly, "Teresa is one I can trust with everything." That sounded even more lame and she dropped the subject for another:

"Mr. Knight has asked me to dine with him. Since he had much to do with the settling of my late husband's estate, I must see him. Therefore I cannot be with you this evening."

She swept back into her room. As the door closed behind her Victorine gave a small laugh.

"Well enough! I think we can do without you, dear Augusta."

She went back to her favorite stand by the window.

"Tamaris, there is fog coming in again. Already the shops show lights and it is only early afternoon. Are there always such mists in this city?"

She was right, as I saw when I joined her. The gaslights of the shops were waging a losing battle against gathering mists.

"Tonight"—Victorine twisted one of the gilt tassels of the drapes—"there should be a full moon. But does one ever see the moon in this damp country?"

She waited for no answer; instead she caught me by the hand, drawing me back to the warm security of the room.

"Let us open all these." She gestured to the parcels and boxes which had been brought up from the carriage. "I want to see my treasures again."

Tissue paper flowed about us as we freed from wrapping scented gloves with embroidered backs, a parasol, lengths of silk which Victorine fingered lovingly.

"Amélie is very clever with her needle. She can use this—and some of that gauze, and these white roses—and put together such a dress! Yes, even that stern-faced brother of mine will have his heart moved to see me in it!"

"Mr. Sauvage is not hard-hearted!" Was it only duty which brought that protest out of me? "All of these are of his providing, Victorine."

She glanced at me, her head a little atilt, her lustrous eyes wide, a smile on her full lips.

"Yes, Alain is most generous." But there was a slight trace of mockery in her answer. "I must remember always to be truly thankful for his generosity. If I am not, then it is your duty, Tamaris, to remind me. And when he returns I shall thank him properly as a good sister should. You shall see!"

I thought it better not to enlarge upon the subject. Again she might well be trying to see how far my control over her extended. But I thought now, more than a little disturbed, that she was not yet ready to accept the family ties my employer wished to tighten. Perhaps there was more that I could do, or should have done. An older and wiser companion should have been chosen for this task.

Her smile widened. "Poor Tamaris, you are so easy to tease. I know well that Alain wishes me to be happy—within the limits of his own world. And this has been a good day. Me, I like San Francisco in spite of the fog. It is not Paris, but it has its own merits. See—I am surrounded by some of them now!"

Amélie appeared then and was overcome (or gave a rather theatrical performance of being so) as her mistress called her attention to this particular item or that. Seeing them so completely occupied, I went to my own room, with more than a little to trouble my mind.

CHAPTER FIVE

Of course I had been tempted to buy during the morning. And to hold to prudence can also leave one with a nagging feeling of dissatisfaction. Prices were high here and one could easily spend on trifles in one shopping tour more than my quarterly pay at Ashley Manor. I must conserve my resources, wasting nothing.

But that was of no account when weighed against the manner of Victorine herself. I must somehow reach her or I was not the mentor Mr. Sauvage needed—and if I discovered that was so I must admit my failure frankly and withdraw as soon as possible. Most of the time, in spite of her flashes of temper, she was amenable enough.

My unease had so little substantial to build on, still it lingered. Wait and see—but I firmly intended upon Mr. Sauvage's return to speak with him, state my doubts concerning my fitness for the responsibility he had given me.

As I turned away from placing my pelisse and hat in the wardrobe, my eyes fell upon my traveling lap desk. There was the journal letter for Madam Ashley. What I would not give now to step into her study and ask for advice. There was—I could not even explain certain formless, vague wishes to myself, and I must by all means avoid fruitless dreaming. My letter—it was unsatisfactory, for though it said so much, yet it revealed so little of what puzzled and disturbed me. But I would complete it now and mail it.

Only when I unlocked the desk, I knew once more my privacy had been invaded. The pages were not in order. My Morocco leather address book, the pearl-handled pen, the thin sheets of India paper suited for such long letters, the envelopes, the small crystal inkwell with the seal cover, wax, my father's own seal—all were here. Still I knew they must have been examined, perhaps even the letter read!

Catching that up I scanned the pages hurriedly. No, my suspicions had not been committed to paper. I had written only of the country and our day-by-day journey across it. There was nothing here that the whole world could not read. But to think that it might have been looked over in stealth angered me, with the same anger I had felt to find my family treasures had been examined.

I rang for Hattie. At least she could tell me who had been in this room during the morning.

But it was not Hattie who answered the bell. Though she was also a Negro, this maid was much younger, more assured, even pert, in her manner, regarding me boldly. I sensed, though I knew I could never prove it, that she was well able to play the spy.

"You wanted me, miss?"

Not only did her manner border on impudence, but her pretty face and lithe, well-shaped body could not be disguised by the coarse uniform she wore. She was a mulatto, I believed, and would be a match for any clumsy questioning I could try.

"Where is Hattie?"

"Hattie's gone." She watched me slyly, as if she expected some other question, perhaps about the desk. I decided it better not to ask any.

"What is your name?"

"I'm Submit, miss."

Suddenly I was inclined to laugh. That meek old Puritan name for this girl was a fantastic misfit.

"Very well, Submit. Will you please unhook me—"

In reality I did not want her touching me, but I had to have some reason for calling her. And I believed she was amused as she deftly unhooked and helped to draw off my heavily draped skirt.

She was perfect in her role, fast, neat, well trained in a maid's duties. When she went to hang my dress in the wardrobe, she clicked her tongue disparagingly and shook her head.

"That there Hattie, she never took no iron to these 'fore they was hung up. Best I do that, miss. The longer these here packing creases set, the harder it's goin' to be to get them out."

I nodded agreement. And the longer Submit moved purposefully about, commenting on this and that in what was now a respectful way, the more she seemed a lady's maid. My imagination had perhaps supplied all those reservations.

While she worked I finished my letter, sealed it. Submit, a selection of my dresses in her arms, left. And she was gone only a moment when there was a tap on my door and Mrs. Deaves entered.

Her hair was in disarray about her shoulders and she carried her brush in one hand as she walked up and down, disregarding my offer of a chair.

"If Teresa would only get here!" She held out the brush, eyeing it as if she were no longer sure how one used it. "She is so clever. Amélie is very good, of course, but her first duty is to Victorine and only Teresa knows just how I like things. Yet—"

Now she stopped to face me, plainly uncomfortable. "I—in spite of my wishes I must speak of something I do not want to mention. Only my duty makes me warn you."

Her self-confidence was once more shaken. Gone, for the moment at least, was that determination to keep me in my place. She began pacing again, her half-fastened wrapper billowing out to display much of her full figure. And her sentences were only half-finished, delivered breathlessly as if she had been running, or was pressed for time.

"It is about Mammy Pleasant. She—she is a fiend! What she has done—no, that I cannot tell you, I can only warn you. Do not have any dealings with her for the sake of your future, your peace of mind."

"But why should I have any dealings, as you express it, with this woman?"

She stopped pacing to face me once again, studying my face as if she were not quite sure what she dared say. But when she did speak her tone again held some of the old cool superiority.

"Exactly. She would have no reason to approach *you*. But she seeks power. It would be much to her interest to cultivate any member of the Sauvage household. I think she will try to reach Victorine. I shall alert Alain, of course. But until his return it is our duty to see that she does not meet his sister. The dear child is so impulsive she would be attracted by the bizarre—"

I made a logical guess. "Does this Mammy Pleasant profess to tell fortunes? Is that her form of gaining power?"

"That—and in other ways. Outwardly she makes a pretense of being a servant, a superior one. But there are those who know her better." Augusta Deaves moved her hands uncertainly. I believed she was torn between the need for warning and a fear which urged her to keep silent.

I knew she was afraid of the woman with the two-colored eyes. And thinking back to that meeting in the shop I was chilled. For Mrs. Smith had plainly been watching me. But my father had not considered her evil, and how could this woman he had dealt with be changed into the Mammy Pleasant of Mrs. Deaves' deep dread?

"Of course, I shall make every effort to keep Victorine from any such contact," I agreed.

She nodded. "But it is well that you will be going soon to Rancho del Sol, well away from this city. And—"

"Madame, there is someone to see you." Amélie came in. At the sound of her voice Mrs. Deaves flinched as if from a blow. But she went to answer the summons, and a moment later I heard her voice raised in warm welcome.

"Teresa! How good it is to see you! Oh, Teresa, I have so missed you—" Then the sound of a closing door brought silence.

I was left to consider her warning. Those who profess to tell fortunes, or those who (as the foolish believe) can summon up spirits, do exert strong influence over the gullible. But to believe that Mrs. Deaves had ever been so beguiled was hard for me to accept. She impressed me as one who intrigued coolly for what she desired, never taking an impulsive step. However, she was a badly shaken and frightened woman.

I did not know whether Victorine would be attracted by such superstitious nonsense; such matters had never been mentioned during our short acquaintance. And now on my guard I would make sure she did not fall victim to any such lure.

How I wished Mr. Sauvage were here! He had not mentioned either that this particular folly was to be encountered in San Francisco, and I needed his authority and knowledge to draw upon. That all cities had crimes and concealed horrors, usually hidden from the class of people I now moved among, I knew.

While my father had shielded me from the sordid life of the waterfronts in many ports, he had never mistaken, as was common, ignorance for innocence. He had, as delicately and carefully as he could, made plain to me that there were certain aspects of life which were both degraded and degrading, people who used vile, low practices to furnish their livelihood. There were streets in cities where a woman dared not walk unless she was already abandoned to wickedness. And vice did not just lurk in squalor either. It was to be found where the outer covering was as fair as in the most happy and innocent household.

Such matters were understood but not discussed. And as long as such a polite covering was maintained, society accepted the status quo. Perhaps in the future there might come a time of greater openness, so frankness and truth could combat evil. But that time was not ours.

I could understand that Victorine, heir to part of such a

great fortune as the Sauvages controlled, would be marked as fair game by someone intent on gain through crooked, ugly means. Yet in the natural order of the circle in which she moved those agents of the dark would not dare to prey openly.

Only my mind kept returning to Amélie, also to that dark figure in the mist-haunted ferry, to last night when Victorine had appeared to lie in a drugged sleep. To accept responsibility alone, I was not fitted for that. Let Mr. Sauvage return and he must decide what should be done. Mrs. Deaves' warning might carry more weight with him than the list of unexplained happenings I could offer.

They were old friends, perhaps more than friends. So, with his sister's safety at stake, she would be more open with him. And she was also right—the sooner we left this fog-bound city for his country estate, the better.

When I entered the parlor later the room was empty. Victorine and the fruits of her shopping had vanished into her own chamber. The door of that was open a crack, through which sounded a steady ripple of that patois I did not understand. I went to the nearest window.

The fog had thickened. Shivering, I drew my shawl closer about me. Perhaps I should ring for the waiter to light a hearth fire. The sight of the flames would be as cheering as the heat. As I moved toward the bell pull I saw the slip of white on the carpet near the door as if it had been pushed under from the hall.

My name was inscribed on the envelope in bold black script. Slipping out the single sheet it contained, I held that close to the nearest lamp.

To the daughter of Captain Jesse Penfold. Since I owe much to your father, I now take pen in hand to warn his daughter. That which you see may not be what it seems. Watch carefully and be cautious. Should you need a friend in the future, as I needed one in the past and found him, send word to Mrs. Pleasant at 92 Washington Street.

Mrs. Pleasant—Mammy Pleasant! I crumpled the note

into a ball, very glad no one was here to see. Memory to balance Mrs. Deaves' warning. If it were true, as I firmly believed, that Mrs. Smith and Mrs. Pleasant were one and the same, I was inclined in her favor. I needed guidance badly. If I only had someone to consult with now. Not Mrs. Deaves—I shrank from discussing this with her.

To allow her to know that in the past I had met with a woman she termed a "fiend" would only provide her with ammunition against me. I must know more—but to whom could I apply? My sex, age, position here were such that the slightest ripple of talk could raise a shadow of scandal. And eager tongues would give the shadow substance. I would serve neither Mr. Sauvage nor myself by raising gossip.

A tapping at the outer door set my heart to beating faster. Almost I could believe that it was the enigmatic Mammy Pleasant herself. But I opened upon one of the waiters, proffering a tray on which another note lay with a gentleman's card. And with distinct relief I read the name "Cantrell."

Though I knew nothing of this young man personally, Mr. Sauvage held him in high enough regard to select him as our escort during his own absence. And I had good reason to see him now to ask him to change my small roll of eastern bank notes into the coins accepted here.

"Ask Mr. Cantrell to come here." Since the note was addressed in both Victorine's name and mine, I felt I could take the liberty of issuing such an invitation.

I should summon Victorine, but I wanted a few moments alone with our caller. Dared I ask him some of the questions to the fore of my mind after I begged his aid in the matter of my funds? I would wait—see if I thought him discreet enough.

Retrieving my purse, I called in to Victorine. Amélie answered that her mistress was dressing, but she would give her the note.

My wait was not long. Mr. Cantrell's interest in Victorine had been marked from their first meeting; perhaps he thought my summons was from her. If he had, he was gentleman enough to display no surprise at my receiving him alone. I came to the point at once, citing Mrs. Deaves' warning about no merchant being ready to take bank notes.

He agreed that this was the case, and offered to turn out his own purse, exchange for me with what money he had on his person, and get the rest from a bank. But my hardly saved sum was so small he was able to cover most of it, laying out gold pieces and the heavier and larger silver coins on a table. When I thanked him, I decided recklessly to seek part answers at least to the questions now plaguing me.

"Mr. Cantrell, there is one question I have good reason to ask. In fact, I wish that I might ask this of Mr. Sauvage as it may be of major importance to him." I gathered my courage as he looked at me with a measure of surprise, as well he might.

Then I plunged. "Can you give me any information about a woman named Mrs. or Mammy Pleasant?"

Surprise in his expression turned to shock, followed by a blankness of countenance which might cover either distaste or wariness.

"Might I ask where you heard of this person, Miss Penfold?"

"I have reason to believe that we saw her today, that she was interested in us."

By the oblique hint that Victorine might be involved I had turned the right key. He nodded.

"Yes, that might be so. Very well, Miss Penfold, but remember what I have to say is largely rumor. This city is a storehouse of many strange stories, and people with very unusual pasts walk its streets. Mrs. Pleasant—outwardly—is a respected housekeeper for Mr. Milton Lanthen. In addition she owns and operates a boardinghouse for some of the highest-placed gentlemen. She has taken a great interest in and shown much sympathy for members of the Negro race.

"Before slavery was abolished she is known to have used certain provisions of California law to free slaves being returned against their will to the South. She contributed substantial funds to the Union cause during the war, and since then has set up freed slaves in various businesses—a laundry, a livery stable, a saloon, and the like. She runs an informal servant agency supplying all types of well-trained servants, not only to hotels, but also to private families."

"This all sounds as if she is an estimable person in every way. Yet your manner suggests that it is not entirely true," I observed.

"The rest is only rumor. She is reputed to have learned discreditable secrets of those people over whom she desires a measure of control. Thus she may bring pressure to bear to further her own ends. But, I repeat, that is the report of rumor. Truth is only what may be proved. However, I would not want any lady of my acquaintance to know Mrs. Pleasant."

"Thank you. Your frankness has been most helpful."

"There is one other thing." Now he seemed embarrassed, as if he were about to repeat something I would find absurd. "She is also spoken of as being a 'voodoo queen.' That is, I believe, a high priestess of some form of mumbo-jumbo—"

"Voodoo!" Such was indeed allied to fortune telling. Had not the Voodoo Queen of New Orleans, Marie Laveau, been supposed to foretell as well as curse? She I had heard of, and a woman of intelligence, retaining in her employ the uneducated and the superstitious, could profitably pretend to occult powers.

"But that is all nonsense, naturally," he added quickly. "And—"

Whatever more he would have said was lost as Victorine entered, a sheet of notepaper in her hand.

"Tamaris," she began eagerly, then, sighting Mr. Cantrell, she greeted him with a smile and addressed herself to him in one of those bursts of childish elation which sometimes made her seem younger than her years.

"Monsieur, for you to venture out on such an evening, even as the bearer of very good news—this is an act of true kindness. Why, outside it is already like night." She gave a delicate but slightly exaggerated shiver. Mr. Cantrell was already completely bemused.

"Amélie shall make us chocolate, such as I am sure you cannot find elsewhere in this foggy country, and you must drink a cup with us. A small reward for such good news! Only think, Tamaris, tomorrow we may flee this wet and dark! We are to go to my brother's home in the country. Mr. Cantrell is to escort us, which is very obliging of him. Now, is this not something to rejoice over?"

She was gay, as utterly charming as she could be when she wished, ushering our guest to a chair, calling to Amélie to make haste. Yet (I grew more and more certain that I knew her very little indeed) I had the impression that her signs of pleasure were all surface only and that she was not as happy as she would have us believe.

I do not imagine Mr. Cantrell found the chocolate as satisfying as Victorine promised. But, since it was she who had poured his cup, he manfully sipped at the sweet contents until Mrs. Deaves joined us.

She made a magnificent entrance (for all my dislike I could not deny that she was both handsome and imposing) in a velvet gown of a deep garnet shade, with a profusion of fringe and beaded trimming. Carrying her velvet cloak banded in fur, there came behind her a tall, thin woman of rather severe countencance.

Victorine's eyes widened in what I was sure was a mock awe.

"*Très chic, chère* Augusta. But before you leave you must hear our good news. My brother has at last sent a message. He wishes us to go to this Rancho del Sol tomorrow. Mr. Cantrell will escort us."

Plainly Mrs. Deaves did not find this news pleasing.

"But it is imperative that I remain in the city at least one day more—there is a matter of business," she protested.

"We understand, Augusta, as will Alain. He has said many times that he knew you could not devote all your days to me and my affairs once we came here. He does not expect such a sacrifice from you."

Victorine's eyelids dropped demurely but that she was watching Mrs. Deaves was also plain. That she enjoyed such concealed sparring I had already learned.

"We shall be very safe with Mr. Cantrell."

Mrs. Deaves hardly glanced at the young man who had arisen at her coming and now stood with chocolate cup in hand.

"I do not understand why Alain did not inform us directly—" the older woman began when Victorine interrupted.

"Oh, but he did, Augusta. He sent a telegram, which Mr. Cantrell delivered. It was addressed to me and to Tamaris, since, of course, we were the two most concerned. He did not mention you, doubtless because he knew you had your own affairs to attend to."

For all my dislike of Mrs. Deaves I was forced to admire her quick acceptance of the situation. Perhaps she did not yet realize the enmity which lay beneath Victorine's courtesy. But she made so instant a recovery that I thought only one well versed to twists of fortune in the past could do so.

Though she made a point of her own by claiming Mr. Cantrell's escort as far as the ladies' parlor below, and he had no excuse but to comply. Teresa draped her cloak about her shoulders, handed her her fan and evening handkerchief. Then without noticing us the maid stalked back into her mistress's chamber and closed the door firmly, just as the outer one shut behind Mrs. Deaves and Mr. Cantrell.

Victorine gave a gurgle of laughter. "How angry she is, our Augusta. Though she tries hard not to show it. She wanted to go with us, to move in as if she already has Alain's ring firmly around one of those fat fingers of hers. But that she will never have—never!"

She laughed again, in a different way. Not the carefree laughter of a young girl who had routed authority, rather a sound which carried anger. Then she changed the subject abruptly.

"What do you think, Tamaris, of this so stiff Monsieur

Cantrell? That he ever tasted chocolate before I cannot believe. But he was too polite to make an ugly face. He is rather like a bear, I think, a big, clumsy bear walking on hind feet. When my brother says 'Up—do this—do that!' he obeys."

Her voice trailed into silence. Then she added in a return of her childish voice, "Tamaris, do not pull your face so—" She achieved an expression of prim outrage which made me smile against my will. "You think I say improper things, such as a *jeune fille,* one of your 'finished' young ladies, would not. But I am me, Victorine! I cannot be cut and trimmed, pushed in, pushed out, to be the proper young lady. I can only be myself." There was a serious note in that such as I had not heard from her before. "I *must* be myself!"

She put down her cup with force enough to produce a sharp click as the china met the silver tray. Then she went to the window.

"A full moon, there should be a full moon tonight. Yet I can see nothing but this fog, this stifling fog! I think I do not like this city."

The intensity of her tone made me uneasy.

"You will be leaving tomorrow," I reminded her.

Victorine presented a puzzle which grew more complex with every hour I knew her. At times she was like the girls I had taught, though she always lacked much of their silliness. On other occasions she became another person, and it was with that one I was uneasy.

However, she might be happy in the thought that here society was more fluid, did not erect barriers too quickly. The criteria they themselves imposed was that those who had arrived in the 1840s and 50s were "founding fathers" if they prospered.

A dearth of women during that period had led to some strange mésalliances which would never have been accepted in the East. There were women now wearing too many diamonds, driving in too opulent carriages, who had held menial—and even less mentionable—stations in life.

The wealth they paraded before each other's eyes was often ephemeral. A mine's rich yield could fail, other chances reduce the wealth of a millionaire within months or weeks. So here was a society where the having—and holding—of money was the measuring stick.

Victorine came from another background, but of a society (even though it might not have been entirely respectable by American standards) which was so old as to be decadent. She was different but here her difference might not matter so much and she could march confidently ahead, or maybe in the raw newness she might unwittingly invite disaster. It was my responsibility to see that the latter did not happen, though I felt as if I myself needed compass bearings.

"Let us order dinner, Tamaris." She came away from the window. "That fog—it crowds against the pane. Amélie—" At her call the maid appeared. "Light the lamps, please, all of them. I do not like the fog."

I saw to it no champagne was served with our meal. And that the wine Victorine considered a necessary part of any meal was only a light one. She smiled as we sat down.

"No champagne? But, Tamaris, in San Francisco everyone drinks that. However"—she leaned over to pat the back of my hand with her fingertips—"this night I shall be good. Were you, Tamaris, in that school of yours always so strict and stern? Tell me again about the school, and how you first lived on the ship."

Victorine made such amusing comments, was so much her amiable self, that I began to believe, with Mrs. Deaves removed, I could establish a firm base for a friendship. And I pushed my worries to the back of my mind with hopes that there they would fade into nothingness.

My companion went early to bed and I sought my own chambers, taking with me some magazines, for I was not sleepy. Victorine had been right, I saw, looking out of the window. The fog pressed against the panes, in truth, like some soft beast striving to get in. That morbid thought brought a shiver with it as I let the draperies fall again.

CHAPTER SIX

That thick mist appeared to muffle sound. In my chamber only the ticking of the clock broke the silence. And that quiet had a heavy, oppressive quality, smothering—pushing my thoughts into dark corners.

I sought sleep which did not come, reading words without comprehending. Slowly I became aware that I was listening—though for what I did not know. Finally I pushed aside the magazines and arose, a little bewildered. I had heard of second sight, but that night I had the feeling I stood on the edge of a vast dark pool into which some unseen, un-understood menace sought to push me.

As I fought my nerves, strove to control my imagination, there came a sound louder than the clock's steady ticking—the soft closing of a door in the parlor beyond.

My own door stood slightly ajar or I would not have heard that. Now I opened it yet farther so I could view a shortened vista of the parlor. By the hall door, hand on knob, stood a figure wearing one of the long waterproof cloaks. This could not be Teresa, she was much taller; and Mrs. Deaves, I was sure, had not yet returned.

The cloak fell back a fraction and I caught a flash of vivid yellow. That was the color of one of Victorine's dresses which Mrs. Deaves had ruled far too strident to be worn. Victorine so dressed, and stealthily making an exit!

Even as I moved to intercept her she slid around the hall door in a manner which could only be described as furtive. I could not pursue her into a public corridor wearing only a wrapper over a nightgown, and could I really be sure it *was* Victorine?

I looked into her chamber. The night lamp burned and I knew instant relief when I saw the bed occupied. Though the sleeping girl had her head turned away. But

71

there was no mistaking the dark hair straying from under the lace-bordered nightcap. Then who——?

Amélie! Amélie wearing one of her mistress's dresses, probably bound for some disreputable rendezvous. At last I would have the proof I needed to remove such an influence from Victorine's life.

And I determined to wait for the maid's return so I could confront her. I heard Mrs. Deaves come in, but I did not try to talk to her. Unless I could make my influence felt by Victorine unaided, I was a failure in my present position of trust, and Mr. Sauvage would have to find someone better qualified.

As the night wore on wearily, so did my thoughts become darker. At the soft chime of one from the clock I perceived the flaw in my plan. Amélie might not return here at all. Her quarters were not with us, but among those provided for maids of the visitors. She might only have come for the dress, thinking to smuggle it back unseen in the morning during the flurry of our packing—and again I would have no proof.

I paced the chilly room, fighting sleep. When the hands on the clock pointed to one-thirty and I was wavering like one drunk, I knew I was lost. Instead I must watch tomorrow for the return of the dress. As I stumbled to bed I tried to plan coherently, but a fog of sleep, as thick as the mist against the windows, swallowed me.

A sharp rapping brought me awake. It took me a moment to realize where I was and there were the bright lines of daylight around the edges of the window shades. Stumbling, I reached the door.

"Tamaris? Are you ill?" Victorine faced me with what I believed was real concern. "It is so late. We feared there was something wrong—"

Late? I was fully roused. Of course, we were supposed to leave for the country this morning! But I had never overslept before. And, if Victorine was as ready to go as her dress implied, her packing must already be done. I had had no chance to look for the yellow gown.

"Mr. Cantrell will be here in less than an hour." Mrs. Deaves, looking as heavy-eyed as I felt, appeared behind

Victorine. "Surely, Miss Penfold, you realize the importance of being ready?"

"Poof—what does time matter?" Victorine broke in. "Take all the time you need, Tamaris. I shall order those rolls you like, and some coffee while you dress. Do not worry about packing; Amélie is very accomplished and she will see to that. We cannot take our trunks in the carriage anyway—they are to follow. But Mr. Cantrell promises they shall be there as soon as we are."

She closed the door before I could refuse Amélie's assistance. And I was forced to admit that if I handled my own packing I would delay our departure. Why had I not attended to some of this last night when I tried to keep that useless vigil? Was I losing the practical good sense I had always prided myself on possessing? Pride, as we know, is a sin.

Amélie brought in a breakfast tray and straightway set about working to fill my trunk and bag, working swiftly, expertly. She offered to dress my hair or otherwise assist in my toilet, but this I refused. When I had finished my rolls, hooked the last fastening on my bodice, she had made more headway than I could have thought possible, pausing once to suggest the taking of the heavier of my two jackets as the day was chill.

It was not the barouche waiting for us this time. Rather a five-glass landau providing more room for a lengthy drive. Victorine was handed to the seat of first choice in the right-hand rear, I took the left, and Mr. Cantrell sat facing us, his back to the horses. There was no sign of fog as the carriage moved through crowded streets, giving way to horse-car and dray when necessary. In turn we were trailed by a larger and less elegant vehicle transporting our luggage under Amélie's guardianship.

The morning was pleasant, though cold. Thus we were glad of the white fur rug over our knees, the velvet foot cushions between our boots and the floor. Mr. Cantrell pointed out sites of interest as we passed. At first Victorine attended to him, then her eyelids began to droop as if her night had been no more restful than mine. But I remained alert enough to give him polite heed.

We stopped at posting stations at intervals for changes of horses. Each new team led out, Mr. Cantrell explained, was of Mr. Sauvage's own stable, kept there with groom paid by him for just such service. So our pace was as swift and steady as the nature of the road allowed. If San Francisco had tried to smother us with fog, the country of the Rancho del Sol, I discovered, presented just the opposite, a blaze of sun.

Though the name of the humble ranch buildings which had once stood on the site had been retained, the edifice now occupying that site was far different. I had seen some of the ancient and beautiful chateaux in Europe, and in addition those manors erected along the Hudson River a hundred years earlier—also the impressive mansions now rising in New York. But this sprawling compound of many styles, all ostentatious and opulent, was such I could not find words to describe it.

On the first morning under its roof we trailed through many rooms, the housekeeper, Mrs. Landron, manifestly taking pride in what she had to display. I already knew that the "rancho" was not of Mr. Sauvage's building. Rather it was the magniloquent expression of one Harvery Pickering, a gold-rich Forty-niner, who had apparently given a captive architect instructions to produce to the last fantastic detail some weird dream.

When fever carried Mr. Pickering away from its forty rooms, a sad discovery followed. To the wrath of his heirs all his estate was the house and the land into which he had poured his wealth. Since an enterprise in which Mr. Sauvage had a major part held the mortgage on the estate, it so passed into the hands of a new owner.

We began our tour eagerly, praising here, uttering the proper exclamations of astonishment and gratification there. But the smothering luxury piled upon luxury soon raised in one only the desire to escape—get away from these miles of marble or polished floors, the league upon league of velvet drapery, of walls covered with silk or painted murals.

There was a Pompeian room and a Chinese room which (except for some treasures of oriental art displayed far too

close together to enhance their clean beauty) was very
much the idea of the "Chinese" entertained by someone
who had never visited that venerable country.

A white and gold parlor possessed not one but two rock
crystal chandeliers, display cabinets of rosewood lined
with rose velvet to hold such a medley of precious trinkets
it would take weeks to make any pretense of seeing them
all.

Walls in another room were painted with a mural of ter-
races and ruins. That was the breakfast parlor, opening in
turn into a glass-enclosed veranda fitted, Mrs. Landron
told us, with proper reverence, with hot-water pipes to
maintain a constant semitropical heat and offering a shel-
tered walk with a conservatory of strange plants and
flowers and an aviary of birds as beautiful as if flowers had
broken from some stems and winged about.

There were too many marvels, far too many. I was
overwhelmed into silence. Even Victorine gave few
glances about her. Finally, when we were shown a very
masculine library, she said, "This is indeed of great mag-
nificence, madame. We are left speechless. And my
brother must be pleased, it is all so well kept."

Mrs. Landron radiated pride. "Mr. Sauvage has always
been satisfied."

"How can he be otherwise?" Victorine smiled. "But it is
just so very much!"

"Rancho del Sol is a very well-appointed gentleman's
residence," Mrs. Landron replied complacently. I thought
she looked upon this splendor possessively, as, being its
first guardian, she had become in a measure also its
owner.

Yet to me it was a jumbled mansion, a series of tasteless
showrooms rather than a home. There were so many
rarities that their numbers destroyed the beauty they
would have provided for the eyes had they been fewer
and better placed.

As we stood in the center hall above which, two stories
high, curved a dome of golden glass to provide a counterfeit sun glow, Victorine fingered the robe of a marble

figure, nymph or goddess, who held high a torch to illuminate the first steps of the grand staircase.

"I am so vey tired," she said in that tone that usually foretold one of those languid periods of hers—which I was not yet sure were the result of real physical fatigue or her expression of boredom. "I think that—"

She was interrupted by one of the footmen appearing with a salver on which rested two cards. Visitors—

Victorine lifted the top card. "Mrs. Arthur Beall," she read, then she glanced to the second. "Mr. Henry Beall. Who may these people be?"

She sounded petulant and I gave her a warning glance. If she had listened at all to Mrs. Deaves' gossip she would remember that the Bealls were the nearest neighbors (if they might be termed so when miles of the two estates lay between us). We must be civil, no matter how inopportune their visit.

"They are our neighbors, remember what Mrs. Deaves said?" Before Mrs. Landron I could not be frank about my charge assuming the role of her brother's hostess. I had yet to see Victorine in the society of her peers and I hoped no whim or carelessness would complicate her local acceptance.

"But, of course. You will show them to the White Drawing Room, if you please. So very kind and thoughtful of them to bid us welcome. Come, Tamaris, let us not keep our first guests waiting."

I sighed with relief. Morning calls never lasted long. And perhaps she was also aware of the need for making a good first impression.

We reached the White Drawing Room only a few seconds before our guests were ushered in. Mrs. Beall was in advance, accompanied by Mrs. Landron herself, with whom she exchanged some pleasantry about the weather. She was a woman of early middle age, but one who used every artifice known to preserve the remains of what must have been truly startling beauty.

Her elaborately dressed hair was of that bright auburn shade decreed to be most handsome for this season, though her skin showed a matte complexion which is more often combined with dark locks. By the left corner of her mouth was a single beauty spot, drawing attention to the ripe, promising curves of her lips.

For she was one of those rare women who, without in the least losing any dignity of manner, exude a physical charm which we as a sex are not supposed to note or admit exists. I have seen only a few women who have it, but with Mrs. Beall it was noticeable and—to me—slightly repellent.

"Miss Sauvage?" She looked from one of us to the other, seeking the daughter of the house.

Victorine did not answer. A glance in her direction instantly disturbed me. She was very pale—had her plea of being tired really been true? She stood by a chair, her hand resting on its back as if she needed some support to steady her. I watched her fingers tighten on the carved wood until the knuckles stood out in knobs. And I had already taken a step, fearing she was about to faint, when she spoke.

"But, of course, you would not know." She laughed and to me that sound was forced. "I am Victorine Sauvage, and this is my friend, Miss Tamaris Penfold." She flashed a smile in my direction so fleeting it was as if she did not see me at all.

"Miss Sauvage, Miss Penfold," Mrs. Beall acknowledged the introduction. "May I present my stepson Henry—"

She had stressed that "step," maybe for the best of reasons. For anyone who wished to cling to the semblance of youth could not have acknowledged this hearty young man as her own.

Hearty he was, thick through shoulders and neck, with a red, full face, and hair so fair that his eyebrows and lashes appeared almost white. He did not seem the type to be paying morning calls, attending ladies in a drawing room. I could better picture him out in some hay field, his shirt sleeves well rolled up those heavy muscular arms. This scion of the Beall name, for all his superfine clothes, was lumpish and awkward. How unlike Mr. Sauvage. Broadcloth and linen did not become my employer too well either, but in the western dress he still possessed authority and dignity. Henry Beall had neither.

He made all the proper responses, conducted himself correctly if stiffly. His eyes, after one sweep over me, never left Victorine. And there was something not too likable in the way he watched her. However, judging by the response of Mr. Cantrell and this young Beall, Victorine might well be the belle of the coming season.

The Bealls did not linger, remaining exactly the correct time, wishing us a pleasant stay in the country with all the conventional polite phrases, suggesting further meetings when we were settled in. But, I noted, Mrs. Beall did not push such vague invitations; it was her stepson who repeated suggestions of future pleasurable outings.

After they had left, Victorine put her hand to her head. "I fear, Tamaris, that I am going to have one of my bad heads." She pushed aside her fringe of bangs, her fingertips pressing against her temples and she did look ill. "The pain is getting worse. I must go and lie down, and Amélie will make me a tisane. No"—she waved me away— "there is nothing you can do, Tamaris. Always I have had these, they come and they go. I know what must be done to help."

Nevertheless I saw her to her bedchamber and rang for Amélie. The maid came so quickly she might have been expecting such a summons, hovered over her mistress with soothing words in the patois. Upon Victorine's insistence that she would now do well enough, I departed to my own suite.

Victorine's room had been all rose satin, a crystal chandelier, a boudoir fit for a fairy-tale princess. But my own rooms, bedchamber, small sitting room, bath, made me uncomfortable. I longed for the neat simplicity, the uncluttered ease of my chamber at Ashley Manor. Here the walls were covered with white silk, topped with a painted fringe of mauve wisteria. There was a white fur hearth rug, all the furniture gilt and upholstered in padded mauve velvet. To me it was all show and no homey comfort.

I had found only one thing to welcome me, perhaps

because it was not new, and rich only in time-dimmed beauty. One wondered by what chance it had found its way here.

It was a worktable of papier-mâché such as was in fashion when my mother was a girl, decorated with an oriental pattern picked out with gold and mother-of-pearl in a design of long-tailed birds and exotic flowers. Since I had arrived I had lifted its lid several times, examining with pleasure the many compartments where some of the original fittings, small carved reels for silks, a matching needlebox, another probably meant to contain beads or pins, were tucked neatly away.

Now surfeited with all the gilt and velvet, I went to that and lifted the lid once more. But—there was something new within, lying almost under my hand.

That one did occasionally use wax to keep very fine thread from tangling, I was well aware, but I had never seen such a sewing aid as this one.

Slowly and reluctantly I worked the small object out of the compartment. In size it was hardly more than the length of my little finger and it had certainly never been made from the clear beeswax usually used for such a purpose. It could have been a miniature candle, for there was a tuft of wick at one end. In shape it had been very rudely molded into a human figure. A ball of head was at one end and indentations outlined arms and legs. In color it was a dull and dirty yellow. And I was sure I had not seen it before.

To the touch it had an oily, greasy feel and I closed the lid on it hurriedly. My innocent pleasure in the table was spoiled. Every time I looked at it now I could not forget that nasty little image and I went to wash my hands vigorously because I had touched it.

Two days later the house which had been a cold museum of all money could buy came alive. I felt a kind of warmth as I gazed into the mirror above my dressing table which had seemed too perfect for mundane use. All because the master had returned. And with his person Alain Sauvage negated the stiff formality, subdued the lavish display, imposed his positive self-confidence everywhere.

My early years since my birth on ship in a harbor of the Sandwich Islands had been spent in a masculine world. For my mother died two days after I was born and my father, producing Mama Lalla, had kept me with him, much to the consternation of the American women in the Islands. I was beginning to remember, after a half-lifetime of fiitting myself as best I could into the ultra-feminine world of young ladies' schools, how men were free. My swift uprooting from Brussels when the coming of war threatened the sea-lanes had been so ruthless and complete a change that perhaps it shocked something inside me, and in that state of shock I had been docile enough to accept other standards, the very confining ones of feminine society, the rules of which I now lived by. Young ladies must be kept away from the world of action lest the precious bloom (which was really ignorance instead of innocence) be destroyed.

I had buried very deep within me my own real self, learning to conform because that was necessary for one in my position. And I was realistic enough to understand that my father's death, the loss of his ship, made that position precarious. Had not Madam Ashley taken me on as instructoress I would have been lost indeed.

Now Mr. Sauvage opened once again a small window into the world of action. He was the only man with outstanding force of character to come into my own narrow world since my father had died. I told myself that this shaken feeling I experienced when he entered a room where I was, or spoke to me, was not founded on any real preference. Yet he changed the world as far as I was concerned. I schooled my emotions fiercely, even as I had in the past hidden grief and loss. I must summon common sense to give me the serenity one in my position must possess.

And that struggle made me believe that perhaps my best solution was to get away, leave even this country where everything was too lavish, too overpowering, as overpowering as the masses of flowers brought in each morning, the heavy velvet and gilt, the marble and mirrors.

The latest cause of uneasiness was the maid Fenton, now busied in the room behind me. I no longer had privacy even in my own quarters. Suddenly this morning I needed freedom, if only for a little while. Victorine made a practice of sleeping late. I arose unfashionably early, so I had at least an hour of my own.

I thrust the last pin into my coil of hair. Fenton had offered the services of a curling iron, but a crimped forehead fringe and the smell of singed hair was not for me.

The drapery of my poloniase puffed out over my thicker underskirt, but the dress was not as burdensome as more fashionable wear. I caught up my shawl and decided on an early stroll in the garden.

By now I had learned the geography of this massive pile well enough to reach a side door and come into the freshness of the day, where the lovely lace of new-hung spiderwebs was still strung between rose bushes. Rancho del Sol? That name made me smile.

Such a name for this mansion was preposterous. Surely its builder had had no sense of humor when he retained the name of the humbler building he had torn down to erect his own dream of a palace. I wished that I could have seen the original rancho. California must have had some history before the coming of the gold seekers—did any vestige of that remain?

"You find this prospect amusing, Tamaris?"

Startled, I gasped and turned. Mr. Sauvage stood a little to my right. How he had appeared so silently puzzled me. He was bareheaded, and in the early morning his thick black hair showed a glint near blue. Again he wore a handkerchief tied carelessly about his throat, and on his feet were not the riding boots I expected, but softer footgear similar to that I had seen worn by the Indian beggars during our cross-country trip. Save that these did not cover the feet only, but extended well up the calf, laced with thongs, and they had pointed, slightly upturned toes.

He was so vividly *alive!* Perhaps I stared too obviously,

as he did not wait for me to answer his question, but thrust forth a foot to display it better.

"Savage wear for a Sauvage. These are Apache boots, better for a long ride than our own. Now, Tamaris, tell me what you find so amusing about this rose garden that you stand here smiling."

Perhaps it was the use of my given name, which had never happened before, that brought me to truthful boldness.

"I was, forgive me, sir, amused at the idea of calling such a stately house as this a 'ranch.' For I understand those are of a rather rough style."

He laughed. "One of our anachronisms, Tamaris. Yes, Rancho del Sol hardly suits, does it? Unfortunately the ranch is a map landmark of long standing, so it seemed wise to continue the name. Tell me, what do *you* think of it?"

I was flustered by his intent stare. How could I say to the master of all this that I had reservations concerning the taste, the overwhelming grandeur, the formality of all those rooms and halls? I hesitated. Of course I could fall back on those phrases I had murmured in answer to Mrs. Landron during the grand tour. But I knew that I could not be false, even in the smallest degree, to this man.

"It is very large—"

Alain smiled first with his eyes, I discovered, before any curve of his firmly set lips showed.

"Honesty is the best policy, Tamaris, I see you have learned that. Yes, it is very large, and it is a treasure house, and it has every possible comfort known to man at the time of its building. But I will share a secret with you—I would gladly change it for the house which once stood here and was near to a hundred years older."

"I wish I could have seen it—" The old house, simple, strong, a part of the land—how did I know all that?

"There are still a few of the old places which have not yet been wiped from the earth so a rich man can have his fancies. We shall go and see one someday."

A queer weakness was growing in me. I had the greatest desire to rest my fingertips on his arm as I had at our

first meeting when he had escorted me to meet his sister.
Another part of me fought that desire fiercely. I *must*
control such strange, wandering thoughts, be the correct
Miss Penfold he employed.

"I fear I am keeping you, sir, you were about to go
riding?" My voice was stiff with control.

"I have been riding. You may think you have risen
early, but in the country some days begin at dawn.
Which"—he squinted up into the morning sky—"is now
some hours behind us. Now I am ready for breakfast—
what about you?"

His fingers closed gently on my arm just above the elbow and drew me forward.

CHAPTER SEVEN

"But this is not the way to the house—"

"You shall discover that there is more than one place in
which one may breakfast. Now Victorine and Augusta pre-
fer to be served in bed. Though on occasion they may come
yawning to the table. But they miss some of the small
pleasures of life—"

I knew that I was disobeying every rule of proper decorum as I allowed myself (though I really had very little to
say in the matter) to be led along a walk bordered by rose
bushes, under an arch cut through the thick body of a
hedge, and so into a small wilderness where stood a small
octagonal summerhouse.

Within was a table spread with a red and white checked
cloth like that of a farm kitchen. And the plates and cups
were not Havilland, but brown and irregularly shaped as
if made by hand. On a neighboring and smaller table were
covered dishes.

"But you are waiting for a guest—" I caught my
breath, and took tight rein on that too-heady sense of
freedom, drawing on common sense, also that virtue which

had been drilled into me for the last half of my life—prudence.

"A guest—you, Tamaris. Learning you seem to be addicted to early-morning rising and walking through the dew, I thought I would be lucky and catch you—which I did!" He laughed.

I thought to him this was merely an amusing adventure, no more than a picnic in the woods. If it could only be so for me! I yearned at that moment for that youthful irresponsibility I had tasted so fleetingly in my venture into the rose garden.

But I had been too long schooled to the knowledge that one was judged in the world not by intent but by outward appearances. The servants who had brought this food, any who might have seen our coming, could and would use their tongues. Invention would lead such witnesses to embroider with "facts" that did not exist. On such a seemingly innocent meeting as this reputations had foundered. I held fiercely to my common sense and training.

In that world where Augusta Deaves lived, a blown-upon reputation was past saving. She herself would need only a suggestion—that I perhaps had made a rendezvous for a "secret" meeting with my employer—to damn me. Prudence must win—not only for my own sake but because of Victorine.

"A pleasant thought, sir, and a kind one." I wondered if my tone sounded as false to him as it did to me. "But you must understand I cannot take advantage of your generous and good nature. How could I play companion to your sister if my conduct caused any whisper? And be sure"—my tension and anger perhaps now made my speech more vehement, anger not at him (for gentlemen are not apt to see the pitfalls among which a lone woman walks carefully in conventional society), but at that society itself which would forbid such a treat—"that my staying would lead to whispers. Men, Mr. Sauvage, are free to do much, indulge their whims and fancies, and enjoy small breaking of the rules. Women are not."

"I did not think that Captain Penfold's daughter would be so missish." His face had turned wooden, expressionless.

"It is because I am Captain Penfold's daughter, sir, that I abide by the rules of proper conduct, even as he did his duty. Petty though such may be, they *are* the discipline a woman must live by. You cannot say 'this may not be done' to others unless you are willing yourself to obey. Since you wish me to companion your sister into society, I must make a special effort to abide by the rules. I am young for the position you have given me, sir, and so must be doubly careful. I can do nothing which, innocent and pleasant as it may be, might lead to gossip. You have engaged me for a purpose and I would not be doing my duty should I disregard it for my own enjoyment."

He had leaned back against a tree, and was measuring me with a look I could not interpret. Though I felt as if I were a strange creature he must classify. Then he shrugged.

"Very well, Miss Penfold. Stern duty it is then. And I shall not ask you again to do anything which will endanger your social acceptance."

He bowed and went abruptly into the summerhouse. His cold formality was that of our first meeting. But that was as proper. I should be grateful; instead I was weighed down by a desolation I could not understand—or did not want to examine too closely.

I went back down the path sure I was right, but no glow of duty upheld warmed me. Instead I felt forlornly alone and, by the time I reached the house, I was fighting tears, so fled to my own suite in haste. Missish I must indeed seem to him. But what did men understand of gossip and how dire it could be? That I had done the right thing I knew, but I was desperately unhappy. Out of all proportion to the incident, I tried to tell myself.

Luckily Fenton had gone and I was able to cry in peace. Though I am not usually one who reacts with tears. In my position those are a luxury not to be indulged in too often, or too long. What if Victorine were to make one of her sudden entrances and demand why I wept?

I had again gained full command of myself when there was a rap on the door and to my surprise Fenton issued

in a footman carrying a tray, which he put down on a
small table she hastened to clear.

The salver bore a bowl, not crystal but actually carved
of ice, and about its rim lay a loose wreath of ivory-tinted
rosebuds. Within were heaped strawberries under a sifting
of finely shaved ice which formed a frost over them. Beside
this was a compote of Belleek, as ivory and perishable as
the roses, fashioned in the form of a fluted shell supported
by seahorses. This contained a mound of powdered sugar.
But there was also a goblet of opaque green and white
glass. Into that the footman poured a small measure of
champagne.

"Fenton—what is this?" I hoped I showed no signs of
my recent indulgence in tears.

Fenton's solid features cracked into a smile.

"The master, miss, chancing to meet me, asked how
you enjoyed your breakfast. I ventured to reply that you
had not, to my knowledge, eaten. He ordered this prepared that you might see what was offered to ladies at
Saratoga last summer. You being from the East, he thought
you might enjoy it. I believe, miss, you dip the strawberries either into the sugar or the champagne."

Did he mean this in subtle mockery? But still I felt a
new warmth in me. Could it instead be a peace offering, a
very generous one? I was going to believe it did signify a
measure of goodwill once more between us.

"What an unusual idea. And so very thoughtful of Mr.
Sauvage. Thank you, Harlett."

I dipped a berry into the sugar, crushed it tart-sweet in
my mouth. I would even try one christened in champagne.

But by afternoon my happy mood faded. I had reminded Victorine that we must return the Bealls' call.
During the past two days she had advanced one excuse
after another, the main one being that she did not feel
well. But she could not disdain social duties forever, so,
pouting, she set out with me in the victoria.

"These so silly cards." She adjusted her parasol, glanced
pettishly at the case in her lap. "Such a stupidity. One
for me, and one for Alain, though he is not with us at all.
Why that?"

"Because," I answered patiently, though I was well aware she meant to annoy, "he is the master of the house and is now in residence."

"In residence! Such formality. Tamaris, did you always know all this, what to wear, what to do? To me it is a very boring game which never comes to an end. What if someone, sometime, broke all these petty rules, spoke as she pleased, did as she wished—what would happen then?"

I thought of that morning when I had been so grievously tempted to do just that.

"It has been done." And perhaps I spoke sharply because of that memory. I added a warning: "Afterwards the consequences were not very pleasant for the one who refused her role in the play."

"What happened? Was it just that she no longer had to make these card-carrying visits?"

"She was not invited to parties which were neither boring nor stupid. Young gentlemen have mothers and sisters who abide by the rules and keep them."

"Stepmothers," she corrected me with a giggle. "Beside this bear-man, this Henry Beall—I do not think him so young. He is too big, too thick—" With her free hand she gestured to suggest Henry Beall's imperfections. "Altogether he is *not* to my taste."

"Perhaps that is so. But you will meet others more to your liking."

Victorine sighed. "I hope that is true, for I am finding this a most wearying afternoon."

She had been so right, I thought ruefully, as we drove away from Fairlawns, having only left our cards at the door.

"So this stepmother is ill," Victorine commented. "We ride through dust and heat just to lay cards on a tray held out to us. Me, I do not believe she is ill at all, she is only more sensible than we are. She wishes to take a little nap, to rest herself, so she says 'My head, it aches. Do not admit anyone foolish enough to call. Say I am ill.' Well, she now has those so important cards and we need not come again."

What Victorine considered a distasteful and wasted

afternoon was not yet at an end. As our carriage entered the drive we sighted a traveling coach before the main entrance of the rancho and Mr. Sauvage handing out Mrs. Deaves.

There came a wrathful mutter from Victorine. "Again that one! Tonight two candles shall I—" she paused nearly in mid-word and then continued: "See how she regards him, as a snake eyes a small and helpless rabbit put into its cage—"

Victorine's analogy was startling. That the larger reptiles have such disgusting ways of feeding, one knows. But she spoke with the familiarity of one who had witnessed such an enormity.

"Tamaris—I swear to you, that one shall never rule here!" She lapsed into French, which she seldom did now. And I had come to know that such a lapse was a matter of either temper or distress.

Still, as our victoria came to a halt, and we alighted in turn, she was all smiles. Tripping lightly forward, she offered Mrs. Deaves the feminine greeting of cheek against cheek. She might have been longing to see her so-dear Augusta as she addressed the visitor.

It was apparent that Mr. Sauvage was as pleased with the new arrival as his sister pretended to be. And we entered the great hall a united party, no matter how separated our thoughts.

I had one flight of fancy when we gathered in the White Drawing Room that evening after dinner.

Augusta Deaves played the pianoforte and Victorine sang some pretty French songs. But what would happen if we were suddenly laid under some spell which would make us reveal our innermost thoughts, concealed now by polite conversation?

The next morning I awakened with a sense of loss. There had been a swiftly faded dream I could not cling to, only I knew that in it I had been happy. As I sat up I thought I knew the reason for dreaming. This was my birthday—though none now living save Madam Ashley would remember. She had always had a tea on this date for me. And, while my father was still alive, there had been a box of small gifts, a treasured letter.

Now there was no one to care. Self-pity was wrong. As penance for that I would allow Fenton to perform the duties of a lady's maid as she wanted to. A good resolve which I discovered was not too much of a cross after all.

To my relief she did not again suggest a curling iron, but put up my dark brown hair very skillfully, with a finish I could never myself achieve. And with Mrs. Deaves here I wanted to look my best—the feminine armor we all don from time to time.

Fenton had laid out a dress of silver gray, banded with soutache braid of a violet shade. And somehow that gave my spirits another lift.

"The master said to tell you, miss"—Fenton gave a settling twitch to the wide bow of violet velvet just above the swell of bustle and drapery at my back—"that breakfast for the family will be in the Green Room this morning."

Heartened by the thought—I did present my best face to the world—I went downstairs. Strawberries in ice again? I hardly thought so.

But another surprise did await me. Victorine sat there and Mr. Sauvage arose to escort me with some ceremony to a chair before which on the table was not only a bouquet of those ivory rosebuds, but several packages wrapped in tissue and tied with colored ribbons.

"You look so astonished, Tamaris." Victorine laughed. "Did you believe we would forget your feast day?"

"But—how did you know?" I felt a little flustered as I seated myself.

"Alain knows everything. How *did* you know, Alain?"

"There is very little about Captain Penfold and his family I do not know since we owe so much to him. The date of a birthday is very easy to learn."

His sister nodded. "Now, Tamaris, you must open your gifts and guess which are from Alain and which from me."

My hands were a little unsteady. It was so unexpected. My father had always made an occasion of this day and now it was almost as if he were close to me, sharing in my excitement. Such special thought for my pleasure was something I had never expected.

My first choice proved to be a richly bound volume of Mrs. Browning's verse. With it in hand I bowed my appreciation to Mr. Sauvage. Victorine clapped her hands.

"The first guess and it is right!"

"Of course." He smiled at me. "Do you not realize, Victorine, that a proper young lady may accept only an edifying book or perhaps a box of bonbons from a gentleman? One abides by the rules." There was no note of challenge in his voice, yet a little of my happiness was dulled. Was he being sarcastic?

Quickly I chose a second package, to find a carved sandalwood box I recognized as one Victorine had bought in the Chinese Bazaar. Within, on a bed of cotton, lay a heart carved of crystal strung on a velvet ribbon. I was enchanted with the pretty trifle, and at Victorine's bidding, fastened it about my throat to admire the way it rested on the frill of my net chemisette.

The third package contained Mr. Sauvage's bonbons. But they were contained in no ordinary box, rather nested in a filigree casket of octagonal shape with an enameled butterfly (so real-appearing one might expect it to flutter away) for a lid handle. While the confections themselves were all topped with candied violets or rose petals, designed to tempt at least a duchess.

I was near tongue-tied over my thanks. Not only were the gifts so attractive, but it meant much they had been given at all. Mr. Sauvage spoke briskly of the need for food now, as he expressed it, the entertainment was over. And then he straightway launched into amusing conversation—to hide my emotion, I thought.

He was talking of having a ball at the rancho, this being the best way to introduce Victorine to society. And there would also be a number of house guests for the important weekend.

Victorine, highly excited, had a storm of questions to ask.

"And we must have new gowns!" She clasped her hands tightly together. "You see, Tamaris, how right I was to buy that gauze, the satin—Amélie shall make me such a dress!"

Her brother laughed indulgently. "You have a vision then in your mind, *chérie?* Naturally you shall have a gown equal to such an occasion; Miss Penfold also."

"But she would not buy anything!" Victorine interrupted him. "She looked, but she would not buy."

"That is easily remedied," he countered. "I have not overlooked such a problem. There is already on her way here from the city the most skillful of Madame Rachell's needlewomen, together with a fine selection of materials. You must both select what is necessary to make the House of Sauvage hold heads high in pride."

"Alain"—Victorine's smile faded, now she had a serious note in her voice—"why do we have so barbarous a name? You are truly a Duc with an old and famous title, so why do you choose to be Mr. Sauvage? Me, I would—"

His indulgent look disappeared. "I am not a duke with any name but my own!" he replied sharply. "Just as I am not French but American. We surrendered that other name and title long ago—it was both empty and useless."

Victorine frowned but did not try to argue with him. Shortly after he arose, pausing by my chair to say, "Miss Penfold, by her talk of shopping Victorine has reminded me that I have been remiss in arranging your funds. If you will join me in the library at"—he consulted his watch—"half-past ten, we can discuss this. Now—I am late and am keeping Wilson waiting."

When the door closed behind him Victorine spoke: "I wish that my brother did not hold these strange ideas. It is true, Tamaris, that in France he would be a Duc. Many times did Madame Varinne remind me of that when I lived with her. It was the same with our father, he was angry with Mama when she once used her proper title, though she had every right to do so."

"But if your brother is an American, he can use no titles except those of common courtesy," I pointed out.

"That he need not be either! Long ago that exile of his family was ended. He could well live in France. There I would be a Comtesse at least, instead of just Mademoi-

selle Sauvage. I hate that harsh name and all it means."
She was in one of her short-lived tempers and I was sorry
my birthday breakfast must end so. But I knew better than
to try to soothe her. She would follow her usual pattern of
retreating to her room, then Amélie would pet and flatter
her into a good humor again.

I gathered together my gifts. The sweet scent of the
roses comforted me, and I resolutely made myself think
of all I had to be grateful for.

When the time came to keep my appointment in the
library there was no one there. Books have always drawn
me and I walked slowly along the shelves, reading titles
printed in gold on the rich leather bindings. There were
many sets of authors' works in full and I guessed that the
larger part of this collection, like the rest of the appointments of the house, had been ordered for show by the
builder. Here were the works of Thackeray, Dickens,
volumes of travels, and the like. But I was delighted to
discover Jane Austen's novels, and those of the Brontës,
which had earlier caused such a stir.

Comparing Jane Eyre's situation as a governess with
my own lot in life made me smile. After all there was no
mad wife roaming Mr. Sauvage's halls by night. Such
melodrama, I thought complacently, existed only in books.
No mad wife—only Mrs. Deaves—

I suddenly put my fingers to my cheeks. There was no
mirror here but I felt quite hot, as if I were blushing. To
compare my lot with Jane Eyre's, even lightly, was to
imply that I had a serious interest in Mr. Sauvage. From
that thought I shrank, refusing to make any honest appraisal of my own emotions. I must compose myself before he did come.

In my slow progress along the shelves I had reached a
position behind a big desk burdened with papers. But in
the exact center of that lay so very strange an object I
stepped closer to look at it.

A small bag of dark cloth rested there; tied to it, black
feathers. It was rudely fashioned, as if by some small child.
But instinctively I knew this was no plaything. I had
thought I was not a fanciful person, having always tried

to curb my imagination, but there was something very
odd—very dark and frightening about this. It riveted my
attention as if it were a living creature snarling up in open
menace.

"What is it, Tamaris?"

Again Mr. Sauvage had surprised me with a noiseless
approach. At my start, he added contritely; "Did I startle
you? Forgive me. But what is it that so holds your attention?"

"That." I pointed to the bag. "It—it looks so queer—
and somehow I do not like it at all."

He rounded the desk and leaned forward. Then, with a
muffled exclamation, he backed away, toward the fireplace, his eyes still on the bag. Groping behind him he
caught at the fire tongs. Only with those in hand did he
again approach the desk.

"You have not touched it, have you?"

His reaction, so unlike that expected of the man he had
shown himself to be, alarmed me. I answered quickly that
I had not.

"Good! Because one never knows—"

But what one did not know he did not explain. Instead,
extending the tongs, he grasped the bag, and so hurled the
thing into the fireplace. A moment later he knelt on the
hearthstone laying kindling to cover it. Only when he had
lighted that and flames arose, did he arise again to his feet.

"What—what was it?" I finally ventured as he stood
staring down into the fire.

"It—yes, it is necessary now, Tamaris, for me to take
you more deeply into my confidence. Since this has happened *here*. As you know, the circumstances of my sister's
early life were unusual. As you have been told, she was
deserted by her mother"—he uttered that last word as if
he found it difficult to say at all—"left with a kinswoman.
This woman had been born and nurtured in the West
Indies where some of the grossest superstitions flourish.
Unfortunately, there many children of the white race are
left much to the care of native nurses and so imbibe
almost from birth belief in such abominations as this
voodoo—"

"Voodoo!"

"You have heard of it then?" Alain's attention switched from the fire to me.

"Before the war I visited New Orleans with my father. We heard stories of it there."

"Yes, you would." He nodded. "The belief was introduced into Louisianna by refugees from the slave uprisings in the islands almost a century ago. Voodoo is not to be lightly dismissed, Tamaris. It is indeed a vicious and deadly thing. For while those who practice it appear to achieve their ends by 'magic,' in reality they have recourse to drugs and secret potions by which they can control others. What I have just burnt is a gris-gris, one of their methods of focusing a curse upon a victim. For all I know some deadly ill might have spread from merely touching it.

"And what its presence here means—" He prodded the burning wood with the poker. There was a puff of yellowish smoke and a strange odor. Now he cried out—

"Get back!" He moved so quickly I was unprepared as he caught my shoulder and dragged me with him to the nearest window, flinging that open, to let in a fresh, cool breeze.

"It means," he began again, "that I am meant to be the target of this debased 'magic.' And I must discover how this came here."

"But why—who would wish you any such harm?" I was very conscious of his touch, far too conscious for my own composure.

CHAPTER EIGHT

There was no light in his dark face, his features were set hard. He could have been one of his own ancestors, a Creek warrior. I pushed away. In this guise he frightened me a little. All that power I had sensed he kept leashed within him might be near a violent outburst.

"While my sister was under the so-called care of this female, she was criminally allowed to meet Christophe D'Lys. He is Madame's nephew by left-hand inheritance, sent to France for education. As are many of the mixed bloods, he is very handsome, ingratiating, subtle enough to attract a young and impressionable girl. Madame fostered their acquaintance, and, when I found her, Victorine actually considered herself affianced to the fellow.

"Being of mixed blood myself, I know the heavy burden this lays upon a man. I did not hold that against him. But when I undertook inquiries I discovered that he was not only illegitimate and half-caste, but in addition he was steeped in the practice of voodoo. The fellow was supposedly a priest of the cult! And I further learned, after I had gotten Victorine out of that vicious nest, he made threats that he would not only claim his 'bride' but summon vengeance on all who separated them.

"I had hoped that in bringing her here, keeping her surrounded by those I could trust, I would protect her. But to find *this!* Now I must discover the breach in our defense and have a reckoning."

Before I thought I uttered a name—"Amélie!"

"What of Amélie?"

To that sharp demand what could I answer—only a few odd happenings? And Victorine was so devoted to her maid, if her brother interfered between them she might turn on him again. Still I could do no less than report what I had seen, hastening to add that there might be acceptable explanations for everything. As he listened, his stern dark face did not alter, instead he nodded.

"While Victorine is so dependent on Amélie you are right, one can do nothing without solid proof. Also, Amélie seems devoted to her mistress. But whether that would make her do as Victorine might ask, even to my sister's eventual hurt, who knows? You were very right to tell me this. Now Amélie can also be watched. And in this house, away from the city—yes, for now we shall say or do nothing."

Though he had asked for no promise I gave one freely.

"And I shall say nothing of this——" I pointed to the fireplace.

The cloying, noxious odor was gone. Alain closed the window, returned to the hearth where he ground the ashes with the poker. Then he fetched a sheet of paper from the desk, used the hearth brush to sweep the ash onto that. When it was gathered to his satisfaction, he folded the paper into a packet, sealing with wax.

"Nothing of this must be left in the house."

I was more than a little surprised. His action, I thought, was not that of a man dealing with a superstition, but rather one taken by a believer dealing with something malignant and powerful.

Perhaps he may have read my thoughts for he asked, "Do you now judge me a superstitious fool, Tamaris? But I have seen——yes, I have seen more than one odd happening which cannot be rationally explained. A gris-gris is the focus of an evil cursing——is it too difficult, then, to believe it can draw harm to it?"

The sea on which I had spent my childhood had legends. I had heard many strange stories. Nor can anyone living deny that sometime in his or her life there has been an occurrence for which there is no logical cause.

"No," I answered slowly, "I think you are right. To be the target of hate or ill-wishing is to live under a shadow. There are many things in this world which we can not understand. I do not think you are wrong to want the ashes of that evil thing safely away from here."

He laid the packet on the desk. "They shall be——soon. But"——now he dropped his brooding intensity of manner to speak briskly——"you came here for another reason." And he explained swiftly that my pay would be given me partly in coin and partly in a banking arrangement. He treated me as an equal in understanding business and I found his attitude a compliment.

The generosity of his offering was in keeping with the life I was expected to lead. Already I had realized that my wardrobe did need many additions. And he repeated firmly that I must order what I desired from the materials

being sent to us, adding that there were two full-time sewing maids on the staff of the rancho waiting employment.

"Those girls will be glad." He laughed, his warrior
countenance completely gone. "Since my sister married
they must find the marking of household linen and the
like dreary. Mind you, select all you need. If there are
any lacks send a messenger into town. I want Victorine
to remain here." He glanced at the packet. "If D'Lys has
the effrontery and tenacity to follow us he can be more
easily detected here on my own land."

I thanked him sincerely for his kindness and generosity,
although that had reinforced the barrier I knew we must
retain. Mr. Sauvage appeared to find my words embarrass-
ing and went to shuffling the papers on his desk, which
I knew was a hint of dismissal. The few moments of closer
communication we had shared over the gris-gris were
clearly now relegated to the past.

Victorine, Mrs. Deaves, Amélie, and two maids were in
the sewing room. Fenton, perhaps excluded from that
charmed circle until my arrival, followed me in. They were
all intent upon a collection of fashion prints displayed by
a very smartly dressed woman.

"Come—look at these, Tamaris!" Victorine was like a
child confronting a collection of new toys. "All these"—
she pointed to the pictures—"are from the Maison Rodri-
gues, no less. Except those from Kerteux Soeurs, from
Meneaar and"—her voice took on a reverent note—"from
Worth. Madame Rachell has sent them to us by Mademoiselle Armtage—"

"You see, ladies"—Miss Armtage bowed to me—"you
can be sure these styles have not yet been seen in San
Francisco, for all the prints have just arrived. I can assure
you they are exclusive."

"Tamaris, what think you of this one?" Victorine held
one of the pictures at eye level before me. "See—made of
the gauze over satin—trimmed with the roses—will it not
be just right?"

Certainly the materials she had purchased would com-
bine well. The pictured gown was plainly designed for a

young girl and was ethereal in its use of a floating overskirt, which in the drawing was tulle. The apron-front drapery and the puffing in the back could well be caught up with the white silk roses of Victorine's selection, each of which bore sparkling crystal dewdrops affixed to petal or leaf.

"Now—you choose, Tamaris!"

I caught the hostile glint in Mrs. Deaves' sidewise glance. But she could not protest as I shuffled through the drawings, which ranged from the fairylike choice Victorine had made to regal gowns designed for dowagers.

My mother had possessed a few pieces of jewelry, none of any great value, chosen for their delicate beauty. And among them I fancied most, and always had, a parure my father had bought her in Genoa on their honeymoon. It was of the marble mosaic much in fashion in Italy, and consisted of a breast pin, earrings, necklace, and matching bracelets of red gold, each set with the mosaics—black marble background, on that in white and green of the same stone almost life-sized white violets among their leaves. Since this would furnish my party jewelry, I would keep it in mind as I made my choice.

I must, of course, have a pattern and material richer than I had ever worn, since display counted for so much here. But I had no longing to be conspicuous. Thus most of the French styles did not attract me. As I laid aside print after print I began to believe that I would in the end have to have one of my eastern gowns copied. Then I came upon one which I studied carefully.

Since I was already more than halfway to spinsterhood (it was my twenty-fifth birthday I had just celebrated) this pattern was more fitting. I could envision it made up in silver gray silk with black lace and perhaps violets. But at my mention of the proper material, Victorine made a face.

"But such is for *old* ladies, Tamaris. You are young!"

I smiled. "Not young enough for gauze, Victorine."

"Most correct." Mrs. Deaves gave majestic approval. Which immediately made me wonder if I were indeed too conservative and would appear a dowd. But I would not change choices now, only said I would consider the materials.

"Augusta is much older than you. And *she* plans to wear gold satin trimmed with hummingbirds!" Victorine announced.

I did not miss Mrs. Deaves' faint frown. To have the difference in our ages so promptly pointed out could not be pleasant. Nor, perhaps, would I myself have relished such a speech had our positions been reversed. But I had no wish to outshine her.

Watching Amélie answering her mistress's excited questions as to whether a cluster of roses should be placed so or so, it was hard to believe that the slim young maid could be responsible for the evil thing Alain had found. And Victorine—since she had thrown off her sullen reluctance to travel during our first days together—when had she shown any regrets or rebellion? She must have forgotten D'Lys in her excitement at new surroundings and people. Perhaps she was actually relieved to be free of the half-caste, content in her role as pampered sister of one of the wealthiest men on the Coast. No, I found it hard to believe that anything might threaten her, still I must not forget the possibility.

Miss Armtage supervised the unpacking of the materials. Though her own figure was short and poorly proportioned, she was an example of how such shortcomings might be overcome by excellent taste in dress, as she moved deftly about, draping lengths of shimmering fabric over chairs and tables, pointing out the beauties of each. While Victorine chose material for a riding habit, afternoon and walking dresses, more elaborate dinner gowns, Miss Armtage made quick efficient notes on an ivory-leaved tablet. I found my own selection. Not the silver gray I had planned, but rather a satin with the color name of "pearl," which was not the pure white kept for the very young, but one possessing a silver overcast. Against it the black lace of my desire displayed tastefully. While from a vast box of silk and velvet flowers, Fenton, aroused to competition with Teresa (whom I was sure she disliked), sorted out clusters of white velvet violets.

Therefore I made other choices too, a dinner dress material of biscuit taffeta, some green and white chintz for a "Dolly Varden." While Fenton, warming to the hunt, picked out laces and some other odds and ends which she urged on me for the furbishing of my existing wardrobe.

The sewing room, equipped with two machines of the latest model (though the maids did the finer sewing by hand), became a hive of activity. Invitations to the ball had gone out and acceptances were flooding in. The famous French caterers of San Francisco had sent their expert to survey the appointments of the kitchen and the dining room where the supper buffet would be laid. Poor Mrs. Landron spun around as if small wheels instead of feet were tucked beneath her spreading skirts, checking this, ordering that, making preparations for those guests who would stay the weekend.

Victorine, having decided on her dress and seen that begun, grew fretful during the lengthy fittings. Several times she retired with headaches and Amélie was called to nurse her. They both made it plain when this occurred my assistance was not welcomed.

I began to be a little anxious about those headaches, for I knew that Victorine took only remedies provided by Amélie, and those always sent her into deep sleep. Yet she awoke again in good health and spirits. But I resolved at the first opportunity to suggest that Mr. Sauvage call in his own physician. Only during these days I practically never saw my employer, save at dinner in the evening, and then I could not speak out before the others.

We received other "morning calls" from neighbors during these days and twice Henry Beall rode over. But we saw nothing more of Mrs. Beall, though she had accepted the invitation to the ball. Henry mentioned the return of his sister from a fashionable school down the peninsula, but, I noticed, he did not speak of his stepmother.

It was very plain he was fascinated by Victorine. Though she, as plainly, gave him no encouragement. I think Mrs. Deaves favored him; certainly she was most gracious when he called.

Our ball gowns were finished and hung in our wardrobes. To Victorine's great delight her brother produced the traditional pearl necklace for a young lady making her first bow to society. Our house guests began to arrive and these I found a varied lot.

Most of the men were business associates of Mr. Sauvage, bearing names which carried great weight in financial circles. Among them were some of the French colony of note in the city. Their ladies all dressed in the height of contemporary fashion, as I had expected. But I detected those differences of background which marked the fluid state of this society. Though their mothers might have to make an effort to move into this elite world, the daughters adapted better. Two of the noted belles of the season accompanied their parents, but neither to my mind could compare with Victorine.

The overflow of accommodation in the main house was taken care of by two guest cottages, in which the bachelors were quartered. And our company was in such numbers I had to make a distinct effort to remember names.

Though Victorine was in truth hostess, Mrs. Deaves, under the pretense of helping her, insinuated herself wherever possible. If the girl was conscious of this encroachment she did not comment. I was proud of her demeanor, for she was on her best behavior and so enchanting. Perhaps the fact that she was the present center of attention brought out the best in her nature.

Dinner on the night of the ball was served in the smaller salon and not prolonged. I think that the ladies would have been satisfied with trays in their rooms while they gave last attentions to their toilets. But we dressed early instead.

Fenton arranged my hair, adding a slight padding which I disliked in the ordinary way. She very artfully placed a violet-adorned comb at just the right angle.

I knew I had very little claim to being more than passable looking, but with Fenton's aid I had never made such a good appearance as I did that night. My mother's parure was the perfect touch, I knew, as I put on the earrings, fastened the brooch to the front of my corsage (which was *not* cut as low as Victorine had urged), added the necklace, and slipped the bracelets over my long gloves.

A bouquet had been delivered to each lady earlier, with Mr. Sauvage's compliments. Mine consisted of the ivory roses, accompanied by a short note of regret that it was not white violets. The fragrant flowers were in a crystal holder united by a chain to a ring one could slip on a finger. My fan was of my father's giving, a brisé one of carved ivory from China.

"Miss"—Fenton sat back on her heels (she had knelt to smooth out my short train)—"you look just lovely!" Her plain face lighted up.

"Mainly your work, Fenton." I gathered my skirt and made one of those grand curtsies learned at Ashley Manor. "To you goes the credit."

"Oh, miss—!" I was surprised at the feeling in her voice. When she had been sent to me I had resented her as a curb on what small independence I thought I had a right to. Perhaps I was uneasy because I had never had a personal maid before. And sometimes she had looked so disapproving, as if the arrangement suited her no more than it did me. But recently we had become closer. And I was aware she took pride in dressing me and that I must be a credit to her.

My skirts whispered on the carpet as I went on to Victorine's suite. There I faced one who might have stepped out of a fairy tale—the princess all little girls long to be. Her hair was dressed loosely, a second string of pearls woven through it. Above the massing of gauze which edged her satin bodice, molded so closely to her young body, her perfect shoulders emerged as if from some lightsome summer cloud. We read of great beauty but we seldom see it as I viewed it that night.

"Tamaris—but that dress *is* right for you after all." She picked up a mother-of-pearl holder with pure white roses.

"Victorine! Never have I seen anyone look so lovely!" And I meant that with all my heart.

She caught up her full skirts and turned slowly about, looking over her shoulder into the mirror.

"Myself, I think that Amélie has done better than ever before. You hear that, Amélie—*très bon!*"

Amélie held a spangled fan in one hand as she watched Victorine with an odd expression I could not read. Was it envy?

A little of my old distrust and uneasiness flooded back. But I would not think of that now; nothing must mar Victorine's happiness tonight.

Mrs. Deaves was as magnificent as I had guessed. Her golden skirts with their trimmings of hummingbirds, the beaks of which were gold, the tiny eyes rubies, had the splendor of at least a duchess. Though I disliked seeing those small birds killed to make dress ornaments. Their use so was a part of the same waste which assaulted something in me all through this house. Gold and yet more gold, red velvet, things which in restraint could be beautiful, but when in opulent parade disgusted rather than pleased.

My dinner escort was a Major Barkley from the Presido, colorful in his dress uniform, stiffly attentive. He was one of the bachelors and his remarks (plainly delivered for the sake of good manners) were based on features of the countryside. Though he unbent a little when I spoke of Mr. Sauvage's description of some of the old California houses which had *not* been razed. He said he had been stationed here prior to the war and grew quite animated in his description of a cattle round-up on such a ranch. My companion to the left was a much older man, who, when we exchanged conversational partners, paid me some too florid compliments, but exhibited much greater interest in the contents of the plate and glass before him.

Even the house had been changed tonight. Now the great hall under its amber dome had a circular seat of quilted red velvet in the center. This formed a ring to enclose a tiered pyramid of red and white camellias, bordered by red and white roses, the fragrance of which was near overpowering. On the balcony at second-floor level a string orchestra had been installed to play soft music to promenade by, and there were divans and chairs scattered about.

The two great salons, where strips of opaque crystal

bearing mythological designs alternated with full-length mirrors on the walls, had been converted to one huge ballroom by pushing sliding panels back into hiding. It was at the entrance to this that Mr. Sauvage stood, Victorine to his right, and me (in spite of my attempt to avoid being so singled out) to his left.

Mrs. Deaves did not form one of our small reception list, though I did not doubt she had fully expected to. She stood instead with others of the house party, a set smile on her lips, talking in a low tone, with feverish vivacity, to her dinner partner.

My discomfort at being so placed on show was such that I found it increasingly difficult to remember names and faces as the guests began to arrive, each lady being presented at the door with a dancing program.

Mr. Sauvage had already filled ours I saw when I had a moment to glance at mine. When our duty in the reception line was finished I was claimed by the Major who, though not too graceful, performed creditably enough in the lancers to music provided by a second and larger orchestra.

If Mr. Sauvage had ignored Mrs. Deaves' wish to be singled out as co-hostess, he was politely punctilious about giving her the second dance, having opened the ball with Victorine and then relinquished her to a younger escort. But when the third, a waltz, began, he bowed before me.

In such a throng, with people continually passing in and out, or going to walk along the conservatory veranda, or sit in the center hall, it was difficult to keep Victorine in sight, especially as all the other debutantes present also wore white. I was trying to locate her when my partner said abruptly, "Are you looking for someone, Tamaris? Do you have some acquaintance here you want to meet?" His tone was sharp with no jesting note in it.

"No, sir. But as you well know my status here is on a slightly different basis than that of your other guests. I am watching for Victorine."

"Duty as always then." But there was a softer note in his voice. "Tonight I do not think you should take that duty too seriously. Think not of Miss Penfold the very proper lady instructoress, the ideal companion-in-residence, but rather of Tamaris who is quite young enough, and certainly pretty enough, to be enjoying a ball."

Only he was so deadly wrong.

Supper was served at midnight and my escort of the last waltz, an amiable young man whose name to this day I cannot remember, proved himself quite adept at selecting from the display of macaroons, blanc mange in fanciful shapes, tipsy cake (and very tipsy it was, too), brandied cherries, jelly trifles, and the like a most tempting plate. Having been ceremoniously seated on the round seat in the hall to await his return with champagne, I had a moment free to check on Victorine.

And I saw her—not nearby, but up on the balcony, where she stood with her back to the silver railing, talking with a man. Some trick of the gaslight caught his face and I started. He possessed a masculine version of Amélie's features! But I must be imagining things—

Before I could rise my escort returned and I had no valid reason to hurry away. Also the young man had left Victorine and she was now seated as if awaiting the same service which had just been provided for me. Who was that man?

I did not really taste the delicacies on my plate, nor attend intelligently to my partner's conversation. I hoped I was not outwardly rude; at least he showed no signs of boredom. But at last I could stand it no longer.

Thanking him as gracefully as I could, I explained I must seek Victorine. It was a lame excuse but he accepted it politely. Perhaps with relief, as I had certainly not been a rewarding supper companion.

As I started up the stair to the balcony I saw Victorine on the move again. This time she sped down a side corridor, the cream Chinese shawl about her shoulders. And she was heading for the stairs at the back of the house. It was up to me to restrain her from any folly. I gathered up my far too heavy and hindering skirts to follow her.

Although the forepart of the house was thronged, here was silence and emptiness. Luckily Victorine never glanced back; she could not hear any trailers. She gained the lower hall and the door there giving on the garden, but not that section where the fairy lights of tree-strung lanterns illuminated statues and walks.

My skirts caught on a bush and I had to halt for a moment. That pause, short as it was, lost me Victorine. But she could not be too far ahead, and this leafy underbrush had only one opening. I shivered as I hurried on, my skirts held as high and close to my body as I could manage. Victorine had a shawl but the night wind was cold on my bare shoulders.

A fork in the path—which way? The garden was so large and the paths had been laid out to wander, crossing and dividing. Perhaps I could never find her. The way to my right led to the lighted section. Now I caught the scent of tobacco; some masculine guest had come outside to indulge in that habit most ladies deplore.

"Miss Penfold!"

I turned my head to see Henry Beall.

"Is there any way I may assist you?" Even the dim lantern light betrayed my agitation. I must be very careful lest Victorine be suspected of some indiscretion.

Which meant I must bear the suspicion of indiscretion for myself. I forced a smile I did not feel.

"You surprised me, Mr. Beall." In my own hearing, my voice did not carry the right note of embarrassment. But perhaps I underrated my powers of dissimulation for now he was smiling, a smile I hated to have turned on me, since it made very plain he thought I was keeping some rendezvous.

"Your pardon, dear lady." The bow he made me was a veiled insult, warming my cheeks with a flush of anger. Yet I could not counter it with the disdain I wished. "But you are very much alone here. May I share your solitude? The moon is bright enough for a stroll or—"

I must find Victorine! But how to rid myself of this unwelcome escort I did not know. There was really only one way and that would confirm all his suspicions. So it must be done.

"You are most kind, Mr. Beall. But, as it chances, I do have an escort due to appear at any moment—"

Again that hateful smile.

"But of course, dear lady. His gain is my loss. I will be but an unnecessary third. But may I inquire if you have seen Victorine? The next dance is mine and I have not found her—"

"She may have retired momentarily, sir. You would better seek her in the house than here." My impatience colored my reply. He smiled more broadly and bowed again.

"Naturally. Please accept my apologies for the intrusion."

I watched him go before I moved on, suspicious that he might choose to linger for no other purpose than to see who would join me. Only when I was sure he was out of sight did I turn into the left-hand path.

The gravel was white in the moonlight and I could hear muted sounds of music from the house. But somehow I seemed cut off from the safe world I knew. I was chilled, worried, and, worst of all, sure I had neglected my duty. Had I kept closer watch on Victorine I might have prevented this midnight excursion.

I paused to listen, and so caught the murmur of voices. Whispers so low pitched I could distinguish only a word or two, and those in that patois which Victorine spoke with Amélie. Only three words I could understand reached my straining ears:

"St. John's Eve."

CHAPTER NINE

Since I was not a Catholic the saints' days meant nothing to me, but the words were my guide as I stole forward. Ahead, as the path turned, a screen of brush still concealed the speakers from sight. Just as I made up my mind to move boldly, I heard the crunch of heavy footsteps on gravel, moving away. Throwing aside all caution I hurried around that curve.

Here was a glade opening around a small pool with a softly playing fountain to feed it. Facing that was a garden bench of wrought iron. And on it Victorine sat, or rather slumped.

Her shawl had slipped to the ground, her head lay back, her eyes closed. I ran to her, sniffing a stranger scent than the rose oil she used as a perfume, something vaguely disagreeable.

"Victorine!" I caught her hands, her flesh was fever hot. She opened her eyes, staring at me as if I were a stranger. And she kept moving the tip of her tongue back and forth across her lips as if she still tasted something she longed to savor again.

Then her eyes focused, and I felt tension flow out of her. Her hands went limp, her head dropped even more. Her eyes were closed now, a grimace of what might be pain distorted her face.

"Victorine! You are ill!"

"Oui"—her answer was very low and weak—"so very ill, Tamaris. Please do not leave me—" Her hands turned in mine, closed with a convulsive, bruising force on my wrists.

"Let me go for help—"

"Non! Stay, please stay. I am so *triste*—my head, it spins so—such pain, such floating—! Stay with me, do not leave me alone!" She continued to hold my wrists with a strength I would not have believed such a frail girl could possess, as if so she anchored herself to safety.

Perforce I stayed. Though I was worried. Certainly these attacks were not just acting to avoid situations she disliked. Victorine needed far more than just the tending of a devoted ignorant maid.

"Victorine? Tamaris?"

I was never so glad for anything in my life as to see Alain come into the glade. At the same time Victorine's grip on me loosened. I caught at her just in time to steady her against my body or she would have slid to the ground. Together we got her back to the house, Alain carrying her, while I kept the bushes from catching at her billows of gown and train. When we brought her into her suite Amélie was there as if she knew there would be a need for her. As she worked efficiently to get her mistress to bed, with what little help she would allow me to give, I knew Alain was waiting in the sitting room. But I had so little explanation for him—

"She is ill." Amélie shot a hostile glance across the bed. "Always she has these—these maladies when she is too excited. Now she sleeps and when she wakes all will be well. It is true, what I tell you!"

I thought that Victorine did now seem to be sleeping normally. But that she needed treatment for such attacks was apparent. However, when I went out to Alain, I thought to discuss this in Victorine's suite might not be wise. Amélie could be on guard in more than one way, not only for her mistress, but also that she not be supplanted here.

"What is it?" I could read Alain's impatience in his tone. "What were you two doing out in the garden, Tamaris?"

I made a warning gesture to the door behind me and answered carefully.

"Victorine was taken with one of her bad heads. She thought going into the night air might help."

His expression changed slightly. He had been quick to catch and interpret my signal, for now he said, "It is well you found her. We must let her rest."

He opened the hall door, then closed it firmly behind us both. Nor did he say anything until we were opposite my own sitting room. Then, with no by your leave, he opened the door of that and waved me in.

I was afraid Fenton might be waiting. But the room was empty, with only a single lamp turned low.

"Now let us have the truth—what happened?"

I began by describing the young man I had seen with Victorine on the balcony and Alain's impassivity became fixed.

"I was wrong then," he interrupted as if he thought aloud. "So *he* did dare to be here tonight! And perhaps— but tell me, how did you get into the garden?"

I made my story as short as I could, but I mentioned meeting Henry Beall. Alain nodded.

"Yes, I met him also. I had seen you from the terrace and followed. It was good that I did."

What had his thoughts been then? That I was so untrustworthy a guardian that I had sought a hidden rendezvous after all my "missish" words earlier? But it was not Alain's scorn or possible suspicion which counted now, it was Victorine.

"You would know this young man again?"

"Yes. He is quite unmistakable."

"Good. I want you to come with me. If you see him, point him out. I have had him described to me but we have not yet met face to face. Meanwhile we shall say that Victorine has been taken ill and is resting."

As we returned to the hall we came face to face with Mrs. Deaves.

"Alain! Where have you been? Judge Stevens and his wife are about to take their leave—"

Ignoring me entirely, she laid her hand possessively on his arm, drawing him with her. I could see his dilemma. Now it must be up to me to hunt alone for Victorine's mysterious escort.

But that was difficult. The crowd, passing back and forth, was never still or confined to one room. How could one search effectively? I tried but speedily discovered that in order not to make myself conspicuous I had to pause now and then for some exchange of civility with a guest. Alain had made a mistake in putting me in the reception line earlier and so given me a quasi-hostess status.

I had reached the glassed-in veranda when I came upon a group of ladies paying court to an older and very stately dame, whom I recognized as the redoubtable Mrs. William Gwin, for almost two decades the leader of local society. Her black velvet and pearls were well suited to her role, and it was plain from the attitude of those about her she was still very much on her throne.

On the outskirts of the small court, which I was endeavoring to avoid, I saw one not as politely attentive as

the others. Mrs. Beall, wearing mauve brocade and a rich
display of diamonds, was looking about as if searching
for someone. Then her eyes met mine.

She edged her way gracefully out of the group and cut
off my escape into the conservatory.

"Miss Penfold!" She repeated my name so sharply I
was forced to pay her heed. "I have not yet had a chance
to speak to Miss Sauvage—"

Why, since in the immediate past she had given every
indication of not wishing to pursue any acquaintance, I
could not understand. But so firm was her manner now I
could not push by without open rudeness.

"Victorine is not feeling well, Mrs. Beall. She has just
retired with a sick headache."

For a moment I thought she was about to challenge my
statement. Then some second thought apparently checked
that impulse and she said, in quite another tone of voice,
"What a pity. She is quite the belle. I have heard many
compliments on her this evening. I trust her disorder is
not serious?"

"Not in the least." I replied with all the reassurance I
could muster. "She is subject to these attacks when she
becomes fatigued or overexcited. This has been an occasion to produce both those conditions."

"Yes, an important night for any girl, her formal entrance into society." Mrs. Beall spoke absently. "Tell me,"
she continued, "you have been with Miss Sauvage for
some time, have you not, Miss Penfold?"

I sensed a method in her questioning and grew wary.
But telling the strict truth is some protection.

"Since she was in New York only." I did not elaborate.

"So you did not know her in France—when she was
younger?"

"No, Mrs. Beall."

"It is odd that she did not come sooner to live with her
brother."

My reticence seemed to force her more and more into
the open. There was a demanding note in her voice. Surely
the story of Victorine's past must be common knowledge.
Rumor and gossip must have played in turn with such an

account. That Alain Sauvage had gone to claim a sister heretofore unknown should be known to all the "old families."

"I know nothing of that, Mrs. Beall," I said firmly.

Though the art which had maintained her semblance of youth was meticulous, yet tonight, kind as the lighting was, she had a slightly haggard look. Now her eyes hardened.

"Of course you would say that!" she flashed. She must have been hard driven for the polite surface of her manners to so crack. "Do you not guess? I have a mother's desire to know more of a young lady in whom my son shows so much interest—"

Her explanation was so patently false she must have realized it even as she spoke. I did not believe that she harbored any maternal feelings for Henry. She did not even try to explain herself further, only stared rather wildly at me.

I was amazed for I read in that look a desperation out of all keeping with what I knew. As if—almost as if in Victorine she had discovered some danger.

She turned away, twisting her lace-covered fan in her hands. Though she might be able to control her expression, those writhing hands betrayed her. I heard the ivory sticks snap. She looked at the broken fan and then gave a little cry and hurried away.

I went on into the veranda. There were people there, though the crowd was beginning to thin, for a dawn breakfast was offered. Others were calling for their carriages. And nowhere had I seen the young man.

Later I met Alain in the great hall where he was bidding guests farewell. He glanced at me and I answered with a slight shake of the head. Mrs. Deaves had at last won her place by his side and was queenly self-confident. I slipped away without trying for speech with him.

The sun was rising when I regained the quiet of my own room. I had paid a visit to Victorine, found her sleeping, Amélie on guard. In the sitting room waited another maid, sent there by Alain to run any errands—or rather to make sure of Victorine's continued privacy, I fancied.

Fenton, who aided me off with my gown, showed consideration by not talking. Ever since I had followed Victorine into the garden this had been a draggingly long night of worry and I was glad it was over.

I slept most of the day, but it was not restful slumber and I carried into my late waking memory of disturbing dreams, so my own head was aching. But by the time I drank the tea Fenton brought me, I was able to better order my thoughts.

When I visited Victorine I found Mrs. Deaves seated in a chair close to the bed. The girl was propped on pillows and, while she looked languid, she had lost the feverish flush. She smiled at me in welcome.

"Tamaris at last!" She drew a small watch out of the embroidered pocket made fast to the inner side of the tester curtain, consulted it, then frowned at me in mock reproof. "You have slept and slept. Twice Amélie went and Fenton hushed her away. Did you take some powders?"

"No. It was the fatigue of a long and exciting evening. But how are you feeling, Victorine?"

She clapped her hands over her ears. "Never do I want to hear those words again! I feel much better, but no one will believe that is so. Now Alain says on Monday we shall go to the city, that I must see some physician there to prove that I was only a little tired. The rooms were so hot I went into the garden, then I walked too fast, and I was chilled—which made my head bad. So all this fuss-fuss—it is for no good reason. This I say to Alain but he will not listen. He puts on a stern face and says that I must see the doctor—

"Very well, I shall do so. Then when Alain learns how foolish are his fears we shall hear no more about it. Always this has been with me so, even from a small child. Amélie knows just what to do to make me feel right again. To speak of a doctor is foolishness."

That she had met someone in the garden I was sure. If Christophe D'Lys had followed her, if it had been he I had seen talking to her on the balcony, it might well have been she promised to meet him in the garden. Those words I had caught—St. John's Eve—I must find a saints' calendar, try to discover the right date.

But now I accepted—outwardly—Victorine's excuse. And I greeted Mrs. Deaves pleasantly, hoping she had enjoyed the ball.

"A most enchanting time. As you must know, Miss Penfold. The garden was beautiful in the moonlight, excellent for private talks and walks, was it not?" Her malice was hardly hidden.

But I was startled, thinking for a moment that she might have witnessed Victorine's secret meeting. Still the malice was plainly directed toward me.

"Mr. Beall is most attentive," she continued in that lazy purr. "Only perhaps I should warn you, Miss Penfold, that while a married lady is allowed freedoms in society, an unmarried one, even of mature years, finds many censorious eyes ready to mark any deviation in her conduct."

"That is well known, Mrs. Deaves." If she had expected some protest of injured innocence from me she was not going to get it. I saw the slightly malicious amusement in Victorine's expression and with it curiosity. Did she wonder what I had been doing in the garden?

"Mr. Beall?" Victorine repeated. "Tamaris—can it be that the so-gallant Henry was that attentive to you last night? But what a disappointment! I had thought him coming here to play *my* cavalier." She gave a mock sigh. "So you took Mr. Beall into the garden, or he took you? Fie, Tamaris, you who always talk so much about being ladylike. Did the moon influence you that much?" Her tone was still light even though it carried a slight sting, but not the malice Mrs. Deaves had used.

"I was in the garden because I saw you leave the house, and I feared, as it turned out rightly, that you were ill. While I was searching for you I encountered Mr. Beall. That is the extent of my excursion into the moonlight."

Victorine laughed. "If he was smoking one of those *très horreurs* he affects, then I am pleased he did not find *me*. For I have such a dislike for that odor. It makes me sick, even sicker than one of my heads. *Pauvre* Tamaris—"

She made such a face I echoed her laughter.

"Oh, it was not quite as bad as that. We were in the open and he had already disposed of the cigar before he joined me. We were only in talk a moment or two. He was in search of you for a promised dance."

"So he said," Mrs. Deaves remarked. I wondered what had passed between her and Henry Beall. If he had hinted that I was engaged in an assignation, she must have welcomed that. But Henry Beall would have suggested that another man was involved, not himself.

At any rate such gossip did not matter now for Alain Sauvage knew the truth. And if Mrs. Deaves wished to make mischief in that quarter she would not succeed.

I spent the remainder of the short afternoon with Victorine. Mrs. Deaves quit our company soon after my arrival with the news that she must be joining Alain, who had promised to take the reins of a coach-and-four (the latest novelty of the neighborhood) and drive a party of guests around the estate. When the door closed behind her Victorine sat up straighter and spoke with some vigor.

"That specimen *d'chat!* Do you not hear it in her voice, see it in her air of triumph? Already she fancies herself mistress here—ruling all—including me! Unless she cannot manage to make a marriage for me with some thick-necked, big-handed son of a miner! I tell you, she shall not have Alain, she shall not!" Her delicate hands folded into fists and she pounded them into the spread of coverlet over her knees.

"I think your brother must be left to manage his own affairs, and I do not doubt he will do that wisely." I answered as best I could.

Though the triumph Mrs. Deaves had shown last night, when she managed to circumvent Alain's search for the intruder, was to the fore of my mind. As well as the fact that she had stepped into the role of hostess to speed the parting guests. But Victorine's present agitation was such that I made haste to reassure her, to remind her that he had not asked Mrs. Deaves to receive, but had put Victorine into that role. Just as he had seated her at the head of the table last night, and led her out to open the ball.

"Yes, what you say is true," she admitted. "But in the

matter of a woman a man may be quite blind, never seeing an open trap she has set. I do not like Augusta, and she is determined to be Alain's wife." She reached a hand under her pillows and withdrew it again, her fingers tightly closed about some object. I caught a glint of gold but did not see what she held, as she brought her hand to her bosom, cupping what she had hidden between palm and body.

Her eyelids dropped, in fatigue I first thought, then I believed because she was lost in thought. At that moment she had withdrawn from me. Amélie came forward and gestured. I found myself obediently rising quietly from my chair to leave Victorine and her self-appointed guardian alone. Now I wanted to find Alain, to be reassured by his presence that the shadows which seemed to be gathering were but figments of my imagination. But Alain was with his guests and I must wait alone.

Victorine appeared downstairs for dinner, a vivacious and charming hostess once more. Perhaps she made the effort fearing that Mrs. Deaves would insinuate herself further into the role of mistress here if she did not. But if she came by effort of will there was no sign of strain about her.

As this was Sunday evening, our amusement was decorous. We spent a few short hours in the White Drawing Room where the two Brighton girls played and sang, the gentlemen edging out now and then to, I was sure, smoke and discuss those matters of politics or business considered too complex for the female mind.

Alain did not make such a surreptitious sally into the night, but remained seated beside Victorine with Mrs. Deaves to his left. I withdrew to the edge of the company, content to sit quietly and relax.

When we drove to San Francisco the next day (or the next two days, as Alain wished to spare Victorine the threat of overfatigue and broke our journey halfway) Mrs. Deaves was still in our company. Victorine muttered about that in a way I hoped that neither Amélie nor Fenton, who shared the coach with us, could hear. She hoped that dear Augusta in Alain's smart turnout would be sick all the way, that ought to make her brother think a little. But if their swifter pace did produce such qualms Mrs. Deaves showed no ill effects.

During these hours I had time to think a few deep and serious thoughts of my own. My sense of duty would not allow me to leave if Victorine was really ill. But some instinct within me warned of a loss of peace of mind if I stayed. I made myself face the truth squarely. Alain Sauvage (I never thought of him any more as "Mr. Sauvage") had become, without my willing it at all, a center of attraction for me, occupying far too many of my thoughts. He need only enter a room for me to be instantly aware of his disturbing presence.

Romantic love as the sentimental novelists were wont to describe it—I had long seriously doubted that such intense emotion ever existed, save in the imagination of those writers. But neither had I believed I could become so aware of the slightest movement of any one man, want desperately to hear his voice, have to restrain myself from making excuses to be with him.

I was, in a way, ashamed of this discovery of my feeling. For it seemed to me that I was afraid of what lay behind some inner barrier. Safety for me lay in detachment, in refusing to allow anyone to pierce below the surface I so carefully maintained. If I were so foolish as to yield to this new feeling I would never again be a real mistress of myself.

For the first time I longed for the advice of a woman older and wiser than I, to whom I could speak without reserve, ask questions concerning this stir of emotion. Should I quit this household before I was too deeply entranced to ever hope for a quiet mind and heart again?

Yet there was no one to whom I could turn. Of all those in the past who had crossed my life, only my father had been close. And, had he been here, this was something I could not have shared with him. I must accept that I had only myself to depend upon. Any wrong choice *I* would have to take the consequences for.

That realization was frightening. I felt as if I were being

borne faster and faster toward some dark danger with no will or strength to ward off the end.

Alain established us once more in the same hotel which we had stayed in earlier. And, since our return to the city, Victorine seemed in perfect health. She was energetic, roaming restlessly about the suite, going from window to window to watch the scene below. Oddly enough she did not suggest shopping, though we took drives each day. Usually we visited the Woodwards Gardens where one could see the famous black swans on the lake and the flowering slopes around the conservatories.

Victorine was content to view such vistas from the carriage alone. And when I suggested a visit to an art gallery, and Mrs. Deaves the theatre, Victorine's answer was always "later." Since she was not ill, I believed she was waiting for something—or could it be someone? She might be apprehensive of missing what she awaited by being engaged elsewhere.

The physician Alain favored had gone down coast and we must await his return, while Alain was caught up in a press of many affairs. During those days I learned of the feverish speculation in mining shares which was constant, not only among men, but women, too. There were astounding tales of washerwomen who were one day at their tubs and the next able to buy diamonds to cover their swollen red fingers.

I wondered if the Sauvage companies were entangled in this gambling. But when Mrs. Deaves once spoke of some investment, Alain answered quite forcibly about the folly of such buying and selling. His interests did not lie in mining alone, and it was during these days that I learned of his power over what might be termed an "empire"— including cattle ranches, lumbering, mines, steam packets, ships on voyages across the Pacific.

On the third day of our aimless city stay he returned at midmorning, bringing with him, as always, a fresh wind to enliven our enervating hothouse of a parlor.

"Your bonnets, ladies, and your mantles, jackets, whatever you need. We have a visit to make!"

So brisk and authoritative was he that I started for

those designated articles at once. But Victorine, as yet unstirring from the divan, asked languidly, "Where do we go?" Her voice sounded resentful as if she would like to say "no" at once but did not quite dare.

"To the *Ranee*. She has just come to anchor, and she carries a treasure on board which will amaze you. Hurry now, I have a carriage waiting."

Perhaps it was the magic word "treasure" which brought Victorine out of beginning sulks. I was more than a little excited as I pinned on my hat. For I remembered —so much. It had been a long time since I had walked a ship's deck, smelled that odor which is a combination of many scents, but would always signify happiness for me.

CHAPTER TEN

As we drove along Victorine asked many questions. But I was silent, relishing the thought of the experience ahead. This was a different part of the city than I had seen, for we entered now the fringe of the infamous Barbary Coast.

The blatant noise reached our ears even through the closed carriage windows. Here, I had heard, hoodlums ran in packs, and the police (specially chosen for strength and courage, carrying both pistols and knives) dared only go in twos and threes. This strip of the city was famed throughout the seas. In filthy lodging houses, the unspeakable drinking dens, crimps followed their trade, putting opiates into the liquor of fuddled seamen, plundering them of everything worth taking, then shipping them out again, inert and oftentimes deathly ill, to fill up the crews of waiting ships.

My father had never dealt with crimps. Twice in this harbor, he had told me, he and his mates had to fight on deck to get rid of them. And his stories of San Francisco portside had made me shudder.

But when we at last stepped on the deck of the *Ranee* I

gazed about with a feeling close to pain. She was a clipper, one of those beauties now, alas, fast being replaced by steamers. No more beautiful ships have ever existed, the dreams of men who had built them, sailed them fearlessly into waters where the American flag had never been shown before. She was one of a dying race and I loved her.

We were met by the Captain and his first officer, escorted below, Victorine complaining over the unsteady footing. But I discovered that sea legs cannot be lost and I needed no steadying hand.

Captain Maxfield entertained us royally. There were boxes of candied ginger, other strange sweets. Yet not so strange or exotic to me. I was surrounded by far-found objects such as my father had once collected. There was a scroll of a Chinese painting, a hideous mask with shark teeth set in its gapping mouth, a Malay kris, its blade pitted by exposure to the salt air.

I nibbled my ginger and gazed from one wall to the next until I was startled from old dreams by the first officer:

"Pardon me, Miss Penfold, but one would think you had been here once before, the way you look about you."

"I have," and then catching sight of his amazed expression, I explained. "No, I did not mean right *here*. But my father was Captain Jesse Penfold and I sailed with him for many years. In fact I was born on shipboard."

"Fancy that now!" But I supposed in my fashionable furbelows I looked far removed from Spartan sea life. "Captain Jesse Penfold? Aye—I've heard tell of him. In Canton it was. He was good friends with Merchant Ho. They still speak of him there."

"I am so glad!" A man should live in the memories of those he had touched. That those of his calling still spoke of him with respect made me proud and happy.

"And it was he who beat off five pirate junks in the Japanese sea, too, I heard tell," Mr. Whicker continued. "Now *that* was a story!"

I smiled. "One which seems to have grown in the telling. I was there, you see. There were only two junks and one must have had a drunken steersman, it sailed so erratically. But their attack was frightening for a while."

"Two—five—what matter? It took a tough man to do that. Those eastern pirates are none I want to meet without a couple of cannon primed and ready and a pistol in each hand. It was a sad loss, Miss Penfold, when those devils of Reb commerce raiders put an end to such a man and his command," he ended frankly.

Again I was touched and pleased, glad to know my father was remembered so.

"Well now, ladies." The Captain, who had been talking with Alain, arose. "Mr. Sauvage thinks you might like to see the cream of the cargo before he turns it over to the bank guards."

He went to a small safe well secured to the deck and brought out a metal box. From that the Captain lifted several trays, lined with raw Indian cotton, which held treasure indeed.

There was one tray of pearls, their luster gleaming against the dull cotton. Below those a second tray held stones from Ceylon, rubies and sapphires, and the third contained jade. Not that jade which is usually exported to the West, but that translucent "imperial" jade kept so closely within the borders of China that many westerners do not know it exists. These pieces were not unset stones like the others, but worked and carved. There was a butterfly, two perfect drop earrings, a bracelet bearing a tiny intricate scene—all of which might have belonged to a lady of the Court.

"That jade—where could you have gotten it?" I asked before I thought.

Captain Maxfield smiled. "Fair come, Miss Penfold, though of this quality you might well wonder. The truth is we were lucky in the Straits. The pirates tried one of those devilish tricks of theirs—set a ship's boat adrift with an upright oar, a bit of a shirt rag fastened to it for a distress signal. Only one of our hands had been in a ship near suckered in by such a ploy some years back. So we let them think we took the bait and then got the dhow as they came in to board us. We found this"—he patted the top of the box with weathered brown hand—"in her captain's quarters. No telling where he had stolen it, could be loot of years. But in any case there are no legal owners, they're probably long dead. So it's rightful treasure trove."

"So it is. After an auction or a private sale, whichever you decide," Alain said briskly, "the sum realized shall go on ship's share. I'll give you a receipt for the box and that will be taken straight to the bank. Tucker himself has agreed to value it. He may make you an offer; if he does, consider it. His jewelry shop is the best in the city."

"We'll leave all that to you, Mr. Sauvage. You take owner's cut anyway."

"Not this time," Alain shook his head. "Spoils of a fight I wasn't in are not mine. You risked your lives, I don't collect on that."

The Captain produced pen, ink, and paper and Alain wrote out the receipt. Over his hunched shoulder I watched Mrs. Deaves and Victorine. The former was frowning but Victorine had eyes only for the gems. There was a kind of hunger in her face—as if she regarded food placed just beyond her reach.

I felt the fascination of the gems also—mostly the jade. Then my mind shuddered away from imagining how those pieces had found their way into the hands of a Straits pirate. I believed that any who wore them and knew of their history could not feel clean.

"Alain," Victorine said as we once more settled in the carriage, "those so beautiful things—who will buy them?"

"Perhaps Tucker. His 'Diamond Palace,' as they speak of it, could afford them. At any rate Captain Maxfield can depend upon him for a fair appraisal. Now you have seen what might be termed 'the wealth of the Indies.'"

"The wealth of the Indies," she repeated dreamily.

"And most of the profit will be wasted!" There was irritation in Mrs. Deaves' voice. "Those men were perfectly ready for you to accept owner's share, Alain. Now it will go into the pockets of ordinary seamen, to be wasted in such places as these!" She waved a gloved hand toward the streets of the Barbary Coast.

"Not ordinary seamen. Very extraordinary ones to accomplish what they did. No, owner's share comes from legitimate trading. This find was the result of their risking their lives. They are entitled to benefit from their effort, if ever men did. That jade—it must once have been the pride of some imperial princess or concubine. How did it wind up in the strongbox of a Straits pirate?"

"In a way I would not care to dwell upon." I spoke my earlier thought aloud.

"Quite right!" Alain returned promptly.

We did not return at once to the hotel; rather Alain escorted us to the famous French restaurant, The Poodle Dog. There we lunched on viands which I had not seen or tasted since I left Brussels on the *India Queen*. It was when we arose after dining that I caught a glimpse of a dark head beside a pillar on the far side of the room, eyes which watched us.

Was that the young man I had seen with Victorine on the balcony? Or was I inclined to see that stranger in any man of the right height and coloring? My glimpse had been so fleeting I could not be sure.

A waiter came hurrying just as Alain was handing us into the carriage. He reached past Mr. Sauvage and handed a folded handkerchief to Victorine.

"Mademoiselle dropped this—"

Victorine murmured thanks, crumpled the linen square to tuck it into the lace undersleeve of her dress. A small enough incident, and an innocent one—but it lingered in my memory.

As we entered the Lick House Alain was presented with a telegram which set him frowning. His mouth became grim and all the harsh lines in his face were emphasized.

"Bad news?" Mrs. Deaves asked quickly. She appeared ready to offer sympathy but I could not imagine Alain Sauvage wishing that, no matter what blows life might deal.

"There is difficulty at the Horseshoe again. I thought that this last time I had made Parkinson see reason. He simply cannot deal well with the men. It is time I made a change there. But this means another trip to Virginia City. I shall make it as short as possible."

"At least," Victorine observed after he left, "he did not send us back to the country. Here there is something to do, to see—"

"But you have not wished to do anything." I was more disturbed at the change of events than I dared display.

Again I was responsible, and if Victorine had only been waiting for Alain to go—what could I do?

"That was because Alain spoke always of the *docteur* and said I must not tire myself by doing things until I saw him. Now Alain is no longer here to shake his head and say be careful. I am *not* ill, as I have told him—all of you—but never does he listen. I have only now and then an aching head which makes me feel queer and giddy. Now I do not feel that way at all and we shall do things without seeing Alain's stern face." She drew down the corners of her mouth in a counterfeit of a disapproving expression.

At least she was not going to start at once, for which I was thankful. For instead she started toward her chamber saying she would rest now. We had had cards left by those who had attended the ball, but had been absolved from the rounds of duty visits by the plea of Victorine's ill health and the fact we were in the city ostensibly to see a physician.

I think Mrs. Deaves chafed at our isolation when Alain was no longer available. Now she might wish to establish contact with old friends and I would be left alone as Victorine's mentor.

Heretofore the girl had been docile enough. But that restlessness which she showed again in the afternoon, wandering from window to window, dismayed me.

Mrs. Deaves withdrew with a bundle of notes she said must have immediate answers. And Victorine's lack of ease reacted upon me; I could not settle with a book nor a piece of needlework. Victorine had made plain from the first that fashion magazines were her only reading. If she had ever opened a book, that had been an act of curiosity to see why others could be attracted to reading.

Though she had clever fingers and could fashion amusing trifles in the way of caps, jabots, and the like from scraps of lace, ribbon, an artificial flower, her span of concentration was short. She would toss her creation aside before it was quite finished, leaving Amélie to add the last few stitches, her interest in it gone.

Now she clapped her hands in that way she always used to summon her maid, a gesture I found too hinting of slave-day customs to like. Though neither mistress nor maid seemed to find it amiss.

"Amélie—bring me the cards." Her order was in the sharpest tone I had ever heard her use in addressing the maid.

While, unlike her usual quick obedience, Amélie did not go at once, I saw her lips part as if to say something, and she glanced questioningly in my direction.

"It is all right, I tell you!" Victorine's impatience mounted. She seemed overriding some unheard protest. Her fingers went to her throat, parting the frills of her vestee to reveal the serpent necklace. "Bring them now!"

Amélie went with visible reluctance. And Victorine selected one of the smaller tables, swiftly stripped it of a vase of roses, a salver filled with calling cards, and a half-emptied box of bonbons. She ended by switching off the crimson plush cover to bare the polished surface.

A couple of jerks brought the denuded table to face her chair, as she kicked the cover into an untidy heap. Amélie returned, a black box in her hand, but she did not present that directly to her mistress.

Instead she stood by the table, holding what she carried pressed against her breast as if she hated to yield it up. Victorine's fixed gaze met the maid's stare. Then very slowly Amélie put down the box. That hideous bracelet with its spider setting was very obvious as she did so. I wondered why she clung to an ornament lifelike enough to bring a shudder from me every time I saw it.

"You may go!" There was a chill in Victorine's voice.

Amélie left slowly. She might be lingering, hoping to be recalled, to have her mistress declare she had changed her mind. If so she was to be disappointed.

Victorine paid no attention to me. She might have been alone in the room as she moved briskly as one repeating an action she had carried out many times before. The lid of the box pivoted to one side at a touch, and she lifted out a pack of cards.

They were certainly no ordinary pack such as might be used for a game of whist. In her white, beautifully kept hands, they were as incongruous as if she had deliberately reached into a gutter for a handful of mud. For their surfaces, as far as I could see, were grimed with ancient dirt. Such a foul deck might have been used for play on the Coast, yet they did not seem to disgust Victorine.

She shuffled three times before she laid the cards out, face up, on the table in a complicated pattern which had no resemblance to any form of patience I knew. Some were horizontal, crossing those laid vertically. And she did not use the entire deck, only a counted number. It was plain this was serious to her, her attitude was one of intense concentration such I had never seen her display before.

A few of the last cards had been laid face down and these she picked up one by one, surveyed, and then stabbed down on the table top either right or left. I was so curious I arose to look over her shoulder.

The usual pips were missing from these cards. Hearts, diamonds, clubs, and spades, there were none of those. These bore instead pictures which were so overlaid by dirt that one could hardly make out the full design, save one was a hand holding a dagger, another a black snake curled around a rod.

Victorine turned over the last card, added it to one of her piles. She scowled and muttered in the patois I could not understand. With a gesture of impatience or anger, she swept the cards into a pile, put them back into the box. Before I could ask a question, she pushed aside the table with such force that it nearly crashed, and stood up.

It was only then that she appeared to remember she was not alone, and turned her head to gaze at me.

"I am very tired, I go now to rest." Her abrupt speech had little in common with her usual half-drawl. And her bearing was not that of one fatigued. Rather her eyes glittered, her body was tense. But the door of her room closed so firmly behind her I was at a loss.

When Mrs. Deaves appeared to say that she was dining with a friend, Amélie came from Victorine's room to announce her mistress had a headache and would want only a cup of chocolate.

"But she was feeling so much better!" Mrs. Deaves was plainly vexed. "Very well, I shall send a note to the Andrews—"

"You need not give up your engagement." I did not fancy spending the evening with a Mrs. Deaves annoyed at the loss of her pleasure. "I shall remain here, of course. And I want no more than some sandwiches and a cup of coffee. Mr. Sauvage left that package of new books that arrived this morning and I shall have plenty of entertainment with those. I shall be near if Victorine needs anything."

She was torn two ways, but her desire for the evening's pleasure won. I sighed with relief when she left. Earlier I had dismissed Fenton so she could spend the evening with her sister, and the sitting room of the suite was very still.

In the book parcel was one of those three-volume novels from England with a most intriguing title—*The Moonstone*. I had vaguely heard of the author, Wilkie Collins, but the book was new to me and I sat down with the first volume, prepared to spend a quiet evening. If I were watched from Victorine's chamber, as I must have been, I was unaware of it.

When the light repast I had ordered arrived there was a second tray Amélie claimed. But I halted her to ask concerning Victorine. She said her mistress was better, had asked for soup and biscuits, but wanted nothing more. And she was so eager to go I could not detain her.

I found my book enthralling, too much so for an evening's reading when alone, I at last decided. Now I felt a

vague apprehension and depression, as if the troubles of
the characters were communicated to my own spirit. So I
put the volume firmly aside and went to bed.

It must have been close to an hour later that, still uneasy, I drew on my wrapper and slippers to make one
last check on Victorine. As I stood in the doorway of her
room I could see her asleep in bed. All was well, I could
retire.

Yet I could not sleep. The memory of those dirty cards
crowded into my mind every time I closed my eyes. Why
had I not asked Victorine to explain them to me? To
handle such filthy things might well cause an illness if
she did it often. The ancient Black Death itself could well
cling to their smeared surfaces.

Did I finally drowse? I must have, for suddenly it
seemed I was back in the cabin of the *Ranee*. But the
friendly Captain, Alain, Mrs. Deaves were missing. Alone
I faced Victorine and there was that in her face which
made her another person—evil.

Her fingers moved deftly dealing out those horrible
cards, not in any complicated design but for two hands of
play. While piled on the table between us was a heap of
jewels from which sluggishly trickled runnels of blood.
So great was my horror of touching those cards she willed
me to pick up that I awoke, found myself sitting up in
bed, my heart pounding.

I did not wait longer than to snatch my wrapper for I
must go to Victorine, assure myself that she was not the
demonic thing I had faced in my fantastic dream, so much
did that nightmare still hold me.

Nor did my feeling of need to lay that illusion fade as I
crossed the darkened sitting room to fling open her door.
There she lay calmly and peacefully asleep. What folly to
be so influenced by a dream! Yet I approached her bed.
Her face was turned toward the night lamp and now I
could see it clearly.

This was not Victorine!

Amélie lay there, wearing her mistress's robe and nightcap. In the dim light, if her face had been turned away,

the illusion might not have been broken. Only the chance that the dream had brought me—

Now I reached for the shoulders of the sleeping girl. My fear was lost in rising anger. What possible trickery was this?

"Wake up!" I shook Amélie with all my strength. "What are you doing here? Wake up!"

My grasp raised her from the pillows. But her head only rolled on her shoulders, her eyelids did not even flutter. I could hear her breathing, heavy, strenuous. As I shook her again I wondered if she could possibly be drunk.

But where was Victorine? And why was Amélie wearing her nightcap and lace-trimmed gown? Why this imposture?

The maid was a dead weight in my hands, gave no sign of consciousness. I let her fall back on the pillows. What was I to do? Where had Victorine gone and why? I fought to control rising panic, make myself think rationally. Was Amélie a party to deception or in some way a victim of it? For her complete passivity awakened my fears.

With an idea of discovering what I could before I summoned help, I lit a second lamp and, with that in my hand, I moved about the room, heading for the wardrobe. When I jerked open the door I had part of my answer.

There was no doubt this had been hurriedly ransacked. A mantle lay on the floor, dresses were in disorder. And two carpetbags stored in the back were gone. A quick check of the dressing table made clear that Victorine's jewel case and some of her toilet articles were missing.

I could think of only one explanation—an elopement. But why had Amélie been left so? I had thought the tie between her and Victorine was such she would have been included in such a flight.

Something lying on the hearth caught my attention as I lifted the lamp higher, a half-burned screw of paper. As I picked it up a yellowish powder shifted from the uncharred portion. There were words written on it. I smoothed out the half-sheet and read in French what was left:

"Enough for—"

I laid it carefully on a table. Enough for what, of what—? Had this contained a drug for Amélie?

Hurriedly I brushed the few grains of powder adhering to my fingers back onto the paper and folded it carefully. It might be well to know what the powder was.

Now I returned to the bed, only to face a new alarm. During the few moments I had been making my superficial search there had been a change in the girl. She seemed to be fighting for every breath she drew, and those labored gasps had longer intervals between. When I touched her forehead her skin was very chill. Amélie must have help and at once!

Putting down the lamp I rang the bell pull, which would summon the night porter. As I stood there waiting for an answer to my frantic summons, there came the grate of a key in the lock of the sitting room door, and that opened to admit Mrs. Deaves.

At the sight of me in the doorway of Victorine's room she stopped short.

"What is the matter?"

CHAPTER ELEVEN

To admit that one has failed in one's duty is never easy, and to do so to Mrs. Deaves, who I knew disliked me, was doubly difficult. But what mattered now was perhaps Amélie's life and certainly Victorine's safety.

I made the story short but before I had finished she pushed past me to see for herself. I would have followed, but there was a knock on the outer door and I answered, to front the hotel floorman I had summoned.

"Bring a doctor, as quickly as you can!"

"There's Dr. Beech, ma'am. He's just down the hall, lives here. If he's in—"

"Get him. If he is not there find someone else—but hurry!"

"Yes, ma'am." He padded away.

Fingers jerked at my arm.

"What are you doing?" Mrs. Deaves demanded.

"Getting a doctor for Amélie—I am sure she is gravely ill."

"Have you gone out of your mind?" she retorted. "Don't you realize what a scandal may mean to Alain? That wretched girl in there is drugged. Left alone she will recover. But if you bring in others that will start all kinds of gossip—"

I shook off her hold. "Did you really look at her? I know little about drugs, but I believe she is deathly ill. She must have help and that as soon as possible."

Brushing past Mrs. Deaves, I returned to the bed. Amélie's breathing was worse, even to my untutored ears. I had never had experience with any serious illness before, but I was sure of the danger now. Mrs. Deaves had followed, to face me across the bed.

"You are a complete fool, and Alain will never forgive you for this. You had better think about where Victorine might be, worry about this slut later. I intend to telegraph Alain—"

"Do!" If she had meant that as a threat, it did not matter. Alain was needed here. This was what he had feared from D'Lys. I only longed to have him walk into the room this instant.

"Be sure I shall tell him *everything*," she continued, paying no attention to Amélie's struggle for breath, just watching me, gloating in her eyes. At that moment I did not care what she told him, all that was important was that he should come.

"Someone is ill?"

Together we looked to the door. A burly man wearing a brocaded dressing gown, his tousled hair standing up like a cockscomb, stood there.

"I'm Dr. Beech. Well, ladies, what is the matter?"

Mrs. Deaves moved quickly away from the bed as if to disassociate herself from the scene.

"I shall go to send the telegram." She spoke to me, not to him, and with her head held high she passed him without a word.

The doctor watched her retreat in some surprise and then turned to me.

"Now then, young lady, what have we here?"

I explained while he made a quick examination of Amélie.

"She's been drugged, yes," he agreed. "We shall need hot coffee, plenty of it. Must get her roused, make her walk if we have to drag her around—keep her moving. I don't recognize the drug but the symptoms suggest a soporific of some type and certainly an overdose."

"I'll get the coffee, Miss Tamaris." Startled, I glanced around. Fenton had come in and never had I been so glad to see anyone. Her angular, upright figure was reassuring. I knew we could expect no help from Mrs. Deaves, but with Fenton I had a steady supporter—until Alain could arrive.

Though Amélie was in danger, I dared not forget Victorine. Where had she gone and with whom? It might be that every moment we used to fight for Amélie would allow her foolish young mistress to get farther out of our reach. Yet I did not see what else I could do. Perhaps when Amélie recovered consciousness she could tell us that which would help.

Fight we did during the next few hours, forcing the hot black coffee down the maid's throat. After the first cup she was wretchedly ill and the doctor found that promising.

"Gets some of the stuff out of her," he explained.

Fenton was a tower of strength, though we saw no more of Mrs. Deaves. We worked hard, two of us at a time leading Amélie about. She moaned, fought us weakly. However, I doubted if she was conscious of her condition. When her eyes did open now and then, she did not seem to know who we were. Or did she pretend that for reasons of her own?

At last Dr. Beech was satisfied she had thrown off the worst effects and we settled her back in bed. I collapsed on the chaise longue, suddenly aware that I was shaking

with fatigue and nervous reaction. As I sat so the doctor
came to me, holding that fan with the hiding place in the
end sticks. He sniffed at the hollow.

"Do you know what was in here?" he demanded.

"That there's nothing of Miss Tamaris'!" Fenton was
at my side in an instant. "You'd better ask Miss Victorine.
This here is *her* room, and that girl is *her* maid!"

"Please, Fenton," I curbed her, though her champion-
ship warmed me. "What is it, Doctor?"

"Something I can't name." He stared at me as if trying
to search my mind. "I've seen, or rather smelled, that
before—but when or where—" He shrugged.

Abruptly he stalked away from me to the bed. Picking
up the lamp and holding it closer to Amélie, he studied
her closely. Her nightcap had fallen off and her black hair
lay in rippling waves across the pillows. The usual deep
cream of her complexion was now yellowish and her
features seemed sharper, as if she had been ill for days.
Setting down the lamp at last, Dr. Beech turned back to
me.

"Is that girl from New Orleans?" I was surprised; what
did it matter where Amélie came from?

"No—from France. Or the West Indies—I am not
sure."

"Yes, she has all the look of *les sirenes*."

I had never heard that expression before. He must have
noticed my questioning look. Though he did not flush, his
eyes dropped from meeting my gaze as if he were embarrassed. "Just a term. Used to describe certain young
women of color." He picked up the fan again. "I'd like
to take this with me."

"Can't you tell me what you suspect?"

Dr. Beech shook his head. "I'm not sure myself. Just a
guess and nothing to discuss with a young lady either.
When Mr. Sauvage returns I would like to see him as
soon as possible."

"Of course."

"Now"—he became the authoritative man of medicine
—"I have arranged for one of the hotel maids to sit with
this girl. You, young lady, had better go to bed also.

Here"—he rummaged in his bag to produce a packet he gave to Fenton—"see that she takes that in a glass of warm milk. Then do not let her be disturbed until she wakes of her own accord."

I had no intention of following his orders, though I did not say so. Having just witnessed the result of a sleeping potion, I would never, I determined with a shudder, take one myself. Also—sleep could not be thought of. We had saved Amélie, but what of Victorine?

That I had failed in my responsibility was painfully true. Also there was little hope of redeeming that failure. But if I could discover some clue before Alain arrived I would have that much to offer him.

In my own room I faced Fenton. I must talk her into helping me, tired and shaky as I was.

"Fenton, we have to find Miss Victorine!"

She nodded, did not voice the protest I had half expected.

"You have been worrying about that all along, miss, that I know. But where do we look?"

Her prompt offer of alliance in that "we" heartened me.

"Someone must have seen her leave the hotel—"

"If you ask a lot of questions, Miss Tamaris, there can't help but be talk. The quieter we keep this the better when she comes home again. This is a town which talks a lot, and when mud's thrown, it's bound to stick—some of it— real hard."

Fenton was right. Yet I was sure that time mattered, that Victorine's danger might be, in another way, no less serious than Amélie's.

"There are people who'd know a little," Fenton continued, hesitatingly, as if she were not quite sure how she should word this.

"You mean the servants. They might not talk to me, but would they to you?"

"That's a way for us to start, yes, miss."

"Then—try it, Fenton! If you are able to uncover even the slightest clue—"

"I'll do my best, Miss Tamaris."

She left and I went to the bathroom, bathed my face

in cold water, which I hoped would help me to think more clearly. Then I hurried to my wardrobe and surveyed the garments hanging there.

From among them I chose a very plainly made alpaca which Fenton had so disdained she had suggested giving it away. Instead I had brought it with me, thinking it acceptable to wear to the shore where Alain had proposed taking us. It was of a dull dark blue with only a little braiding in black, made with a shorter "walking skirt"—what we had referred to at Ashley Manor as a "rainy-day dress."

If I were to venture forth to search for Victorine I must be as inconspicuous as possible. Wearing such a dress, a waterproof cape for a wrap, my hair plainly caught back under my oldest hat, perhaps I would not be remembered.

Where I would go and how I did not know. No lady of standing ventured out alone. If she had no other companion she took her maid. But there might be reasons why I could not take Fenton. I brought out my purse, counted out some silver and gold coins which I tied into a handkerchief and pinned into the seam pocket of my dress. Then I put on my stoutest shoes, though even those were meant for carriage travel and not walking.

So dressed, save for hat and cape, I returned to Victorine's room. There was someone visible in the half-light by the bed, bending over the sleeping girl. I saw a hand slipped under the top pillow as if in search.

"What are you doing!" I demanded.

She straightened with a start and I saw this was Submit. As she turned to look at me I was astounded by her expression.

If fear had ever looked at me from human eyes it was at that moment. The hand which had been under the pillow curled into a fist as if she now grasped some object. I thought I caught a glint of gold.

"What do you have there?" With a hasty step I reached her side, caught her wrist. She tried to jerk away, then stood quiet, her face still a mask of terror.

"What have you?" I repeated, pulling her hand into the full light of the lamp.

"Look then!" she spat out the words, opened her fingers.

The spider bracelet fell onto the bed. Against the soft pink coverlet it looked even more loathsome.

"*Z'araignée!*" Submit actually spat now. A drop of saliva struck not far from that distasteful thing.

"You were taking it!" Why did she wish to steal an object toward which she had so great an aversion?

"I take it because it is evil. She is evil—but not so much as—"

Then her torrent of speech dried as if she had been choked into silence. Submit was in the grip of fear and, I thought, judging by her expression, I would get little more out of her now.

I went to Victorine's dressing table, found a handkerchief. That I threw over the bracelet, picked it up with the lawn between my fingers and it, for I shrank from touching it otherwise. Why anyone had designed such a horrible object was a mystery to me. That Amélie had worn it had added, I believe, to my dislike for the girl. Had I been too deeply prejudiced by so small a thing?

Our fight to save Amélie's life had taught me pity. Whatever else she was, she was the product of a heritage which carried a heavy burden. How dared I judge anyone more straitly than I did myself? I held the wrapped bracelet in my hand, tried to think of what must be done. But I was so tired, and I could not make a clear decision.

"What you do with that? It is bad—very bad—"

"What were *you* going to do with it?" I counterquestioned.

"Take it to—" Again she stopped short. Then, knowing she must give me some answer, she added, "I take it where it do no more bad things. Then she"—Submit pointed to Amélie—"she can do no more bad either!"

"Submit—" Was there a chance to learn here something about Victorine? In this hotel most of the servants were Negroes; would they talk to Fenton? Submit was plainly shaken, in such an emotional state she might answer me more freely. "You know Miss Sauvage is missing?"

She replied with a swift nod.

"Could you find out whether anyone saw her leave the hotel tonight? Let me know if she was with another person, or went alone, possibly even *where* she went?"

All expression was gone from her face. She turned on me one of those blank masks those of another race use when they refuse communication. I had seen this with the Chinese, and in the Islands with the Polynesian people. Fronted by that I knew the uselessness of further probing.

"What you do with that?" Ignoring my question, she returned to her own, pointing to the bracelet.

"I don't know. Keep it, I suppose, until Amélie asks for it."

"It will bring you bad luck, very bad luck. It's nothing for a lady like you to have. Give it to me and I shall make better—you will see! Keep it and bad things will happen to you."

Though in that prophecy she was wrong as I was later to prove.

For the time being I put it into my inner pocket as she watched me slyly. Apparently she believed that, having disdained her good advice, I now courted misfortune.

Sure I could get nothing more out of her now, I went back to my own room. Unable to sit quietly waiting for Fenton, I paced up and down. I thought of the police, but to consult with them would mean exposure to the very kind of scandal which would ruin Victorine. That decision must be left to Alain. When could he—would he get here? Should I send a telegram also—not to make excuses for myself, but to impress upon him the gravity of the situation? Though I was sure I could depend upon the fact that Mrs. Deaves would have already painted as dark a picture as she could.

A light tap on the door sent me hurrying to let Fenton in.

"What have you learned?"

"A queer enough story, Miss Tamaris. Someone was seen leaving here, yes. But not Miss Victorine—they say it was Amélie."

"But it couldn't have been!" Then a sudden thought came to me. "Victorine in Amélie's clothes?"

That suggested a plot well planned in advance. Would Victorine drug her own maid, with whom she appeared to be on such good terms, put on the girl's clothing, leave in disguise? While they were of a height, there was the matter of Victorine's fair skin. No—it was impossible.

"Those who saw her said it was Amélie," Fenton repeated. "She went out the service entrance and got into a hired hack waiting there."

"When?"

"At a little after nine o'clock is the nearest I could make out."

Then she had been gone for several hours before I found Amélie. And now it was the next day. Victorine could have left the city, by ferry, carriage, even a ship!

"They were sure it was Amélie?" I repeated. "But I don't see how they could mistake Victorine for her—even if she wore Amélie's clothes."

Fenton coughed.

"You know something more?"

"Miss Tamaris, there are ways of darkening the skin. If a person had a mind to change her appearance she could do that easily enough."

"But that would mean Victorine has been acting a part for days!" I felt dizzy enough to catch at the back of the nearest chair for support. Now I faced the idea of two Victorines—one the lighthearted girl of quickly changing moods, the other a devious stranger. Which was the true one?

On that point much depended. If Victorine had been coaxed into this by another, she might be already regretting her rash actions. By now she could be frightened.

However, if she had planned this herself, then none of us had understood her character. Even Alain had been deceived. Victorine could be anywhere, yet we did not want to hunt her as if she were a criminal in flight.

"You might look around her room, Miss Tamaris—"

Fenton's suggestion was good. I could not just sit and wait. Wait for what? Only the arrival of Alain, when I would be forced to admit I had failed the trust he had placed in me.

Though I had a strong distaste for prying into drawers, searching the private belongings of others, this I must do. I went with Fenton, to discover that Submit had disappeared. Amélie was alone, which was directly against the orders the maid had been given.

But I was glad I would not have to search with her watching me. Fenton went into the bathroom, I turned first to the small desk.

Victorine, as I well knew, was no letter writer. I had never, during our weeks together, seen her at such employment. Now I found no address book. The drawer was empty of paper and envelopes. But in a small wastebasket close by was a crumpled wad of paper, beside it a scrap torn roughly into four pieces. I placed both finds on the desk, smoothing out first the crumpled sheet.

From it came a distinctive perfume, Victorine's. This had been carried in close contact with her person for some time. It bore a crude drawing.

That was a heart depicted with thick black strokes. From a point between the lobes sprang a bar resembling a sword, the hilt of which down-curled at both ends. While from the meeting point of sword and heart were upward shooting lines of red, unpleasantly suggesting blood spurting from a fatal wound. Last of all, from the pointed tip of the black heart, weaving upward to rest against the sword hilt, its forked tongue extended in threat or defiance, was a serpent of gold.

For all its crude delineation there was ugly power in the drawing, as if it had been done for a dark purpose. Beneath the design was a single short sentence in French:

"Tonight at nine."

I laid the drawing temporarily to one side and set about fitting together the torn bits. There was something so distinctive about the writing that I had a feeling I had seen it before, where and when I could not remember. This, too, had a single curt sentence, but in English:

"Be satisfied, for there will be no more."

"Miss Tamaris." Fenton came from the bathroom with

a bottle in her hand. "I was right," she told me triumphantly. "This is a stain for the skin—"

Then Victorine *had* planned this. That drawing which had been so crumpled—

A mind picture came from my memory, the waiter at The Poodle Dog bringing her the handkerchief. How quickly she had balled that up and put it in her sleeve. In the restaurant—the young man I had seen beside the pillar—had he drawn that disturbing picture, sent it to her under the very eyes of her brother? Had he indeed been that dabbler in voodoo, Christophe D'Lys? And was this some compelling symbol of that wicked belief? Now matters seemed to fit together—yet it was all guesswork on my part.

When Amélie aroused she must be carefully questioned. Until then she should be guarded. If she had purposefully been given an overdose of the drug she could still be in peril. But that was all too melodramatic. I could not believe Victorine would commit *murder!* She must have mistaken the power of whatever potion Amélie had, willingly or unwillingly, swallowed. I must not imagine horrors.

As Fenton set the bottle down before me, the wide oversleeve of her dress caught the edge of a small pile of notes, sweeping them to the floor. These had been sent to Victorine wishing her a quick recovery. They had been brought in yesterday by Mrs. Deaves who had insisted Victorine reply to each.

There was among them a cream-white half-sheet which caught my attention. I put that beside the torn one from the wastebasket, comparing one with the other. To my mind there was no question that both had been written by the same hand.

The sentiments were couched in very formal language and the name signed at the bottom—

Mrs. Beall!

"What is it, miss?" Fenton was scooping up the rest of the notes. "Did you find something?"

"Nothing I can understand," I admitted. I had Fenton get a larger envelope from my own desk. Into that I put the note from Mrs. Beall, the torn sheet from the waste-basket. I was about to seal this when I saw that other half-burned bit from the hearth which I had totally forgotten. The powder in it should have been given to Dr. Beech, but it was too late now. Instead it went into the envelope with the rest, and I wrote Alain's name across the outside.

I had retained the drawing, for I wished to confront Amélie with that when she awakened. My head was aching cruelly and I was desperately tired. Yet there was also a kind of feverish energy in me.

Now I must appeal to Mrs. Deaves, learn if she had had any answer to the telegram. How long after receiving it might we expect Alain? I had no idea of distances. And by the time he arrived, where would Victorine then be? We must do *something!*

"Miss Tamaris." Fenton pulled my attention from my own dark thoughts. "Please, can you not rest now? There's no way to follow Miss Victorine—"

I shook my head, feeling stupid and dazed.

"There *has* to be, Fenton, there has to be! Or I don't know what will happen. She"—I nodded to Amélie—"may hold the key to the whole thing. She must not be left alone. Please, Fenton, will you watch with her and call me the minute she rouses?"

She was, I could see, unwilling. But when I added that she was the only one I could trust to do this, Fenton appeared reconciled. Why she had so wholeheartedly embraced my cause I did not know, but that she had done so left me deeply grateful.

Back in my room I laid the envelope for Alain in plain sight on my desk. As I did so a slight noise startled me. Submit had slipped in without knocking. Her drab uniform was partly covered by a shawl, and she wore an old-fashioned bonnet pulled forward to hide much of her face.

"What are you doing here?" Since the scene in Victorine's room I was wary of this girl, sure that she knew something she would not share. Now, to my amazement and deepened uneasiness, she raised one finger to her lips, signaling silence, and brought out her other hand from beneath her shawl, holding an envelope for my acceptance.

Victorine! She must be using this method of getting in touch with me. That was my only thought as I eagerly snatched at the missive and tore it open. But the message was not from the girl I knew.

If you wish aid in your search for the missing, it may be that the undersigned can supply that. Come with Submit, since our meeting must be private, and she will be your guide.

The stilted writing was odd enough. However, it was the signature which surprised me the most.

"Mary Ellen Smith."

CHAPTER TWELVE

The strange "Mammy Pleasant" whom Mrs. Deaves had labeled a wicked woman, whom Mr. Cantrell had warned me against, but whom my father had treated with respect. This was the second time she had offered me aid and now I weighed my own memories against Mrs. Deaves' outburst, and Mr. Cantrell's ambiguous words. Of the three I chose to believe memory.

"Where do we go?" I asked the maid.

"To *her* house—on Washington Street." Submit tucked her hands under her shawl.

So I made my choice, perhaps foolishly and hastily. But it seemed to be such a chance as I had prayed for since I had found Victorine gone. I dropped the note on my desk beside the envelope marked with Alain's name, took up my hat and cape.

While there was no clinging fog, a light drizzle of rain made me pull the waterproof closer. We had gone out of the service entrance of the hotel, using back corridors. A hired hack waited and I climbed into its musty interior, which smelled of horse and stale cigar smoke. Though Submit had given no directions to the driver, the carriage moved on as soon as we were seated.

I shrank back as far out of sight as I could. The bad weather was a good cover; there were few on the street or sidewalks. Still I had a strange feeling of being spied upon.

Submit seemed to share my desire for invisibility, huddled into her own corner. I longed to ask questions, about our destination, about the woman who had sent me the note, but some instinct told me the girl would not answer.

Since I did not know the city I had no idea of direction. The pull up hills, the sharp descent down again, was manifestly difficult for the bony horse between the shafts of the hack. To my relief the driver did not use his whip. Instead he favored the patient plodder so we did not go very fast.

It was hard to curb my impatience. I was sure I could outstrip this rattletrap conveyance on my own two feet if only I knew the way. I made myself think not of wasted time but what I might ask in way of help.

How "Mammy" Pleasant might aid I could not guess. I began to believe I had been very rash in coming and was about to demand to be returned to the hotel, when we stopped before a three-story building, one a little more pretentious than either of its neighbors. I caught sight of the sign on the lamp post—Washington Street.

I fumbled for the handkerchief in which I had knotted my money, wondering how much to pay our driver, when Submit shook her head.

"*Her* man brought us—you do not pay."

Traffic in this street was light. The pavement was deserted as Submit put her hand lightly on my arm to urge me to a door which opened at once, as if we had been watched for. Warmth, the smell of tobacco, an opulently furnished parlor off the entrance hall to my right, greeted me. But I had only a glimpse of those rich furnishings, of the fire on the hearth, before the girl who had opened the door beckoned me on. Submit remained behind.

The doorkeeper was white, and wore a wrapper as

frilled and belaced as any Victorine indulged in. Her light brown hair was dressed to allow long curls to lie on her shoulders. Had I met her elsewhere I might have thought her the pampered daughter of a respectable house.

She did not speak, only gestured me to follow her up the stairs, to walk along a carpeted hallway above, moving swiftly as if we must get out of sight. At the final doorway along that corridor she knocked twice and stood aside for me to enter alone.

The door had been opened by that woman I had last seen in the ribbon shop.

"Mrs. Smith?" I ventured.

She smiled and her smile was warm.

"Once I was Mrs. Smith, Mrs. James Smith. For some years now I have been Mrs. Pleasant. But since you knew me by my earlier name, I used it to introduce myself. Come in, Miss Penfold."

The room into which she ushered me was elegant. I looked about me curiously, since I had not the least idea of the nature of this establishment.

Striped wallpaper in tones of oyster and pink covered the walls. There was a black marble fireplace before which stood two chairs, their frames of carved rosewood, their upholstering a pinkish-purple velvet. Between those was a table holding a tray of covered silver dishes. Velvet drapes of oyster gray were pulled completely across the windows, and what light there was came from a low-turned gas jet and two lamps.

My hostess was a woman of presence, just as I had remembered her, the magnetism she exuded easy to feel. She wore a full-skirted dress, old-fashioned in cut, but of a rich plum silk, with delicate white lace collar and cuffs. These were matched by a mourning cap, a heart-shaped piece of lawn. Jet earrings and a jet pendant contributed to her general somber clothing, yet the effect was one of elegance, perhaps more tasteful than the highest fashion could now display.

She slipped the waterproof from my shoulders, took my hand to draw me closer to the fire. A scent of roses clung to her rustling skirts.

"You do remember me." That was a statement, not a question.

"Yes, you came to the *India Queen* to talk with my father."

"Captain Penfold risked much to help my people. I owe him a debt I had then no way of repaying. Perhaps I can discharge that now in service to his daughter."

"Your note—you said you could give me news of the missing—" I settled only on the edge of the chair to which she had guided me, trying to read some answer in her pleasant, placid face.

She was removing the covers of the dishes on the tray. Then she poured into a small liquor glass something from a bottle fretted with silver.

"Drink this, my dear. It is wild clover cordial, of my own brewing. You need sustenance of body as well as peace of mind." Her voice soothed, invited trust.

Yet what did I know of this woman? That long-ago meeting, the outburst of Mrs. Deaves, Mr. Cantrell's caution. Still, when I looked at her, I could not doubt she meant me well.

I sipped the drink. The taste was odd but not unpleasant. The warmth of the fire drove out that chill which had been within me since I first found Amélie hours ago.

Now my hostess poured me a cup of coffee, uncovered a plate with crisp bits of bacon and eggs scrambled together. I began to eat, first because she urged me, and then because the food was very good and I was near famished. All the while she said little, smiled that relaxing smile.

I have met many women who have some claim to authority and position, but never before one who possessed such an assurance of certainty that what she desired would be, that there was nothing which could stand against her will.

"You are seeking Victorine Sauvage," she said when I refused more food and had relaxed a little. "That is what we shall now discuss."

My caution had not been entirely banished by this restful room, the personality of my hostess. Now I asked boldly, "How did you know Victorine had gone?"

Mrs. Pleasant's smile did not alter; if anything it deepened.

"Child, there are eyes and ears everywhere. And tongues to repeat any news out of the common. Also—but of that we shall speak later. It remains I can learn what you wish to know. If Miss Sauvage is still within the city, it will be reported to me. If she has left, the manner and direction of her leaving will also be discovered. However, such a search requires time. This is a large city, it has many places where people who do not wish to be discovered can remain hidden.

"Under this roof I have guests of standing, members of the city government. Captain Lees of the detective force, for example—"

"No!" I interrupted. "Not the police, unless Mr. Sauvage so decides. The scandal of an open search—"

She inclined her head as a queen might nod. "That is understood. When Mr. Sauvage returns he will be at liberty to do as he thinks best. But it may be some time before he does return."

All my anxiety flooded back. "I know! If we can only find her soon—I have a feeling that we must—for her own sake!"

"Time may be of major importance," she agreed with me. "I shall alert my people. Since those under obligation to me work in many places around the city, they see and hear much. When the word goes out that we seek a certain girl, they will watch for her."

"She—her appearance may be changed. My maid found a bottle of skin dye. Victorine had made herself look like her maid Amélie—who is a quadroon."

"And she has gone with a man."

"How do you know that? Have your people already found her?" I half started out of my chair.

"No. But in such cases there is always a man at the bottom of the mystery. Perhaps you had some warning that this might happen—is there a man against whom

Miss Sauvage had been warned? Perhaps forbidden to see? Let me know all you can."

Would I be betraying Alain's confidence if I told her? But what did that matter if a few words would lead to finding Victorine? So I repeated what I had heard about Christophe D'Lys.

"Voodoo," Mrs. Pleasant repeated. "And from those islands where it remains very strong."

"There is this—I found it in Victorine's room this morning." I brought out that much creased bit of paper with its strange design. She took it from me and her expression changed. Her benign smile was gone. Instead her lips tightened, her eyelids drooped. When she looked up from the paper to me again there was a cold scrutiny in those mismatched eyes.

"Ezili Coeur-Noir," she said.

"What do you mean?"

The intent gaze was once more on the paper. "Better you never know, child. But if this is what—no!" She arose.

"This shall not happen, not in *my* city!" That accent on the possessive in that sentence might be unconscious, but it was quite revealing. Her queenliness came from a sense of power, I knew with a sudden flash of insight. And whatever that power was based on, she was confident in her control.

"It is part of the voodoo belief?" I persisted.

"What is called voodoo, yes. Now—you must remain here for the present while I make certain arrangements." But still she stood regarding the paper. "This raises—" Again she broke off, then continued, with her first warmth of tone. "I shall return as soon as I can. No one must know you are here. Such a house as this is not recognized by the ladies you move among. Do you understand me? You must not, for the sake of your good name, be seen by any of my guests." Her warning was seriously meant, I could see.

"But I can't stay here—"

"You can and must, until you can leave unobserved. Did I not say that I owed your father a debt? I shall not involve his daughter in any action which will blacken the Penfold name. Talk is cheap, as the old saying goes. There is always a lot of idle talk here, mainly mud-tinged. We shall be what we can to find Miss Sauvage, though it would seem that she has ventured into very dark ways indeed."

Mrs. Pleasant did not give me back the drawing. She still held it as she left me. A moment later I was sure I heard the turn of a key in the door lock. Was she making sure I would not be intruded upon by one of her famous "guests," or was I to be kept secure to save me from flouting her warning? The fact was that at that moment I could not have fled anyway. My limbs were as heavy as my eyelids, and a languor, born of fatigue and nervous exhaustion, pushed me into a dream-filled sleep.

When I awoke I was not in the chair by the fire, but lay at greater ease on a divan, a shawl over me. I was still drowsy but not so much that I did not see Mrs. Pleasant once again by the tea table, her head resting against the chair back. She was intent upon a small object she held in a pair of tongs.

A pair of tongs—as Alain had held the gris-gris he had burned! Alain! I sat upright with a muttered exclamation and my hostess turned her head to look at me.

Then, as if she did not want me to see what she had been holding, she thrust the tongs' burden into the very heart of the fire. Again I was reminded of Alain's action. Where was he? Had he returned to find me gone? I must get back to the hotel as quickly as I could.

"Victorine—what have you found out about her?"

"Only a little. She is not with the man of whom you spoke. He is here in the city, however, and is being watched—well watched." Mrs. Pleasant's voice was decisive. "It is my belief he has hidden her someplace. That we must discover before he realizes his presence is known."

"You can do that?"

"Given time—yes." She spoke with such confidence I believed her.

"Time—how long have I been here? Alain—Mr. Sauvage—has he returned?"

She smiled and worked her magic again. I was soothed, reassured.

"It is five o'clock. And Mr. Sauvage had not arrived. Submit reports the telegram missed him in Virginia City. He had already left to visit another mine farther north. But a messenger has been sent after him."

"I must get back to the hotel—" I pushed away the shawl still covering my knees. Though I would not admit it, I felt a little giddy.

"You need not worry. I have sent a note to Mrs. Deaves. She knows you are not only safe but are striving to find Victorine."

Mrs. Deaves—who had called this quiet, smiling woman wicked. If Augusta Deaves thought I was in league with "Mammy" Pleasant what story would she bear to Alain? I stood up to look for my cape and my hat.

"Now you are disturbed, but why? You have nothing to fear from Augusta Deaves. She understands now that she must aid instead of hinder you."

"But she spoke as if she hated you!" I was so amazed I blurted that out before I thought.

Mrs. Pleasant's gentle smile never changed. "She has no reason to hate me, child. I have pointed that out to her but she will not believe me; mainly because fear feeds fear. Sometimes people indulge in foolish actions and someone learns of their folly. Then follows fear of exposure. However, I know many secrets and keep those well. Mrs. Deaves has no reason to fear me, every reason to aid you and Miss Sauvage. She will do all she can to help.

"As for your leaving here—that cannot be done as yet. My guests are arriving, and you must remain unseen. Later we shall provide a way for you to go unnoticed. Also, it is better you stay until we learn where Miss Sauvage is so we can bring her out of hiding. Perhaps by this time she will be better advised of the character of

D'Lys, will be very grateful for being found. If he has not gone too far—"

"You mean taken such action that she will have to marry him?"

"That—or other matters." Mrs. Pleasant did not enlarge on the second part of her reply.

So I was forced to be content while she left and returned shortly thereafter with another tray of food. It was a superbly cooked meal, such as to tempt even a small appetite. But I chafed at my imprisonment.

I even took to listening at the door after Mrs. Pleasant left again. There was the sound of laughter, muted voices. Once a woman sang a sentimental ballad in a languishing voice, to be paid with a crackle of applause. The door had been locked again, but this time Mrs. Pleasant had been frank about that, saying she did not want anyone to intrude upon me.

I kept thinking of my own folly, that intermingled with my worry over Victorine. I shrank from picturing what Alain's return might bring. For my own part in this bizarre happening there could be only censure.

Mrs. Pleasant presented an enigma I could not solve. She had summoned me to a house where she admitted I must not be seen, yet her promise of aid was, I was sure, honestly made. Her discussion of Mrs. Deaves, was there a hint of blackmail in that? And to this add voodoo—

Amélie had been drugged nearly to death. Was Victorine a second victim, controlled by another's will? I had heard of strange drugs which produced hallucinations—could such hellish devices be part of voodoo?

I found my patience wearing very thin by the time Mrs. Pleasant returned.

"You have learned something?" I demanded even before she closed the door.

"A hint only, but one we can act upon. If she *is* in the place suggested to me, we can bring her away. However, that hint came to me through several sources and such rumors can be false. But I am told she believes herself to be safely hidden until D'Lys comes for her, and she is entirely devoted to him. I have no key to compel her to come away, save force, and that would bring unwelcome attention. All I can do at present is make sure she can leave if she wishes. Do you understand?"

"Where is she?" That speech had been so full of half-hints and implications it irritated me—I wanted the bare truth.

I think she was weighing the need for being frank against reticence before she answered. Perhaps it was because I was my father's daughter she did answer.

"She is, according to report, at the Red Rooster. That is a parlor house—a *French* parlor house."

Though her accenting of the "French" meant nothing to me (I was not *that* worldly wise), I guessed at the meaning of the other term.

"But then—she—" I was filled with such horror that I could not speak coherently.

"No, she is only in safe keeping there. That is all, I swear."

"And you are not entirely sure she *is* there—"

"I am as sure as I can be without seeing her myself. When this D'Lys returns—my people have lost sight of him—I do not know where he plans to take her. Nor do we know when he shall return."

"Then we must go to her. She knows me—will listen to me certainly. She cannot be utterly lost to all that is right, she is so young—"

"If she will not listen"—Mrs. Pleasant spoke with a deliberation which gave her words deeper emphasis— "you must take measures to get her to go with you. Once we can bring her here, D'Lys cannot bother you."

"But we must take her back to the hotel—"

"To do that before Mr. Sauvage returns would be folly. If you cannot convince her, can you keep her prisoner in her room there without courting the very notice you do not wish?"

Her logic was right. But the path ahead seemed to me to lead deeper and deeper into trouble. Yet I had to agree, if reluctantly, to her proposal.

"You cannot come with me as you are. You must be no young lady, but rather someone likely to be seen in

such a place. Not—" she read aright my start of re-
pugnance—" one of the regular habitués. But it is customary that the maids in such houses be of Negro or mixed
race. Many of them have been hired through my agency
by the keepers of such establishments. Thus tonight I
shall simply be calling on an acquaintance with a maid
she might or might not want to hire. That will introduce
us to the house. If Miss Sauvage is there, it shall then be
your duty to persuade her to leave with us. If she refuses—
there is another way—"

She crossed the room to where stood a tall cabinet, a
beautiful piece of Chinese design, with a double front
panel inlaid with mother-of-pearl. Taking a ring of keys
from her seam pocket, she unlocked those doors. Within
were two sections of narrow drawers, and she chose
from one a paper packet.

Having carefully closed and relocked the cabinet, she
advanced to the full light of the lamp, placing the packet
on the table. For a moment she regarded it intently and
then nodded, as if in answer to her own thoughts.

"Do not touch this," she cautioned. "I shall be back
very shortly."

So swiftly and soundlessly did she move, she might
have vanished as do the characters in some fantastic
story. Then she was back, a handkerchief in her hand.
This she spread flat on the table before she tipped onto
it the contents of the packet, a saffron yellow dust. Turning up the corners of the linen square she tied those together to form a loose bag.

"If she refuses to listen to you, you will have this. Be
ready to loosen it quickly—so—" She inserted one finger
to prove how easily a corner could be loosened. "Then
throw the powder into her face!"

"What! But what will it to do her?"

"If she is under the influence of D'Lys as we suspect,
breathing this will break his control over her. She will
become, for a very short time, like one who is sleepwalking. You can lead her by the hand, and she shall be
as obedient to your direction as a small child—"

"But what is it?" I shrank from the idea of using such a weird weapon, even if Victorine's future depended on it.

"It is a powdered herb, or rather a mixture of herbs. The effect is not long lasting. And it is harmless, that I swear to you."

Such was the tone of her voice that I believed her. Only the thought was so strange I hoped that I would not have to put it to the test.

Mrs. Pleasant brought out a second handkerchief to wrap the first. Then she spoke briskly.

"You must darken your skin and I shall bring you a bonnet to help your disguise. Take down your hair so it can be tightly netted under that."

Though I shrank from all this I knew it must be done. Unhooking my bodice I allowed her to pat a soft wad of cotton, first dipped in a bowl of dark liquid, over my face and throat. When I looked in the mirror as she busied herself netting my hair as tightly as she could, I saw how much the darkening of my skin transformed me. I could indeed now pass as one of mixed blood.

The bonnet she had ready was akin to the face-concealing one Submit had worn. But added to it was a fringe of wiry black curls sewn within, so that when its strings were tied beneath my now brown skin, I had hair to match my complexion.

My own waterproof cape was discarded in place of one more worn and shabby. But my dress, she decided, would do. There came a discreet tap at the door as she submitted my person to a last searching gaze.

"Our hack is here, it is time to go. Oh, you have forgotten!" With an exclamation of annoyance she caught up the handkerchief bundle and thrust it upon me. "Tuck that in your sleeve where you can reach it easily. Your father was a man of great courage and resolution. You are not unlike him in looks; if you share his qualities of character, call upon those now."

We descended a back staircase, passed through a kitchen filled with delicious smells where my companion paused to inspect the contents of various pans on the stove, speaking to the cook in charge of them. He was a stout man who paid no attention to me huddling back in the shadows.

"This business," Mrs. Pleasant announced as she pushed upon the back door and we had only the faint glimmer of a single yard lantern to guide us to a high board fence, "must be resolved as soon as possible. It is only by luck that Mr. Lanthen and his family are away from the city. Were they here now, I would have to be at their house—and they are due to return soon."

At her push a section of the fence swung like a door and I held my skirts tightly against me to squeeze through in her wake. Beyond, in an alley, waited a hack. It might have been the one which brought me here; I did not know.

Nor did Mrs. Pleasant give any directions to the driver. But he set off as if he knew exactly where to go. The drizzle of the early day had stopped, but dampness was heavy in the air. In the light of the infrequent street lamps pools of water glittered in the gutters. And now there was more traffic in the streets through which our conveyance twisted and turned.

Ahead I saw a gleam of light, fire red, not at ground level, but in the air. Now we advanced more slowly. A carriage ahead had pulled to a halt and two men, their voices loudly jovial, alighted, to enter the door under that beacon. Now I could see the light formed a rooster of bright scarlet. There was certainly no mistaking the sign.

But we did not stop before the front door. Instead our hack continued with a sober clip-clop to the corner of the block and turned left, carrying us into another dark alley where the driver at last reined in. Mrs. Pleasant got out.

"Hold up your skirts, girl!" she bade me as I were indeed a would-be maid. "No sense in going to see Madame Célie all draggle-tailed."

The warning was necessary. Here the pavement, which I could only dimly see, was noisome, the smell noxious. I watched my footing as best I could, reaching another fence where my guide opened a gate. Then we were in a small littered yard. Luckily the far wall of that was badly rotted, for there was no second opening; instead we had to squeeze through a gap to reach an area paved with brick, more stable footing than the alley had allowed.

"Be quiet, and stay a little behind me," Mrs. Pleasant cautioned in a whisper.

I was just able to make out the outline of a door in the house wall. A single stone step was between that and the yard. Mrs. Pleasant set her feet firmly on that and knocked on the door with a series of small taps.

The portal opened and we came into a narrow back hallway, lighted only by the candle of the woman who greeted us. Of her I saw little save she was Negro and wore the cap and apron of a maid. Nor did I catch the words Mrs. Pleasant murmured to her. She turned and led us to a stairway down which filtered some light.

From the front of the house came the sound of a parlor organ, laughter, and talk. There was the smell of strong scent, the fumes of wine, and the spice of burning incense.

CHAPTER THIRTEEN

At the top of the stairs opened a second hall carpeted in thick red stuff, lighted by gas jets (turned quite low) in the form of gilded cupids holding aloft torches. The maid continued to the front of the house where there was the head of a wider stair, up the well of which came much louder sounds.

She opened the door of a room which must face the main street and waved us in. Thus I found myself in surroundings my untutored imagination could never have pictured for me. Here the red carpet was overlaid by a scattering of thick fur rugs dyed a golden yellow. Light was provided by amber- and topaz-banded lamps. There were no signs of windows, for crimson drapes of velvet fell, in gold-fringed folds, to hide the outer world.

Overhead the ceiling was frescoed with nude golden goddesses depicted showering trails of overblown roses. But it was the walls which astonished me the most. Mirrors ran from floor to ceiling in panels, the door through which we had entered being concealed by one such. All were framed in gold and between them were four life-size pictures of nude women painted without any restraint of taste. Each was plainly meant to represent a different type of beauty, one brunette, one blonde, one with brown hair, and the last with red.

The bed was very wide, its deeply carved headboard nearly touching the ceiling. Across that headboard played cupids holding more gold roses. While the sheets and pillowcases, revealed by a partly folded back red velvet cover, were of gold satin.

There was a marble-faced fireplace equipped with a gilded screen. Even the fire irons had been treated with a wash to counterfeit that same precious metal.

About were several chairs, all of gilt, with padded crimson velvet seats and backs. And the atmosphere had a thick, cloying scent which made me a little faint. I longed to go to one of the concealed windows, push aside that smothering weight of velvet, and open the panes, let in the night air. There was no sign of Victorine.

"She is not here." I looked for the door, now so cunningly hidden behind one of the mirrors that I felt trapped.

"She is here—but not in this room. Be quiet, leave all to me."

Mrs. Pleasant seated herself placidly on one of the chairs as if she were in her own sitting room. The calm dignity with which she moved, the elegance of her dress, put to shame this gaudy chamber. I averted my eyes from the walls, the bed, looked straight at the fireplace. How could Victorine come willingly to such a place? What had happened to her?

The mirrored door was flung open with such force as to suggest that the woman who entered was in a far from amiable temper. Small, she wore a dress as red as the carpet. And that garment was so betasseled, beaded, and sequined in gold that she glittered with every movement.

Her bright chestnut hair was built high into the most elaborate style. Small diamond stars, anchored on almost invisible wires, were entrapped in that edifice, sparkling with every movement of her head. Bracelets thick with the same stones ringed her plump wrists, and a necklace was fully displayed above a bodice cut so low as to be hardly decent.

"Vat you vant now?" Her eyes held the same hard glint as her diamonds as she planted herself before Mrs. Pleasant. She spoke with a thick accent, her voice huskily hoarse.

"Some words with you, Célie."

The woman snorted angrily. "Eet ees time for vork, not for talk. Come een zee morning as always."

"When you shall be deeper in trouble than you are now, Célie?"

At Mrs. Pleasant's question the woman stared. She might have been about to protest and then her eyes narrowed, her painted mouth closed. A moment later, in a much lower voice, she asked, "Vat you mean—trouble? Me—een trouble—"

"Right now you have under this roof a young lady of good family, taken from her relatives and friends. One word of that, Célie, spoken to Captain Lees—and with the anger of a very important family to spur him on—"

"You are wrong! I 'ave no von as you say—no von!"

"Perhaps you have been told a false story. That might just save you when Captain Lees comes, if you can make him believe it. But knowing him, Célie—and knowing he will be spurred in this case to do his whole duty—do you want to risk it?"

"Lees! Ha!" Célie laughed. "Vat do I care for him? Do you know who comes here? Lees vould take a look into my parlor—then he vould run, like a puppy, vith his tail between zee legs!"

Mrs. Pleasant smiled. "Come, come, Célie." She might have been warning a boastful child. "You know the Captain as well as I do. I tell you in this case the pressure which can be brought to bear is such that none of your valued clients would dare lift a finger in your behalf."

Célie had been studying the other's face, which now wore its most benign expression, as if she were trying to assess how much truth there was in that threat.

"You know ziss?" The bombast was gone from her voice.

"Would I be here at this hour if I were not certain? We have been acquaintances a long time, Célie. Because of that I have come to warn you. What story you have been told, I do not know. But the truth is exactly what I have said. If it were known that this girl was under your roof it would rock this city from top to bottom. We have come for her. Once she is away all will be forgotten."

"He said—she ees his wife—" Célie bit her full lower lip, rubbed her hands together. "He vill be most angree—"

"There are those who will be even more angry, ones who have the power to make that anger felt. Keep her and you will have no house, perhaps you shall even finish your days in prison, Célie. You know well enough there are those in this city whose wills can supersede even the law."

"She has said ziss also—zat she ees his wife."

"Which he doubtless forced her to say. I have brought one with me who knows her well, can persuade her to go with us." Mrs. Pleasant gestured toward me. For the first time Célie glanced in my direction.

"Ziss von—she ees only a maid—"

"A maid, yes. But one who knows enough to make your guest remember who and what she is. Let them be alone for a space, then we shall leave and you will have nothing to fear."

"Except him! And he ees a bad man—a veree bad man."

"He shall also be taken care of, I promise you, Célie. Captain Lees dislikes troublemakers, he shall be informed."

"Ah, you have an answer for all!" Célie flung at her.

"Except what you have already been given, Célie— the gold paid for this service. Better return that and be sure of a less troubled future. I would advise no greediness in this case—"

Angry as the woman was, for some reason she did not set her will against that of my companion. As she turned abruptly to the concealed door she said, "So. Let eet be. Come viss me—you!"

It was me she addressed and we went back along the cupid-lighted corridor, to a continuation of the back flight of stairs.

"Up—eet ees zee first door." She went swiftly away, her heavy skirts whispering over the carpet.

I groped my way up, feeling unequal to the task ahead. However, when one is faced by a disagreeable or dangerous duty, it is best to move without delay.

A single gas jet gave light enough to see the door. I turned the knob, more than half expecting to find it locked. It was not and I entered.

"Christophe!" A name, murmured softly, reached me.

Victorine sat on the edge of a bed, wearing only a filmy wrapper which made her look as wanton and shameless as those dreadful pictures below. When she saw me her eyes went wide.

"Who are you? What are you doing here?"

I had forgotten my disguise. Now I swept off that bonnet with its fringe of false curls.

"It is Tamaris, Victorine. I have come—"

She stared at me, then tensed, her mouth twisted in a ugly way. This was not the Victorine I knew. Only I was given little time to assess the stranger for she burst out, "Go away, do you hear me—go away! I do not need *you*. Where is Christophe, what have you done with him? If you do not go I shall scream and scream. Then, when they find you here—you shall be sorry, you pinched-faced little cat my brother set to watch me!"

She laughed in so wild a way that I thought of drugs. If Amélie had been left to die, then perhaps Victorine had been given something which had turned her brain. My horror of that was so great that for a moment I could not answer at all. Then I knew that I must depend upon the weapon Mrs. Pleasant had given me. Otherwise I could never get Victorine out of this terrible place.

The handkerchief was in my hand. But I must get closer to the distraught girl before I could use it.

"Victorine"—I strove to hold my voice steady—"truly I mean you no harm. We have been so worried—you left us without a word—"

"You lie, Tamaris." Again she laughed. "All you worry about is that Alain will blame you because his plans are spoiled. He hates Christophe, he swore we should never be together. But Alain is not *le bon Dieu!*" Again came that wild laughter. "There are many things he cannot control, for all his money and power. Now I stay with Christophe. And when *she* knows what is due me she will pay more and more. Alain shall also give us money—you will see. Christophe is not a nothing Alain can sweep from his path—he knows much. Alain shall pay, more and more and more—"

The hysteria in her voice was plain. I had myself under control, knew what I must do.

Then Victorine began to repeat words strange to me, allowing her robe to slip from her shoulders until she was nude to the waist. She reached beneath her pillow and pulled forth that serpent necklace, fastening it about her throat so its evil head hung between her breasts.

Her preoccupation with the necklace gave me the chance I needed. Moving swiftly, I flipped the handkerchief in her face. The yellow dust struck her cheek and chin, adhering thickly to her skin. Victorine gave a startled cry which turned into a cough as she inhaled or swallowed some of the powder.

As she continued to cough her hands fell into her lap. Now she stared straight ahead, her eyes vacant.

"Victorine?" I spoke her name gently as I drew the wrapper up about her. If she heard me she made no answer.

"Victorine!" I endeavored to awaken some spark of recognition. "You must get dressed, we have to go quickly."

Slowly she arose. "Get—dressed," she repeated as might

a puppet. Still staring ahead, not even looking at the garments for which she fumbled, she did dress. I tied laces, buttoned, and hooked as fast as I could. For a moment I could only think that she was manageable now.

I was in the midst of hooking her bodice, while she stood like a doll, when the door opened. Terrified by a faint creak, I looked over my shoulder. Had it been D'Lys I would have been lost, but Mrs. Pleasant stood there.

She studied Victorine and nodded as she picked up from a chair a hooded cloak. I made no attempt to order Victorine's hair, which still spilled across her shoulders. But with the cloak on and its hood pulled up, she was well hidden.

"We must move fast," Mrs. Pleasant warned. "The virtue of those herbs does not last long. If she rouses the house we might be in trouble."

I needed no other spur. Together we urged Victorine down the stairs and she went like a sleepwalker. During the rest of our journey through the house we met no one; perhaps Célie had arranged that.

Our charge had to be led across the yard, pushed through the fence gap. Mrs. Pleasant moved with quick energy. I wondered in what strange undercurrents of this city she swam. That she might have two sides to her character I already believed. But her help tonight was beyond price.

The hack still waited in the alley. Three on its seat was a tight fit as we put Victorine between us. I hoped we could continue to manage her when the effects of the powder wore off.

How late was the hour I did not know. There were no open shops about, and most of the houses we passed had a secret, well-shuttered look. As if what lay behind their windows were no normal life.

I had intended to defy Mrs. Pleasant and return with Victorine to the hotel. Now I knew that I could not do that. However, I clung to a thin hope that Mrs. Pleasant might relent and agree with me even yet.

"I do not see how we can get her back to the hotel—"

"But we are not taking her there, child. For the time

being she will be much better at Washington Street. No one will know she is there. And as soon as Mr. Sauvage arrives in the city, he will be notified and can come for her. He will be able to provide a believable story for her absence and carry it off."

That Alain was capable of that I had no doubt. I should have felt an overwhelming relief at such a sensible suggestion. Except that I could not forget that I had not fulfilled my trust or my duty. That we had had to enter *such* a place to find Victorine—

Célie's talk of her marriage to Christophe, that must only have been an excuse he used to enlist the woman's aid. Though perhaps the girl might even believe she had gone through a form of marriage. If so, Alain knew how to deal with that. But if even a rumor of this night's work ever reached those circles in which Victorine was to move—she was lost.

Thus I was not relieved, only tormented by a sense of anxiety and foreboding, as I once more entered Mrs. Pleasant's own domain.

We did not return to her sitting room, rather climbed a second flight of stairs to the third floor. There our hostess showed us into a bedroom which was not luxurious, but comfortable enough to suggest she treated her maids—if this was a maid's chamber—very well.

I steered Victorine ahead of me. But, as Mrs. Pleasant closed the door, that sound acted on my charge like a waking bell. Victorine twisted out of my hold and swung around. In the light of the lamp Mrs. Pleasant carried her face was contorted with fury, her crooked fingers reached to score the flesh of my face.

"Let me go—!" Her voice scaled into a screech.

Mrs. Pleasant moved swiftly behind her. As we struggled, my strength was not enough to save me from a smarting scratch on the side of my chin. But our hostess seized and held Victorine's upper arms.

In Mrs. Pleasant's grip Victorine still fought. But the older woman was even able to clap one hand over the girl's mouth, reducing her cries to muffled sounds.

"Over there." Mrs. Pleasant gestured with her head.

"The bottle on the shelf. Sprinkle a few drops on a handkerchief and hold it to her nose—quickly!"

Victorine's struggles were now so violent she dragged Mrs. Pleasant back and forth. I hastened to obey. But when I turned back, bottle and cloth in my hands, she stopped fighting. Above Mrs. Pleasant's muffling hand her eyes lost that feral glare which so frightened me.

"She is better now. Victorine, I do not want to use this, I only wish to help you. If we let you go, will you be quiet, listen to us—please?"

She nodded. Mrs. Pleasant released her. But, though the girl did not scream, nor try to attack me again, there was still something in her expression which did nothing to relieve my fears. She now regarded us with the kind of arrogance one in full authority might affect toward menials with whom she planned to deal in her own fashion and in her own time.

Still saying nothing, she glanced from me to Mrs. Pleasant. One hand went to her throat, lay across the serpent necklace, either to shield it from sight, or as one touches a talisman to gain courage.

Then, speaking in a stern voice, Victorine repeated a phrase of what sounded utter gibberish to me. Mrs. Pleasant looked faintly amused. I knew that I was witnessing a battle of wills on a plane I did not understand. One to which Victorine had come with full confidence, and from which she expected only victory. Once more those strange sounds issued from her lips with the cadence of a ritual chant.

Mrs. Pleasant pointed to the hand Victorine had folded about her serpent necklace. Now she replied with a phrase which she did not speak loudly, yet her intoned words drowned out Victorine's chant.

I saw the girl silenced. She shivered, both hands raised protectingly over her serpent. Her expression became that of a trapped animal, her eyes no longer steadfast on her opponent, but darting from side to side. She might be in a cage, frantically seeking escape.

Mrs. Pleasant stepped back toward the door. Before she touched the knob she reached inside her seam pocket, brought out what looked to be a common piece of chalk. To my surprise she stooped, to draw on the drab strip of carpet a series of figures as crude as a small child might make. Then, never glancing at me, she quietly left, shutting the door behind her.

Victorine stumbled to the bed, more fell on it than sat. She raised her hands to her face, covering her eyes. Believing she was weeping, I went to her. The purpose and meaning of that exchange, of Mrs. Pleasant's final action, were mysteries. But if Victorine would turn now to me perhaps some good could be gained from this terrible night.

Tentatively I put out my hand to touch her shoulder. She shivered, dropped her hands to look up at me. With her darkened skin she was so unlike the Victorine I knew it was like facing a stranger. Also there was a subtle, unpleasant alteration in her expression.

"Tamaris—Tamaris who is always right, always correct, always the lady!" Her voice was very low. "Tamaris!" She pointed a finger at me in an odd fashion, as if she so indicated me to something unseen now sharing this room with us.

But that was only a morbid fancy, though I found myself looking around.

"You have interfered grievously, Tamaris. So the black cock shall crow for you, and the white shall die. Though perhaps that you will not see. And He Himself"—her hand went once more to that sinister necklace, her fingers stroked the enameled scales—"shall come forth from the grave to—"

"Victorine!" I interrupted that eerie singsong. "What nonsense are you saying?"

She smiled. And for the first time I understood how a smile could be more terrible than a frown.

"You do not know, do you? But *she*"—now she pointed to the door—"does. She thinks she knows so much. But beside Christophe's knowledge hers is nothing!" Victorine made of the last word a passionate cry.

Fancies—my mind was too full of strange fancies, born of this dreadful night. Was this voodoo, this belief in the dark spirits from the unknown continent of Africa, grafted within the new world by slaves who needed to call up all possible vengeance against those who held them in bondage? Was voodoo at the core of Victorine's danger? Had she willingly, or under the influence of others, become so enmeshed in the wicked belief that she turned from those of her own blood and race, appearing now in spirit, as she did with her darkened skin, to belong to another people?

In spite of myself I shrank back a step. Once more she smiled in that hateful way.

"You begin to feel it, do you, Tamaris? Already you sense the power of the Great One. Shall I make you a 'horse' for the riding—so that a Loa can enter your body and wear it as you do a dress, use it as you would a piece of clothing? When that Great One leaves you, you must face what *you* have done, and with whom! Do you think my brother would then allow you to so much as touch the sole of his dirty boot? You watch him with those great eyes of yours, you think nobody knows your silly little secret— that you have a liking for him. But after a Loa is through— you shall be as the mud of the gutter. The Great One likes such sport with those who deem themselves 'good.' " The word "good" she uttered as if it were an obscenity.

Now she leaned closer and began to speak with some of her old vivacity. But such talk. She used foul words I did not understand, then would smile evilly, or laugh, and define them. I covered my ears, but that did not stop her talking, smiling, laughing—

This—this was not Victorine! The old tales of possession by evil spirits might thus be proven true. No young girl could have learned the filth she spouted as she swayed back and forth, her hands clasped about the serpent.

How long that continued I could never afterward remember. Finally the door opened and Mrs. Pleasant returned. Seeing her, Victorine was silenced. I was crying from overwrought nerves, the fear of the *thing* which seemed to me to be now wearing Victorine's body.

Mrs. Pleasant carried a tray on which sat a decanter

of ruby Bohemian glass and two small glasses. She put this down on the chest of drawers.

"I have received a message. Unfortunately Mr. Sauvage has not yet been located." As she spoke she poured from the decanter into the glasses. "He is being diligently sought by those who have reason to be grateful to me. There has been much trouble on one of his properties, stirred up by someone who wanted him away from this city. As soon as he is found he will be brought here."

Picking up the nearest glass, she brought it to me. "Drink this. You will find it will revive your nerves."

I was so haunted, so sickened in mind, that I obeyed her without question. I was sipping again that drink she had said was distilled from clover.

"Now to sleep with you. No"—she caught the anxious glance I turned upon Victorine—"you need have no worries here. She will be very safe."

It was as if I had not known a bed for days. I staggered toward the one she showed me and fell across it without even removing my clothing. Before my eyes closed entirely I saw Victorine standing, Mrs. Pleasant gripping her arm firmly. That utterly hateful smile was back. The girl raised her free hand, fingers spread widely apart. Between those she spat at me, as if she threw some curse and such hate as I could not believe that I had aroused in anyone.

Perhaps some of that ill-will did follow me into sleep. For my dreams were such as to bring me, panting in terror, to half-wakefulness. Though I could not remember what had frightened me.

And each time I so awoke I was only vaguely aware of the room in which I lay, as if the dream had been more real. Then I would slip back, in spite of my feeble struggles, to face some ordeal again. When I roused the third time it was day. Someone shook my shoulder and I looked up into a face I knew, but which I was too sleep-drugged to put name to.

"Miss! Miss!" There was urgency in the voice so I finally fully roused.

"Submit?"

"Miss—listen—" She fell to her knees by the bed so that her whisper sounded closer to my ear. "There is trouble, big trouble. *She* says you must help—"

Abruptly I sat up. Someone had thrown a cover over me but I still wore my underclothing, though my dress had been removed.

"What is the matter?"

"You got to help, miss. Wake up—listen!"

"I am awake and listening." I looked around. Victorine was nowhere in the room.

"Where is—?"

"Please—no time to talk now. Listen—*she* says—put on this!" Submit brought a bundle up from the floor, shaking it out to display a flannel nightgown made for someone who wore a garment several sizes larger than mine.

"But first—"

She dropped that fantastic robe on the bed and turned to a small table where a sponge, towel, and basin waited. "Let me wash you. Hurry, miss—there ain't much time."

CHAPTER FOURTEEN

She was quick and deft. I saw the sponge show brown where she bathed away my skin stain. When that was done she produced a nightcap, tied it firmly on, and then pulled the gown over my head.

So far I had not asked questions because there was such an urgency in her actions. But now I said, "You must tell me why—"

"There is a man, he come lookin' for a girl. We show him girl who is sick in bed. He sees she's not girl he's lookin' for—he goes away."

Christophe D'Lys? But how had he tracked us here and why was Mrs. Pleasant allowing him inside her door? Had Célie talked once we were gone? And for me to play a role—I was sure I could not. Though I had no time to protest and, even if I did, Submit was not the one to whom to do so.

She emptied the stain-tainted water into a slop jar. A moment later thrust the towel and sponge into the wash-table cabinet and slammed shut the door.

"*She* says to tell you that the young lady is safe hid. But if he sees a sick girl, then he think those who tell him things are wrong. He won't hang 'round watchin'. You is sick, miss—remember now—real sick."

As I slid down in the bed, the voluminous folds of the gown wrapped around me, I wished I could pull that garment up over my head also. However, the best I could do was to turn my face away from the door and hope to present the passive appearance of a bedridden sufferer. The room was none too light, as the single window was some distance away.

"Remember"—Submit paused beside me to deliver a last hissing whisper—"you is real, real sick!"

I needed no such reminder. I *was* sick, from nervous fear, my chilled body shivering. For the moment I could only lie and wait, praying my ordeal would be quickly over.

My hearing, perhaps because I strained to catch the slightest sound, was acute. I picked up now the thud of footsteps in the hall, knew those approached my door. That was flung open, and I lay so tense my muscles ached with strain. I must remain passive, outwardly unmindful of what was happening.

"You see, massa"—Submit's voice, humble as I had not heard it before, slipping back into the speech of the slave days when she had been property, not a person—"this here's the girl. She's one of them who entertains the gentlemen, but she's mighty sick. You can see that for yourself, massa—"

I held my eyes closed. The tread neared the bed. Then my chin was cupped by a hand, my head turned. I was startled enough to open my eyes and so found myself looking straight up into a face I shall never forget. Though I had better reason later to have it etched into my memory for all time.

This was the young man I had seen with Victorine on the balcony. He was handsome with a delicacy of feature which was almost feminine. But the narrow line of mustache, the small, pointed imperial on his chin, proclaimed his sex. His brows slanted oddly above his most arresting feature, his eyes. They were unlike any other human eyes I had ever seen for their color approached amber yellow, with the pupils abnormally large and dark.

My rising fear led me to better acting than I might have produced otherwise. I gave a little moan, closed my eyes against that piercing regard which raked over me as if he searched not only for my identity but for my very thoughts.

He withdrew his hand and I allowed my head to roll away on the pillow.

"You see, massa—this here's like no girl you was askin' for. Mrs. Pleasant, she ain't gonna take kindly noways to your comin' in to see if we're tellin' lies." Submit was fast sloughing off her humbleness. I deduced from that she believed our ordeal near its end.

"I shall speak with your mistress in due time." He had a trace of accent.

At least he *was* going. I heard the door close, the sound of footsteps retreating down the hall. Then I sat up in bed. The sooner Victorine and I were out of this house the better. Surely Alain must be found by now, on his way to us. With his arrival the whole nightmare would be over. I had no doubt Alain Sauvage would be well able to handle Christophe D'Lys.

Submit had not returned as I completed dressing, fastened my hair into order. But when I tried the door I found that locked. Had Submit done so that no one might intrude? But even if it were done for my own protection I resented it. We must get away. Christophe D'Lys was not one to give up easily, I suspected. And how far Mrs. Pleasant was willing to go to hide us was another question.

I began to speculate as to what did lie behind her efforts for us. She had stated she owed a debt to my father; that I could believe. But she owed Victorine nothing. And— If only Alain were here!

Wishing was not going to bring him. Until he did arrive

the responsibility for Victorine was mainly mine. I could not shift the burden to Mrs. Pleasant. So my first duty now was to find Victorine and hope she would be more reasonable.

This was no time to wring one's hands and call upon Heaven after the witless fashion of those heroines of a novel. Rather this was a moment to summon my own courage and fortitude, to think clearly.

The mere act of dressing was wearying, and I realized I was very hungry. It was then that I saw a tray bearing covered plates on top of the chest of drawers.

What I found when I lifted those covers was an odd mixture, as if someone had rummaged among the remains of a banquet. There was a crab shell stuffed with meat mixed with sauce, garnished with a sliver of hard-boiled egg. Some beans appeared cold in another savory dressing, a slice of ham beside them. And there was also a pecan tart. An odd collection for breakfast, but, as all which I had been served in this house, expertly prepared so I ate to the last crumb. The glass of wine I did not touch. Perhaps the clover cordial had produced my earlier drowsiness. I wanted nothing now to dull my wits.

So heartened I faced the problem of getting out of the room. Submit had not returned, and there was no visible bell pull nor button. Short of hammering on the locked door, or calling out the window, I saw no remedy.

Curiosity drove me to a closer inspection of the room itself. I was cautious about approaching the window. There was a curtain across the panes but the material was thin. It would not do for any watcher below to see a "sick" girl moving about. I was taking pains to avoid passing close to that when chance led me to a new discovery.

Though I had put on my stoutest shoes before I began this expedition those had never been intended for such hard usage as the past hours demanded. As I turned, a loose heel caught in the carpet, throwing me against the wall. And under my right hand a panel moved!

Startled, I pushed away in haste. But the pressure I exerted to do that made the opening even larger. When I faced about I saw a low narrow doorway.

A few cautious experiments proved that this hidden door opened so easily I could not believe it concealed a forgotten way. And the age of the house was not such to suggest those ancient passages intended to make a reader's flesh creep. Since there was no latch or fastening on either side I thought I dared explore, at least for a short way. But the bulk of my skirt was too much to enter such a narrow passage.

Greatly daring, I discarded my bustle, the draped skirt of my dress, pulling my cloak about me for decency's sake. Arming myself with a candle, I ventured in. The passage *was* narrow. I had been well advised to shed my clothing first.

The way ran, as far as I could determine, for a short distance paralleling the hallway. Then I came to a steep stair where the flickering candle was of little assistance. Here I moved with the utmost caution, feeling for each step slowly.

I descended so to the second floor, hoping there to find an exit. A murmur of voices halted me abruptly. Shielding my candle, I eyed the dark before me carefully. Now I saw a glimmer of light and crept to a peephole. Though my view was very restricted, I found myself looking into the very parlor where I had stayed on my first visit to this house.

The chairs before the fireplace were well within my range of vision and those I saw so clearly I was sure my vantage point had been planned to focus on them.

Not only could I see, but I could hear. And sheer astonishment held me rigid.

Mrs. Pleasant sat in the chair in which I had seen her, gracious and hospitable, a gentlewoman entertaining a morning caller. She radiated sympathy.

Facing her, in the other chair, was a woman who was far from any ease of body or mind.

Mrs. Beall!

Though she wore a dress plain enough to be the street garb of a working woman, and a bonnet of the same old-fashioned shape Mrs. Pleasant favored, its heavy veil now flung back to reveal her haunted face, I knew her past any mistaking. That face which had owed so much to skillful art was ravaged, aged. She might just have tottered forth from her bedchamber after a serious illness.

"I tell you, this cannot continue!" Her voice was hoarse as if she had spent long hours crying. Just so her eyes were red, their lids puffed and swollen. "She is—she—is—"

"What she is," Mrs. Pleasant said quietly.

"What I have made her, is that what you would tell me now?" Mrs. Beall twisted her hands convulsively together. "I swear to you I had no choice! It was all the fault of that vicious lottery. I was so desperate. Jaime had died so suddenly, there was no one I could turn to. Mr. Sauvage had made it plain he would do nothing further for me—not after he learned about Jaime. Then everyone began talking about this wonderful chance for gold in America—a lottery of shares, only those who wanted them had to come here to claim them. The Emperor himself was taking a chance, they said.

"Jaime's brother came to me with money to buy a share. I believed he meant it for my good. It was only later that I understood—they were afraid, Jaime's family, that I would make a claim for Victorine—cause a scandal.

"Jaime had asked them on his death bed to make provision for me, but that I was never told then. They thought if I remained in France I could—I did not know. *Bon Dieu,* how could I know that those in power planned another use for those cursed shares—to rid themselves of anyone who might prove to be a problem. In the old days French kings had their *lettres de cachet*—you could obtain one of those by favor, use it to remove an enemy, imprison him without trial for life.

"And Jaime's family used the share in the same way to do away with me—send me overseas to starve, or rot. What did they care?

"For a little while I dared to believe that I was fortunate." She laughed wildly. "I took Victorine to my cousin—to expose so young a child to the dangers of such a voyage would be wrong. I would make my fortune here and then return for her. All would be well for us again. I dreamed like the fool I was—how I dreamed!

"Then when I reached here came the awakening. The lottery was a hoax, there was nothing at all. Me—to keep breath in my body I became—no, I will not say it! I, who was a lady of quality, of name—what was I here? Something my kin would draw their skirts aside lest they touch mine. I knew I must forget Victorine, who was at least safe, forget who I had been—

"You found me in that cursed house, gave me hope and a new life. I was no longer 'Fifi,' no, again I was safe—almost. But I could not go home—it was too late. I sent money secretly, and I heard from time to time—Victorine was well, she was happy. Then the Sauvages heard of her. What could I do, save wait for the day when life would again crash about me, push me back into the slime. I saw her—and she knew me, knew me with hate. I could read that in her face, her eyes. She wrote to me, those little notes, each aimed like a knife point at my heart. She—she had become something which is—I cannot find the words to say what she now is. Only when I look into her face, under that angel seeming, I see evil, that hateful devil which lurks in her. And I wait—for what I do not know—save that for me it will be disaster!"

Mrs. Beall's fingers twitched. As she had earlier broken her fan, now she tore a handkerchief into strips, unaware of what she did. I was too astounded by what I heard to think, I could only listen.

"James—he has been very good to me. He is proud of me—*me,* who was what I was when you found me, took me out of that den and gave me fresh hope. One dreams of romance when one is young. One says one 'will die for love' or some such nonsense. But me, I would rather die right now than let James ever know the truth of my past, all that I did and was! And if *she* continues to watch, to prick me with her demands—that I shall do, I vow it! I have given her all that I can. To give her my jewels, or sell those to raise money, would make James suspicious. He notices such things more than most men. He takes pleasure in seeing me wear the gifts he has given me.

"Henry is not my friend. I have known that from the first. He watches me, strives to find some story to my disrepute to report to his father. I have been so cautious, so circumspect. You cannot believe how I have had to weigh every word, every act, while James is away so that no tales can be carried. For years it has been so—and now this! I cannot stand much more. If *she* wants my death, she shall have that. For I am wrung out of strength—I who have endured so much—"

The note of hysteria which had been in her voice earlier was gone. But now one could hear the determination of a woman who had made a decision, see that in her face. I believed Mrs. Beall meant exactly what she said, that she proposed to choose death over a life which had become unendurable.

Mrs. Pleasant leaned forward, caught those frantically plucking hands in her own, held them still as she looked directly into the other's eyes.

"You shall do nothing, do you understand—nothing! No more will be asked of you. Action on the part of others will remove the danger you fear. I mean this. You are to go home; there you will say you are ill. Lizzie will bring you a potion from me to soothe your nerves, give you a restful sleep. I have stood your friend before, I shall again now. What is past is gone and forgotten. No one shall stir ashes to raise a ghost. Go home, sleep, do not fear. You have my promise of protection."

She spoke quietly, slowly, as one would to a frightened child. It was as if new strength and courage flowed from her into the woman whose hands she held.

Mrs. Beall raised her head. That wild, hunted look was gone. She began to nod, agreeing with what she heard. Her comforter drew her to her feet, gently placed a mantle around her shoulders. Then Mrs. Pleasant led her visitor from the room, and I was left to try to understand.

There appeared to be no other way out of the passage which came to a dead end a few paces farther on. I returned to the upper room, thinking of what I had heard. Much of Mrs. Beall's confession I did not understand, but she had acknowledged Victorine as her daughter! It was difficult to believe that the older woman had so cut herself off from the past that she now appeared fully American. She spoke English without the least accent.

Now the significance of the note I had found in Victorine's room was made plain. The daughter had been demanding money from the mother, and that note had accompanied what Mrs. Beall meant to be a final payment.

All I had learned of Victorine during the past few hours was enough to overturn my confidence in my ability to judge character. I could only assume that the girl was so deeply under the influence of D'Lys that he had corrupted her, young and innocent as she appeared.

If we could free her from D'Lys, take her away—perhaps she could in time become the lovely girl nature intended her to be. But only Alain could eliminate D'Lys.

He must come! So fiercely did I long to see him that I walked up and down the room praying. I had never prayed so for anything in my life—save for my father's safety, and then my prayers had failed.

My father had not been a churchgoer or outwardly, by the standards of the day, a religious man. He had early broken with the narrow faith in which he had been bred. And his wide reading and traveling had raised doubts concerning many of the rigorously upheld tenets of churchmen. But he had never denied a belief in God, or that there was an influence for good in this world, working to combat the evil that we need only to look about us to perceive at its deadly work.

Honesty, courage, and compassion were the virtues by which he judged his fellow men. By this standard he had raised me. I had gone to church during my years at Ashley Manor, and I had found much to admire in those who believed in the stated creed, as well as a narrowness of vision and a harshness of spirit in others, which, to me, was intolerable. I lived my own inner life, not by piety in the conventional form, but rather by my father's teachings. In every situation needing moral judgment I had tried to think what he might do.

Many times I failed. Doubtless through the rest of my life I shall continue to fail. For that is the burden we all must bear. But that I keep on trying is the important thing.

Only with Victorine I sensed an evil I had never before faced. The nature of my wandering life when young had made me far more aware of certain phases of existence than was common for most young ladies. The degradation, open lust, and crime of the Barbary Coast existed, I knew, in most other cities. Just as I knew that in some beautiful homes, among supposedly cultivated and upright people, there was also cruelty and lust concealed under the covers convention decreed must not be lifted.

There are dreadful acts committed when moral barriers fall and people give freedom to their basest passions. I did not know what vile swamp Victorine had been drawn into, but it was not of the world I knew. And its influence lay now like a coating of black filth over her white skin.

Alain had strength of will, courage, determination, and, I hoped, also the deep compassion necessary to free his sister from this morass. If we could keep her from D'Lys until Alain returned—

Mrs. Beall's reliance on Mrs. Pleasant had been complete, she had spoken of aid in the past. I must hope that the mistress of this house would now be *our* good angel. Of one thing I was sure—she could control Victorine where I could not.

I redressed in the garments I had laid aside when I entered the passage. My watch was back in the hotel, there was no clock in the room. Though it was day outside I did not know the hour. To stay here, unknowing of what had happened to Victorine, whether Alain had returned— that I could not bear any longer.

As I started for the door determined to pound on it until released, it opened and Mrs. Pleasant faced me.

"Victorine?" I asked first.

"Asleep. Come and see—" She beckoned me across the hall to a room twin to the one I had occupied.

Victorine's head, the stain still darkening her skin, rested quietly on a pillow. She wore a nightrobe such as Submit had brought me. There was no wardrobe in the room, or sign of other clothing. As Mrs. Pleasant followed me out she locked the door, slipped the key onto a ring swinging from her belt.

"She is safe. The part you played earlier was well done. D'Lys is gone. Not that he would have found her. But there were those in his employ who would have continued to watch outside had he not been deceived by you."

"I thought he could not trace us here."

The faintest crease of a frown appeared between her well-shaped brows.

"Yes. That matter interests me. But now I have good news for you. Mr. Sauvage has been reached, he is on his way back. He should be here in not too long a time if matters go well—"

"What matters could hinder Alain's—Mr. Sauvage's arrival?"

"There is nothing certain in this world, child. We do not know enough about D'Lys. I am most concerned that he was able to trace us here. And he is not alone; my people report he has others in his pay, how many we do not yet know."

I shivered. It might not be wise for Alain to come to us here—not alone anyway. That he could handle D'Lys were the West Indian by himself, that I could believe. But suppose he was set upon by D'Lys backed by supporters?

"Alain—he must be warned! If they return to watch this house—D'Lys may know him by sight, but he knows D'Lys only by description."

Mrs. Pleasant gave me an approving nod. "You have perceived one difficulty. But my people have been alerted, they know what to expect when they bring Mr. Sauvage here. However, there is another matter I wish to discuss with you before such a meeting."

She led the way down the stairs to her own parlor, where she waved me into the same chair Mrs. Beall had occupied. Almost, I thought fleetingly, as if it were now my turn to confess and throw myself on her mercy.

However, she busied herself poking up the fire and did not break the silence. In spite of the aroused flames the room had the damp chill I had come to associate with the city. Spring here was not sunshine and warmth. Having urged the fire to great efforts, my hostess turned to survey me from head to foot.

"You have none of the baby-faced beauty which is favored nowadays."

That was a startling remark, and by it she gained my full attention.

"But you have learned how to make the best of yourself," she continued judicially. For a moment I might have closed my eyes and thought myself back at Madam Ashley's.

"This is not an easy world for a girl who has neither wealth nor family at her back. One needs a husband and an establishment. I am speaking thus frankly, giving you the same advice I would a daughter of my own if she were in your place.

"Mr. Sauvage is not only unmarried, but he has shown no inclination toward that state. However, never before has he displayed more than polite courtesy toward any young lady. He has been the despair of most of the matchmaking females of his acquaintances, so that his singling you out at the first ball he has given in years has been a matter for conjecture among those who had cherished ambitions—you wonder how I know this? Gossip is borne by the wind here.

"Your name has been on many lips since that night, child. After such a marked gesture, it is easy to believe that you have intrigued his interest. Thus you have the best of chances to fix that interest enough to achieve a permanent relationship. Though you may need some unobtrusive and discreet help, for you have already attracted ill-will by all this."

I stiffened. My shock at her bold words must have been easy to read, for she paused, though she did not cease to smile.

Also I was alarmed. Though I had once warned Alain that idle tongues would seize upon any departure on my part from the most correct conduct, I had not foreseen that we might be the subject of gossip because of the ball, probably malicious gossip, as Mrs. Pleasant had implied.

"I do not believe," she now continued in the same

matter-of-fact way, "that you are altogether averse your-self to a closer and warmer relationship with the gentle-man in question."

CHAPTER FIFTEEN

"It is not my place to entertain any such idea." I took refuge in a hauteur I hoped would quench any further com-ment. And I was still trying to deny to myself that what she said was the truth. I dared not allow such thoughts to beguile me into humiliating self-betrayal.

Mrs. Pleasant's smile only deepened. I was no match for her and I knew it. My pretense of composure was a lie even as I spoke and I was so ashamed. How transparent I must be that she could so read me. It was true I thought about Alain far too much for my peace of mind. But I fought to repress such thoughts. To have an impossible dream discussed in this manner denuded me of all pride. Worst of all, had others noticed my preference, had I added to gossip by some fault of my own? I felt a burning flush creep up my cheeks, and that shame aroused my will to conceal, to battle for my pride.

Was she also hinting that I listen to her advice on how to entrap Alain? To think of such a sordid scheme revolted me so much I felt ill. What true woman would rejoice at gaining a victory by such ends? Nor did I believe Alain's interest in me was fixed as she averred. Not that that made any difference in my resolve to refuse to listen if she con-tinued in this strain.

"There are ways, child." She might have been reading my confused thoughts aloud, disregarding my revulsion. "As I have aided others to obtain their desires in such matters, I can do so for you, and with greater reason. No, do not give me the answer which is now on your tongue. Take time to think before you speak. Mr. Sauvage will be grateful for your efforts on behalf of his sister. You can easily make yourself indispensable to him."

I shook my head vehemently. "I do not want it so!"

She was not in the least moved by that quick, hot denial. Instead, smiling gently as she would at some fretful child, she arose.

"Stay and think, think well, dear. Submit shall bring you tea. And perhaps later I shall have some more news for you."

Thus she left me, with indeed much to think about. And few of those thoughts could I face calmly.

Submit brought me food, but with that something else, a note she slipped from the pocket of her apron as she set the tray down. When she was gone, remembering the peep-hole in the wall, I removed the envelope cautiously.

Going to the hearth, making sure my body was between the paper and the wall, I knelt down as if to warm my hands. The missive was without salutation.

I warned you not to trust M. If you do so, you have not only assured your own bondage, but perhaps that of others. It is her desire to control us all. There are many men in this city whose indiscretions have already given her a hold over them. There are others who believe that they had reason to show her gratitude, until, after accepting her aid, they too have become enmeshed in her intrigues. She has long wanted some hold over A.S. If you allow him to be drawn into some plan of hers, or have dealings with her, you have condemned him to become one of her puppets. In the end she always demands her pay, and that can be a slavery such as she delights upon setting on the white race—whom she has long considered her enemies. If you have any gratitude in you or any feeling for A.S., do not allow him to bargain with her. Stop him from this fatal folly.

As there had been no salutation, so there was no signature. Mrs. Deaves had taken what precautions she could to protect herself. But I recalled her agitation at the meeting in the shop. She herself must be one of those entrapped in such a net as she described in her warning.

Perhaps I would have dismissed all this as the outburst of a woman who wanted me out of her life, had it not been for the interview just past. I, too, had been offered aid. That Alain Sauvage was a man of the first consequence in San Francisco there was no denying. I had only vague ideas of his financial holdings, but believed them to be impressive.

Thus, if Mrs. Pleasant had the motives this note accused her of, to add him to the list of those owing her favors would be a major coup. And if he came here, protected by her people, to claim Victorine, she might then well dictate terms.

However—suppose he was warned before he came? My faith in Alain's ability to handle any situation was great. He might well be able to counter any scheme of Mrs. Pleasant's then. I had only Mrs. Deaves' note and Mrs. Pleasant's offer to me, but these were warning enough in my present disturbed state to seem formidable.

Wadding the note into a ball I dropped it into the fire. I already knew the back way out of this house. Though where I might be in relation to the hotel I could not guess. My money was still in my pocket and that could buy me transportation. If I could reach Alain before he came to get Victorine—

My guilt in the whole sorry matter gnawed at me. What my inattention had begun I must do all I could to bring to an end. Then I would admit that Victorine was beyond my control or aid. The sooner Alain had her in firmer charge, the better.

My confidence in Mrs. Pleasant was shaken. That she had done much I would be the first to admit. But what was going to be the final price of her services? If any must be paid, I alone and not Alain would do that.

For so long I had had no advice I could trust, being forced to rely only upon myself. Dimly I realized the danger of that, but when there was no other way—I must do as I thought best and hope it was not arrant folly.

At the moment I must play a passive role, since I could not rid myself of the idea that I might be under secret observation. I seated myself, uncovered the dishes on the tray, and made a good meal. Having finished, I went to one of the windows, lifted a little the three layers of drapes and curtains, to obtain a very limited view of the street.

It had begun to rain again and was dusky out. What better cover dared I hope for? Now was the time to move, or perhaps I could not sustain my courage long enough to try. Was I still locked in? I did not remember hearing a click of key.

Under my fingers the knob turned. I went quickly to the back stair, hearing a stir of life below. But the upper hall was empty as I entered my late bedroom. Swiftly I donned the cape I had worn the night before and the face-concealing bonnet, pausing only to rip out the curls sewed within its brim. I wished I had my own cape and hat but did not know where they were.

Thus clad I eased open the corridor door and halted to listen. Here the murmur from below was only a thread of sound. Crossing to Victorine's room, I found that door still locked. I was certain Mrs. Pleasant would make sure the girl would not vanish again; she was too valuable, if a bargain was what my hostess really wanted.

Step by step I descended the back stairs, pausing many times to listen, half expecting at any moment to see Submit or Mrs. Pleasant. What I would do when I reached the foot, I was not yet sure, for I would not find the kitchen quarters empty.

So—I must go through the front door. The sounds grew louder. I froze, holding to the stair rail with both hands as a white-coated waiter with a loaded tray passed below. He did not glance up—I was still safe.

If dinner was in progress, perhaps the front stairs were better. I returned to the second-story hallway and sped, as lightly as I could, in the opposite direction. Once more I began a cautious descent. The voices were muffled, per-haps by a closed door. Now I was in the lower hall. Lamp-light beamed from the large parlor. I heard a woman's light laugh, the lower rumble of a man's voice, as I ran for the front door. No one called after me. The door was un-latched and I whipped through it into the open.

Rain beat at me and the force of the wind made me

gasp. I gazed up and down the street in despair. No sign, of course, of any hack to hail. There was nothing to do but to walk, to try and find an open shop where I might discover a man or boy to summon such transportation for me. As I trudged along my helplessness began to frighten me. I did not know these streets, where I could find aid.

Through the rain the street lamps, set so far apart, gave out only a very limited and misty radiance. I reached the small circle of light around the nearest when out from the shadows behind me I was seized by my upper arms and held fast in spite of my frantic struggles. In that moment the shock was so great I could not find voice to scream.

A man appeared before me as if he had arisen by some dark magic out of the streaming pavement. My unseen captor behind had me so totally a prisoner I could no longer move as the shadowy form before me caught at my bonnet, pushed that roughly back to bare my face to the light.

"This is the one!" I did not see his face as he made that hissed identification. He wore one of the wide-brimmed hats favored by ranchers, and he had on a waterproof, the shoulder cape of which was enfolded about his throat and the lower part of his face. But his voice I knew. D'Lys! I was weak and sick with fear.

There sounded the clop-clop of hooves along the deserted street. A hack pulled up and I was tossed into it roughly, more prisoning hands waiting within to seize me. With measures so expert as to suggest this was not the first time this action had been followed, I found my cape looped about me and fastened so I could not move my arms. And, though at last I tried to cry out, a thick bag was pulled down over my head and shoulders. It was so vile-smelling and stifling I feared I would smother.

D'Lys had been waiting. But what did he want with me? I could not think coherently as we rattled along, only endure and hope that soon I might be able to breathe more freely.

Perhaps I did faint, for when I was again aware of what was happening I was no longer in the hack but being carried. I heard a blare of music, too loud laughter. Shortly afterward I was dropped on the soft surface of what could only be a bed.

"Vat you do?" A woman's voice, one I had heard before, though in my present near unconscious condition I was too dazed to remember where or when.

Then that vile-smelling bag was torn away from my head. Thankfully I drew in a deep breath of air. The woman had leaned over to view me—

Célie!

"Vy you bring ziss von here? Vat you do?" Her accent thickened with each word.

I did not know whether or not she recognized me. She had turned her head to address someone else. D'Lys stood there. He had not removed his hat, but he had shrugged the cape away from his face.

"I do what I came to do." He added a term in a language I did not understand but I took it to be a foul one, for Célie's face, under its thick coat of paint, went rigid.

D'Lys laughed as if he were thoroughly enjoying himself.

"You would like to use your little knife on me, Célie? Is that in your mind, *chérie?* But no, you would not really want to do that, it can never be, can it, my pigeon?"

With light-footed grace he came to her, caught her wrist in one of his slender brown-fingered hands. If anger had been her emotion it was now wiped out by pain. She tried to pull away, but she did not cry out.

"You did wrong, Célie, did you not?" Still he smiled, watching her with those yellow eyes which had not the slightest trace of human feeling in them. "Did you not?"

He made her cry out at last as she fell to her knees, her arm, at an awkward angle, still in his torturing grip.

"Oui, oui!" She made that word a plea.

"But you will not do so again, will you, Célie?"

He released her so suddenly she fell against the bed. I saw deep in her flesh the print of his fingers. Now she was moaning, but he allowed her no time to nurse her bruises. Instead he reached down and caught her shoulders, pulling her to her feet again against him.

"You shall listen to me carefully, Célie, and you shall

do just as I bid. If you do not—" His smile was an evil promise.

She whimpered in his hold. *"Oui, oui—"*

Letting her go, D'Lys stepped back a pace. "Now you see, *chérie,* it is really very easy. I am never unreasonable, but a most accommodating man. I like all things done in friendship and peace. We shall now be friends again, Célie, and you shall do what you can to aid me—exactly as a friend should.

"It is most needful that Victorine be returned to me. She is, of course, my so-dear wife. But she is of importance to me for other reasons. This Sauvage—he is a great man here, they tell me, so great a man he cannot be injured. But those who tell me so, they do not know Christophe nor what he can do, eh, Célie?" His voice was the soft purr of a ruthless jungle hunter, never did he raise it.

At that moment I shared the terror that soft, almost caressing voice evoked. Célie's eyes were held by his, her mouth hung a little open. She had the vacant look worn by Victorine when she had been under the influence of the powder Mrs. Pleasant had supplied.

"Bon, they know not Christophe, but they shall learn. By the power of Damballa, I, who am the Voice of Baron Samedi—the Prince of Death—ah, these whites shall learn!" There was a deadly force in him. *"Bon.* To the business at hand. For one can dream of the future, but action now must bring that dream to life. You shall go and find me such a messenger as can be trusted, one that yellow bitch Pleasant cannot control. Go!"

Célie left us in a sleepwalking fashion. I cowered, for now he turned those yellow eyes upon me as his smile deepened.

"Miss Penfold—" He noted my start. "But of course I know you—the companion, the wardress of my dear Victorine—set to guard so that she does not come to me, her rightful lord. I have much to thank you for, Miss Penfold, in that you walked straight into our hands this night. Now you have given me that with which I can bargain. You shall rise." He leaned over me, jerked to loosen the cloak binding me. "You shall go to that table—"

He pointed to a small gilt-legged one on which stood a vase, two glasses, and a bottle. With a sweep of his hand he sent all those crashing to the floor, the wine dribbling from the bottle to the carpet. From his pocket he took a folded sheet of paper, smoothed it out, and produced a black crayon.

"You shall sit—so—" He moved a chair to the table on which he had laid the paper and crayon.

"Why?" I struggled against the mesmeric influence his voice exerted.

"Why?" D'Lys repeated. "Because, first of all, I say that you do this. Secondly, your actions may, just may, save your life. You shall sit and write as I tell you."

I had witnessed his brutal handling of Célie and I knew that for the moment I was helpless. My best course of action would be to present the appearance of one wholly cowed to submission. Which I could not honestly deny was far from the truth. So I went and seated myself as he ordered.

"Now you shall write thus—" He stood on the other side of the table, setting on me that compelling, yellow-eyed stare. Only inside me my will was strengthening. That he intended me any good, whether I obeyed him or not, I felt was a false hope.

To Monsieur Alain Sauvage:
    I am now in the hands of him who wishes to be reconciled to his lawful wife, Victorine D'Lys. I shall remain so until Victorine is free to join her husband. I am told that the time for arranging this to-be-desired reunion is limited, and the consequences for me, in case this does not occur, shall be dire. Instructions will be sent you as to how to effect the exchange.

The crayon was greasy in my hold and the writing of necessity bold and coarse. But I put down each dictated word. That Alain Sauvage would accept such instructions I thought impossible. It might be that I could hope for no rescue unless Mrs. Pleasant's people would move on my behalf.

It was ironic that I must now pin my very faint hopes on the very person I had come to distrust. And her payment might come high. But I could only face the future one step at a time, and hope—

"He will not agree," I said, as indifferently as I could.

"No? But that would be then such a pity for you, Miss Penfold. Now, to make him understand the better—" The lamplight flashed on a knife in his hand. From whence he had drawn that blade I could not have said. Before I was aware of his intention, he snatched off the net confining my hair, so long locks fell about my neck and shoulders.

D'Lys cut off a length which he wrapped around the note, using it as he might a cord.

"Now I shall leave you for a space, Miss Penfold. Pray to your white-skinned god for aid if you wish, not that he shall answer you. But it is always well to occupy yourself so. If Monsieur Sauvage wishes you well, he will say 'yes.' If he proves stubborn, it will be so sad for you."

He went out the mirror door. As that slammed behind him I could not mistake the click of a key. I was indeed a prisoner.

Now there welled in me such terror that, had I lost control, I would have screamed and thrown myself at the mirrored wall, hammering at the glass until that broke. I fought one of the hardest battles of my life, forcing myself to continue to sit in the chair, to try and think beyond panic and fear.

As I looked helplessly about me those monstrous painted women on the walls seemed to titter and jeer. In the old days my father had armed me with a derringer, made me practice with it until I was a fair shot. And he had also trained me to think that I might someday, in some way, have to defend myself physically.

But that weapon had remained behind on the *India Queen*. I thought of it longingly. But memory would not arm me, I must seek something I could use here and now.

My hand went to my seam pocket. I still carried that bag of money. Would bribery serve here? But who to bribe? If I dared reveal that small store it might be wrested from me. With it was the spider bracelet. I re-

membered Submit's reaction to that. Suppose I showed it
to some maid—

Mrs. Pleasant had said the maids here were Negroes,
sometimes supplied by her. If I could see one—get my
message out. (That it could serve me, I doubted, but I
would keep it ready.)

Now I studied the room. The vulgarity of its furnishing
made plain its use, catering to the lusts of those with
money enough to tempt Célie. She had boasted to Mrs.
Pleasant that those were not lesser citizens of this city.
Could I appeal to such men? Shame them into coming to
my aid? But how could I? I could guess that screaming
here would not cause comment nor arouse the house, even
if my voice carried beyond the walls of this room.

In those mirrors I saw only too clearly my bedraggled
person, my loose hair, my face smudged by contact with
that vile bag, my clothing plain and creased, flounces torn.
I was no person to raise quick belief.

There I was reflected and reflected, two, three, a dozen
of me. If I could only summon all those mirrored mes to
stand shoulder to shoulder—I realized that I was perilously
close to hysteria.

Always those leering, horrible pictures, their voluptuous
forms made to intrude upon notice, their sly eyes watching
me. I tried not to glance at them as I still searched for a
weapon. The fireplace—those gilded fire irons—!

Fearing that I might be spied upon through some wall
peephole, I arose and tottered so I almost fell. My will was
strong, but now my body could not match it. There was an
instant of vertigo and I clutched at the back of a chair. The
floor wavered under me like the deck of a storm-tossed
ship.

The unsteadiness passed but it left behind a residue of
foreboding that it might strike again. I moved slowly as I
might walk across a bog, crossing to the fireplace. The
heat was almost stifling in this closed room, but the fire
had fallen away to ash-encrusted coals. Stealthily I withdrew the poker from the stand, held it against my side so
the drapery of my overskirt concealed it. I went back to
the chair and sat down.

How long I maintained the vigilance I do not know. One enters such an ordeal with highly keyed nerves and an alertness of senses. But as time passes so does the fine edge of that alert. I began, in spite of myself, to be lulled, slightly off guard.

I had seated myself to face the hidden door, so no one could come on me unseen. And I tried not to think of what might be happening elsewhere, but rather concentrate on my own trial.

Time seemed endless, I could hear the ticking of the clock, raise my eyes now and then to where that stood on the mantel. It was a timepiece in keeping with the room, the dial upheld by a fat, petulant-faced cupid. The hour was now close to midnight.

Would they just leave me here?

I stiffened; a sound had interrupted the ticking, the turning of a key. Since I must now give the impression of one who felt herself to be without protection or resources, I allowed my shoulders to slump.

The door was flung open and Christophe D'Lys lurched in, caught his balance to walk more steadily. He had laid aside his hat and waterproof to show broadcloth and fine linen. In one hand he carried a champagne bottle, his fingers hooked about its neck.

His face was flushed, his eyelids drooped to half conceal those yellow eyes. His lips looked very red and moist, and his tongue moved ceaselessly across them as if he savored something which gave him pleasure.

Though his entrance had been that of a half-drunken man, now his movements suggested he was in full control of his body. He set the bottle down, half turned from me.

My grip tightened on the poker. I had never struck a blow in my life. My resolution would be now tested if I could defend myself so. I arose, hoping to give the impression of one shrinking in fear, backing away.

"White—white meat—" That much was in English. Then D'Lys lapsed into the patois Victorine and Amélie had used. I could guess what he said and it made me sick, but I must not allow that to weaken me.

"Soft white meat—for the eating—" He did not appear

to address me even though he again spoke English. "In the old days—the days of fire and knives and blood when my people arose—the soft white meat—they ran—the masters, the mistresses—they squealed—they tried to hide. Papa Ricardo, how often did he tell me how it was then, and he grew younger with every word. White meat—they were ours!"

D'Lys was caught up in a world of his own. His head swung back and forth, his tongue tip played in and out, a flicker of pink on his lower lip. As a snake might show its tongue, sway—a snake!

CHAPTER SIXTEEN

I continued to edge back, away from the door. He watched me—or did he see *me* at all? His disjointed English faded into those other sounds. His words were hissed.

Step after slow step he followed me. I did not believe I would have more than a single chance, and I must make the most of that. Everything depended upon my being able to choose the right moment.

"Now I shall feast of white meat—what will it matter? This one is already Damballa's and who else but His Mouthpiece has the right to eat?"

He pounced like a great cat. Almost I failed. For his advance had been so slow I had been partially deceived into believing he was drunk. His fingers closed on the edge of my bodice and he ripped that down with great force, tearing open my clothing as if the materials were the thinnest paper.

At the same moment I swung the poker, brought it, with all the strength of arm I could muster, against the side of his head. My breath came in harsh gasps, for a long second I could not move, only stood there, staring down at what now lay at my feet. D'Lys had made no sound. But that other noise—the hollow thud of the blow—would

I always remember that? His flailing arms, his clutching hands, caught in the velvet cover of the bed, dragging that down to fall across his body.

His body—! I shuddered, hurled away the poker with revulsion, wiping my hands on my skirt. I thought that, too, I must carry with me always, the feel of the gilded metal.

D'Lys made no movement, no sound. I could not bear to touch him to hunt for any signs of life. I felt I dared not let myself fully comprehend that I had killed this man with far less pity than I would have felt toward a mad animal. To me he was less than any animal.

Somehow I tottered to the dressing table, found, amid the welter of trifles, pins to make my bodice decent. My legs were so weak under me, I was shaking so badly, I could not be sure I was physically able to crawl out of this room. Nor did I underrate the perils of this house. But I must try—

Back to the bed I wavered, making a wide detour around the body, caught up my cape and pulled it around me. Then I started for the door. But I was never to reach that.

The mirrored surface swung. In the aperture stood Célie, and behind her another, a monstrous caricature of a woman, a fitting part of this nightmare. Though she was decked out in garish finery, a strange aping of fashion, she presented more the appearance of a man striding about in grotesque masquerade, save that her mountainous breasts strained against the lacing of her bright green satin bodice.

Célie was a small woman; this giantess reduced her to the proportions of a child. For the newcomer must have been more than six feet in height, thick-bodied to match her size. Her face, under an elaborate dressing of bright red hair, was raddled, her nose veined with red almost as bright as her hair, her mouth wide, her eyes protruding, giving her a froglike mask of feature.

The reek of strong scent and stronger drink hung about her. I longed for the poker, but that láy across the room where I had thrown it.

"What's all this?" In contrast to her giantess form the

woman's voice was high and shrill. She prodded Célie on the shoulder with the tip of a ring-laden finger.

But Célie was staring at what lay on the floor. She shuffled forward and stooped to pull away the cover. D'Lys' head was turned toward her, a dark stain on the carpet beneath it. She cried out.

"He's dead!"

"Is he now?" The shrill voice held only interest, no horror, nor surprise. As if such scenes of violence were not uncommon in her world. Then she looked to me.

"How did you down 'im, gal?"

Célie, backing away from D'Lys, trod upon the poker. With a cry she pulled her skirts about her, edged to one side to display the weapon. The giantess stamped forward with a ponderous tread, picked up the metal length, to swing it back and forth.

"Nice little toothpick, Célie. You oughta be more careful, gal. Somethin' like this means bad trouble."

"Non!" Célie moved back against the wall, as far as she could get from the tumbled body. *"Non,* eet vill not! Ziss house, eet ees mine! I shall not lose eet, all vat I have in ziss world! I did not vant zat von here. Zat she makes trouble ees no my fault." Her courage was flowing back. "No von shall know—"

"He's here and he's dead, Célie. How you gonna fix that?"

Célie stood with the knuckles of her right hand pressed to her teeth. It was plain she was thinking furiously.

"No von must know," she repeated. "He must be found on zee street—away from here—struck down by a thief. Zat vill be eet! Such has happened before."

"An' just how does he git away from here, Cel? That pore critter ain't likely to git up and walk, now ain't that so?"

"He can be taken. Jasper and—" she swung to face the giantess—"and you, Bessie. You could carry him een one hand!"

"Wal, now, Cel, that there's an interestin' proposition, it truly is. An' what do I git for playin' your little game?"

"Plenty. I know you," returned Célie grimly. "You can

take her!" She pointed to me. "I vant her mouth closed, see zat she never talks to zose who can make me trouble. Use her eef you can. Eef you can't"—she shrugged—"do as you vish viss her. She ees supposed to be a lady— might be a new attraction for your place, Bessie—bring een new trade."

I was in such a daze of horror to hear them discussing me so, as if I were an object for barter, that I could not protest nor move. The giantess tossed the poker back on the floor and reached me in one stride. Her puffed hand closed like a vise on my chin, a grip which could not be denied, and she pulled my face to the light, inspecting me, her foul breath in my face.

"She ain't much of a looker, not as how m'lads like 'em. But being as she's untouched goods, yeah, I could work up a little extra for her for a while. So I take her—an' what else, Cel?"

"A veek's takings," the other returned promptly. "You know vat zat runs to here, Bessie."

" 'Deed I do, Cel. But we'll just make that two weeks, if you please. An' me to count the tokens when I come to collect."

Célie did not protest. Her shrug agreed. It was then that I found my tongue.

"You can't do this! Mrs. Pleasant—my friends—"

Bessie laughed. "Gal, from now on you has just one friend, that's me." She thumped herself between those huge breasts. "You be a good little gal, don't make no trouble, an' all'll be nice an' friendly. You ask any of m'gals, Bessie treats 'em right if they don't give no trouble. 'Course you go in for tricks like this now"—she waved at the body—"an' I'll git real annoyed. An' git me annoyed, gal, an' you'll wish you hadn't. I got m'ways of handlin' them what does. Just to make sure you ain't goin' to give me trouble now—" She stripped off my cape and I was a child against her great strength as she twisted my wrists behind me, secured those with a stocking Célie tossed her.

"Now"—Bessie turned to eye the body—"this here's gonna be a poor gentleman as can't handle his drink. I'll just take him down an' put him in my own carriage, seein' that he gits safely where he's goin'. No need to bring Jasper into this, Cel. Fewer knowin' the better. I've the Dummy drivin' me tonight an' what he knows never matters none, since he ain't got no tongue to blab with."

Bessie had some difficulty getting the limp body through the door but I guessed from her brisk competence this was not the first time she had done something of the sort. When she was gone I took the chance to appeal to Célie.

"You know Mrs. Pleasant is a friend of mine. Why should I ever talk? I killed him. Do you think I want to suffer for defending myself?"

She had been engaged in folding up the coverlet, showing a housewife's anxious care. Now she faced me, her face hard with hate.

"You! Eff Mammy Pleasant learns vat has happened here I shall never have any peace. He vas zee only one who could stand up to her and now how he ees gone. She's a devil, a devil! She know everything and she can curse zee life out of you, make you vish you vas dead, only you just go on living. I have seen her do zat to zose who crossed her. Do you seenk I vill risk zat?"

"But if I told her you held me here against your will. I saw him hurt you, force you to do as he wished—"

"Hurt me?" She struck me across the face, viciously, without warning. "Of vat do you speak? He vas a lover such as you do not know. Me, Célie, he vanted. Such men do not vant your kind. They vant us who give their bodies full pleasure. I never know a real man ever until zat one came to my bed, and you keeled him! I do not forget zat. Bessie, she shall make eet for you so zat you vill not forget eet either—vhile you live."

I was caught in a trap I could not hope to escape. The horror of what was before me was so great my courage broke. She must have read that in my face for she laughed.

"*Oui*, Bessie shall school you—and she has no fine house as ziss—she does not entertain gentlemen as come here. *Non,* her place ees on zee Coast, perhaps you do not know vat zat means. Listen—you—"

She poured forth words like blows, making it very clear what sort of a dive Bessie maintained, and what duties would be forced on me there. So that at last I could keep from screaming only by the greatest effort. That last small rag of self-respect I clung to. I must not let this woman hear me beg for mercy.

All too soon Bessie returned. She took up my cape again, draped it about me to hide my bound arms.

"Now will you walk quiet and nice like the lady Cel says you be, gal? Or do I use this on you an' you leave here sleepin'?" She held one of her huge fists before my eyes.

Conscious I might have a thin chance, taken unconscious I would have none at all.

"I will go quietly," I managed to say.

Bessie's wide mouth stretched in a smile. "See, she's gonna be a good gal, Cel. We ain't gonna have no trouble at all, we ain't."

Her massive bulk towered over me, her hand was heavy on my shoulder, both pushing me along and holding me captive. So we came down into the lower hall of the house where there was music and talk sounding from the other rooms. I prepared to scream. Surely there were those there who, even in such a house, would come to my aid were the truth known. Bessie, however, might have read my mind. Her hand went from the shoulder to the nape of my neck gripping that so painfully I nearly lost my footing.

"I can choke the breath right outta you, gal, just as easy as not," she whispered in warning. And I did not doubt she could carry out that threat before help could reach me.

We went on out into the night. The rain had stopped, but clouds still banked the sky. The lurid red light of the sign spilled like blood to show a waiting closed carriage.

"In with you, gal." Bessie lifted me easily, shoved me into the interior. As she settled herself beside me the springs gave an audible creak. We moved off.

"We'll make a stop on the way—to git rid o' him." In the light of a carriage lamp I saw Bessie's thumb signal to the back of the carriage. "Dummy'll dump him."

Under the cover of the cape I fought feverishly against the stocking bonds. But Bessie knew her knots as well as any seaman. I got only chafed skin out of the struggle.

Any hope for escape must come when I reached the den Célie had so graphically described to me. But that I *did* have any hope—

To surrender, to accept that nothing but black evil awaited me, that I could not do. I must be alert for the first chance fate offered. Yet, as we moved on at a steady pace, I could foresee no opportunity.

We came to a stop and Bessie inched forward on the seat, squeezing me painfully into a corner as she put her head close to the window to peer out. For several long moments she held that cramped position, then settled back with a nod.

"All right an' tight now. Dummy's unloaded him. We'll be on our business, gal."

Across her words cut a sharp cry from behind the carriage, a wail to make a listener shudder. Bessie gasped and wheezed.

"That Dummy! I told him to watch it. Leastways he's got sense enough in his head to git goin'." For now the carriage lurched along at a pace never meant for city streets.

Again we heard that cry, but from farther off. Bessie produced a handkerchief, mopped her face, streaking the paint and powder so heavily caked over her coarse skin.

"Got away from 'em. They can't beat Dummy when it comes to drivin'," she observed. "Got sense, too. He'll take the long way round to git back—that'll throw off any as wants to follow. But that yell now—never did hear nothin' jus' like that before—did you, gal?"

Her elbow nudged me in the ribs with force enough to bruise. I gasped out, "No!"

"Sounded 'most like an animal o' some sort. Nasty kinda noise—"

The carriage began to slow. I saw more lights, other vehicles passing us. If only I had my hands free, was able to throw open the door. But if I tried to scream Bessie could silence me at once, have a plausible story for any who investigated.

We made several turns and the noise became nearly a steady roar. Garish lights were all about us. We must be within the boundaries of the Barbary Coast, and who here would help me?

Our carriage pulled to a stop and Bessie puffed and panted her way to the pavement. It was only because she turned to speak to the driver that fortune favored me as she looked up and called, "You done right well, Dummy."

Thus I had a chance to see two men beyond her. They wore sea clothes, one an officer's cap. He had a tight grip on the arm of the slighter and younger man and his voice was raised loud enough for me to hear.

"Don't be a damned fool, boy. This is the crimps' own hunting ground. Come back to the ship now. Or you'll find yourself shipping out on a Bluenose under a bucko with your pockets to let—"

That was Mr. Whicker, the mate of Alain's ship, the one who had known about my father! And Bessie was no longer in reach to gag or choke. I thrust my head and shoulders out of the coach door, into plain sight, and called with all the strength I could summon, "Help! Mr. Whicker, help!"

He swung around. Would he recognize me? Perhaps in my present disheveled state he would not. But, after an instant of surprise, I saw his eyes widen—only it was too late.

I also saw the blow Bessie aimed at me, and in my cramped position I could not dodge. Pain exploded in my head and then there was nothing.

About me was darkness and pain gnawed at me, but I was once more conscious. I was so sick that the slightest movement made me retch, brought an answering stab through my head. For a long time, I did not know where I was—or who—I was only aware of the pain and sickness.

Slowly I was able to see a little more. There was a lighter space to one side. My eyes were drawn to that because it was a small escape from the terrible smothering dark.

There was worse than the stench of my own sickness, such odors as I had never been forced to breathe. I tried to move and discovered that my wrists were still knotted together, that I lay on my side on a pile of stinking rags.

So—I had failed in the one small chance I had been offered. As my mind moved sluggishly, that was my first thought. So deep was my physical misery that the future no longer mattered. I heard a small bleating sound monotonously repeated, and realized that cry was my own, nor could I control it. So far had I been reduced to a dumb and suffering animal that I had no will or resolution left. Had someone come to kill me at that moment I would have waited without protest for the blow to fall.

How long that period of dark and pain lasted I did not know, nor what forces had been set to work through the night and early morning. Nor, at that moment, would I have cared, for nothing beyond my own misery had any meaning.

I must have lapsed into unconsciousness several times. The last time I opened my eyes the light was pale gray and the window, over which hung a sleazy curtain of filthy cloth, was completely visible. To turn my head was such agony that I dared not attempt it more than once. Before me on the other side were only grimed boards, a stained wall over which insects scuttled.

My pile of rags lay near the middle of that cubby. There was a door opposite and nothing else.

But outside the window there moved a vague shape. The pane was so thick with dirt it could have been painted over. A sound—I watched dully, uncaring.

The sound grew louder, there was a crash, a tinkle of glass falling inward. A moment later an arm swept aside the rotten fabric of the curtain which tore like a spider web. Someone was climbing in.

I watched apathetically. This seemed to have nothing to do with me, my pain and misery. With the window open there was more light in the room and the man who had entered straightened to his full height.

I heard him give a sharp exclamation as he knelt beside me. Now I could see his features. Though my eyes blurred when I tried to focus on them clearly. I—knew him. He had a name—only I could not remember it. And that last small failure, that I could not remember, brought tears to my eyes, running unchecked down my bruised cheeks.

"Tamaris! Good God above, what have they done to you! Tamaris!"

I cried out in pain at his touch. He flinched back and then returned to cut the bonds about my wrists. There was no feeling in my hands, which lay wooden and lifeless.

"Please—" I whispered. "Please—my head—it hurts so—"

"Yes." He did not try to touch me again. Rather he went to the window and whistled. Then he leaned out and I heard a murmur of voices.

After he returned to kneel by me, taking my numb hands into his, rubbing them so that the agony of returning circulation made me cry out. But his fingers pressed instantly on my lips and he leaned close to whisper.

"My brave girl, you must help me a little in order that I can help you. We cannot get out save through the window. Whicker has gone to round up some more of the crew. When he comes you must be strong enough, brave enough, to move—"

I could hear his words but they were like meaningless noises. He was hurting me, that was all I understood. If he would only go, allow me to slip back into the darkness where the pain did not reach. But that he would not do, his voice, his touch, kept me conscious.

"Alain!" That was his name. I had remembered his name!

"Yes, it is Alain. Be still, rest, gather all your strength so we shall be ready when Whicker returns. We have sent for the police also. You are safe—safe—"

Behind his head I saw the door of the room begin to move. I struggled to cry out a warning.

"Be still—rest—" He smiled at me. Smiled! When behind him—

The massive bulk of Bessie—I remembered now. With her others. She held a poker in her hand. No, that was wrong—I had used a poker. So this punishment had come to me—this lying in hell. But why should Alain be here? Now Bessie leaned over him ready to strike—

Somehow I found my voice. "Alain—behind—!"

He swung about without getting to his feet. Strong as he was, how could he defend himself against the giantess? I could see what she held was really a hammer. She shouted in that shrill voice, "Git 'im, boys, when I lay 'im out. Jo'll pay top price for the likes of this boyo!"

But she was not to knock out her prey so easily. Alain dodged, and I saw a pistol in his hand. Bessie edged back from that threat, her men also giving way. Then they divided forces, Bessie to the right, the others to the left. Alain could not defend himself from two directions at once.

Where my own peril had left me defeated and witless, his brought me strength. I edged along the rags of that noisome bed, flung myself at Bessie. My crooked fingers caught in the drapery of her dress at knee level.

Her arm swung down but the hammer did not thud home on my head or Alain's, rather to the floor. Bessie, overbalanced, staggered back. Outside the door there was a thunderous crash. By the force of her own unwilling retreat she had carried supporters with her.

Alain was on his feet, now he stooped and drew me up. My head throbbed with such pain I was afraid I might faint. And with the agony was vertigo which sent the walls of the den in a sickening dance around me.

Shielding me as best he could with his own body, Alain backed to the window, his pistol aimed at the door. Though we could hear shufflings beyond, they had not come to attack again.

"We must get outside," he said. "There is more room there and Whicker's men can't be too far away."

"Git 'em, boys!" came Bessie's cry.

Alain fired. The crash of the shot was deafening. A scream answered, then sounds as if they were moving out of range.

He had me at the window but I could not help myself. I felt a dull anger at my own uselessness, and that anger strengthened me. But it was not lack of will, rather lack of strength in limbs and muscles which hindered me.

"I cannot climb out—"

"Hold on!" His one-handed grip on me tightened. "Can you sit on the sill and drop out?"

How simple—of course I could and would do that. I fell rather than sat on the sill. Alain lifted and I was able to swing my feet over and down. As he kept watch on the door, I fell from the window, leaving him behind.

This was an alley even more noisome than the room. The jar of my striking its slime-encrusted pavement nearly shattered me. I fought faintness, I must remain alive and conscious. This I must do or Alain, too, might become a victim.

I pushed up to my knees. Then, leaning against a scabrous wall, vilely damp, I somehow stood upright. Though I dared not move away from that support.

"Alain—" I wanted to call to him that I was all right, that he must join me. But all I produced was a rasping croak.

I slid along the wall, my goal the window. Perhaps if he saw me he would come. Why was he not already here? There had been no sound of another shot. But those within had knives—

"Alain!" I saw nothing but the window.

So it was that when they closed about me it was a shock. Whicker's men? One glance told me no. They were strangely alike, the three of them, small and thin, dark of skin, moving noiselessly. Their faces were blank of expression, only their eyes were alive. Those regarded me dully. Still it was plain they were determined on my capture.

CHAPTER SEVENTEEN

As, for the last time, I forced out a weak cry of "Alain!" the centermost of those three who had closed in upon me threw something straight into my face. I gasped, coughed, choked, trying to breathe through the dust clogging my mouth and nose. And I was still coughing and helpless when they laid hands on me. They pulled me unresisting down the lane, my will gone. I could no longer fight as they pushed me into a cart drawn by a pair of mules.

Two of the strangers spread bags over my body. Then we jolted off, and I was a prisoner within flesh and muscle where not even my voice would obey my frantic commands.

The cart bumped along and I could hear the clamor of the Coast all about. Then those sounds dwindled and I knew we must be drawing out of that section of the city. Who were these men? Followers of D'Lys? D'Lys was dead. Was that why they had tracked me down—in order to take vengeance? But how had they known where to find me?

I had seen too much, endured too much. That confidence born at Alain's coming seeped away. And what had happened to Alain?

That Bessie could and would summon reinforcements, of that I was sure. And then perhaps he would suffer the fate she had threatened, of being knocked out and shanghaied aboard some ship. From there he could not escape. All because of me.

My thoughts were heavy burdens as the cart creaked on. But being in the open revived me somewhat, or else the spark Alain had ignited had not wholly died. Although my body still lay limp, my mind cleared. And I began a silent fight against what held me captive. Since I had surely been kidnapped for some evil purpose, I must expect danger at the end of this journey.

Alain found me at Bessie's somehow. But I could not hope for another such miracle. I could only pray for his own escape.

We passed through very quiet streets now. Our goal must be whatever hiding place D'Lys had found, the one Mrs. Pleasant's people had never discovered. Finally the cart bumped to a stop. My head still ached, but now the pain was not so intense.

Those sacks over me were thrown aside. Hands closed

on my shoulders and, with unusual strength for their slender bodies, two of the men swung me down to the pavement. The day was well advanced and we were in a thick-walled courtyard with a single gate the third man was barring. Along two sides were buildings, on the third some open-fronted sheds in which horses stamped and snorted. Leaving me to stand, still unable to take a step on my own initiative, my captors unharnessed the mules and took them to the sheds.

The windows of the house section were covered by thick wooden shutters. And the doors, with the exception of the nearest, were not only closed, but had boards nailed across them. Soil drifted from what had once been flower beds and there were fresh animal droppings everywhere. Deserted as the place might look at first glance, it was plainly in use.

My captors returned, the one in the lead taking my arm to pull me forward. I was a puppet in his hands, though my mind struggled to break those bonds the choking dust had laid upon me.

We entered a vast kitchen with a hearth capable of taking a good-sized log. Hung over a fire, dwarfed in that cavern, was a pot on a chain. And from that steam arose.

Standing near, a long-handled spoon ready, was a woman who turned such a seamed face in my direction it was like meeting Death (if Death might be of my sex) engaged in a grotesque parody of a household task. Wrinkled and withered though her face might be (her hands were veritable claws), she was dressed in the brightest of colors. Her wide skirt was a red which clashed with the brilliant orange of her blouse. And twisted around her head, hiding all but a wisp of gray fluff over her forehead, was a blue scarf.

She dug into the pot with her spoon, brought that back up to her chin, dribbling contents over blouse and skirt. Holding spoon at lip level, she blew on it vehemently, sending more of the liquid flying. Then, extending a pallid tongue, she lapped, as might a cat, at what was left.

Apparently the taste did not suit her, for she turned to

the table behind, clawed up a thick pinch of dried stuff and tossed that into the pot. Then, slamming the spoon on the table, she hobbled to meet us.

Though her shoulders were so bent she had to screw her head up at a painful angle to face us, she had once been a tall woman. And it was plain she ruled this household, for the men waited for her to speak first.

I could understand nothing of what she said. Her language was a thick and gutteral one, some of the words delivered with a hissing intonation. But it must have included dismissal as all three men left.

Now she peered straight at me. Around her gaunt neck was a chain of small polished bones and from this dangled a huge spike, like a monster tooth. Her skin was very black, but had a grayish overtinge as if powdered with ashes, adding to her appearance of extreme age. She raised a claw finger, crooked it to beckon.

"Come!" She croaked in French.

I was drawn forward like a dog on a tight leash. We went out of the kitchen into a much smaller room in which there was only a large packing case placed against one wall. To that she pointed with the order: "Sit."

Again that which held me made me obey. She hobbled back toward the kitchen, having made no attempt to secure me. Apparently she was confident that I remained a helpless prisoner.

The men returned, were fed by bowls of the pottage and rounds of coarse bread. Having eaten, they did not again go outside, but passed into another section of the house, that behind the boarded shutters.

Time dragged slowly. But I began to feel that weird bondage was waning. With great concentration of will I was able to make a single finger on my right hand respond to my bidding. A finger, then my hand raised an inch or so from where it lay helplessly on my knee.

So spurred by a small victory I strove to move my toes within the wrecks of my shoes. If I could stand, walk—I could get out, for I did not believe that the old woman had the physical strength to oppose me.

Only, before I could achieve more than a small beginning, she came back, one of the men behind her carrying a large hamper. Dismissing him with a jerk of the chin (he scuttled away as if he were very glad to go), the hag began to unpack the hamper. There were gourds with stoppers, a length of white cloth she did not unfold, a bowl which she placed on the floor, getting down on her knees with a grunt of pain to do so.

Into the bowl she sifted the contents of several small packets, stirring them together with the care of a master cook, using a white paddle instead of a spoon. Each of the packets she so emptied was hung with feathers and pieces of yellow bone.

Having finished, she arose swiftly to her feet and came to me, gesturing me to stand. My freedom was still too limited to defy her. There was a noise at the door and two of the men came, tugging a tin bath in which water sloshed. She pointed to a position on the floor not far from the bowl. They set it there and retreated as quickly as their comrade.

Now the crone caught at the torn draperies of my dress. "Off—all off," she ordered.

Not lingering to see if she was obeyed, she went to the bowl, stooped to pick up a gourd, drew out its stopper, and sniffed the contents.

My fingers fumbled at the pins in my torn bodice. In spite of all my awakening will I could not resist her order. Slowly, clumsily, I dropped my clothing piece by piece, revolted by my own actions, unable to stop.

Meanwhile she poured into the bath the contents of more than one gourd. The odor arising from the intermingling of those liquids was sickly sweet.

I dropped my last garment, standing as I never had in anyone's company during my adult life. And I was hot with shame.

The woman had brought out a paddle with a longer handle, stirred the water vigorously, the cloud of scent rising. Nor did that dissipate, but seemed to hang directly above the bath like a fog.

"Come—" Again she crooked a finger.

I went unwillingly, the spell (which was all I could term it) still holding.

"In—"

I stepped into the bath. The water was warm, oily against my shrinking skin. At another sign I squatted down and she came closer with a white cloth. So armed, she bathed me, washing even my hair, and I had to endure it, though her touch, like that of the water, aroused in me a sick revulsion.

When she seemed satisfied with her labors, she left me sitting in the water, the scent now wedded to my skin, my hair, so I feared I would never be free of it. With its cloying intensity it carried a suggestion of evil so pronounced I felt myself stained and defiled.

The crone left the room, to return with a lighted splinter of wood which she inserted into the bowl, blowing at it in small puffs. A strong smell of incense aroused. When this was alight to her satisfaction, she ordered me out of the bath and brought me to the bowl, standing me directly over it, the basin between my feet, the curling yellow smoke weaving an envelope about my body. As the water before it, it made me feel unclean.

She made no effort to dry me; perhaps the smoke was intended to do that. Leaving me imprisoned in its cloud, she shook out the folded cloth she had earlier taken from the hamper. It was a garment of sorts, very wide and loose, sewn to it at random bunches of feathers both black and white. While on the front was traced a crude design in black paint.

The smoke was dying away, but she left me there until the substance in the bowl was only ashes. She checked now and then so I felt as if I were a pot on the boil. When the last tendril of smoke vanished she lifted the bowl from the floor, holding it with a black cloth between it and her fingers.

Into the warm ashes the crone dipped a brush made of black feathers tied together, catching up the powdery stuff. With that she painted my breasts, outlined below those symbols I did not understand, working until all the ashes were used. The marks clung paint-wise to my still-damp body.

Having so completed her task, she withdrew a step or two to view her handiwork. Whatever she saw must have pleased her, for she set aside bowl and brush, to pick up the white garment. With the ease of one who had done this action more than once, she spun this over my head. It was so loose she had no difficulty in lifting one of my inert arms after the other to insert into the wide sleeves. With a little grunt she withdrew a second time, to survey me up and down. Then she clapped her hands and called out.

As if they had been waiting, two of the men returned to lug out the bath, while she repacked the hamper. Both men made a wide circle around me, avoided even looking in my direction—as if I were now an object to inspire fear and awe.

When they had gone the crone shuffled to the pile of my discarded clothing. She picked it up and searched each piece, finding my money, weighing also the handkerchief I had tied around the bracelet, but not opening that. Rather she made a sound of pleasure and stowed the purse in the front of her blouse.

But as she stooped once more the handkerchief clattered to the floor and unwound so that the spider bracelet lay in plain sight. Spying it, the woman started back, her mouth gaping open to show toothless gums.

She did not reach to pick it up; rather she went into the kitchen and returned with that large spoon she had used earlier. Creaking to her knees, she made hard work of catching the loop of the bracelet around the spoon bowl.

Once obtained without touching it, she held it close to her eyes. Then she placed it, spoon and all, on the top of the case and came over to me. Grabbing one sleeve of the robe, keeping the material between her hands and flesh, she raised my right arm, bared it, and sniffed along the skin. I felt her whistling breath. Letting that fall, she did the same with the other.

"You wear *z'araignée*—"

She did not seem to expect an answer. Now she stood, plucking at her lower lip. Then, muttering to herself, she went back to the case and reached for the spoon handle.

"*Z'araignée*," she repeated. From her own neck she took the bone necklace, rattled it furiously over the bracelet. Her muttering held the cadence of a chant as, from somewhere within her clothing, she produced a length of thong, looped that through the bracelet, turning the ornament into a large, awkward pendant.

Back at my side she flipped up the robe to drop the thong about my neck, settling the bracelet between my breasts before she covered me again. Once more I was then ordered back to the box. My head was still swimming from the effects of the incense. This time as she left the room she closed the door, but I did not think she locked it.

Only I was not alone. I watched, and could not escape, horrors which crept from the corners to squat before me, gibbering, pointing with hands which were not hands, mewing noises which were never speech.

I thought I had gone mad, or would soon. But some hard core deep within me repeated over and over that these were but illusions, things born out of that vile smoke.

Things like demons from old Bibles illustrated by Doré capered there, the darkest fears of childhood put on life. I closed my eyes, yet still they were imprinted on my lids. Also—when I dared not watch, surely they crept closer. So I must look again to make sure—

I was far past tears. Fear tensed my body into one rigid ache, and the garment I wore might have been spun of ice I was so cold. I do not know how I continued to keep a small fingerhold on sanity. But I fought in the only way I knew—first with the memory of my life with my father. Instead of seeing phantoms, I tried to picture him standing on guard as he had so often during the savagery of a storm. And this time another was shoulder to shoulder with him. Deepening into life for me came Alain Sauvage, for he was of the same breed.

With Jesse Penfold's blood in me, the shaping of my

childhood his, how could I not fight? I forced myself to center my attention upon a single one of those demons born of fear and hallucination. Then I willed to see through its misshapen body to the wall of the room, to remember who I was and that I could not be so vanquished by the tricks of devil worshippers.

Whether I had some innate barrier against complete surrender to their drugs, I do not know. I have since heard that the reactions of unbelievers cannot be as enduring as those of true worshippers who expect to see and feel what is not of this world.

I did not break, if that was what they expected. Rather I gained command of myself. Once more I could raise my hands, though those shook and trembled so I could not use them. But my legs remained numb and lifeless.

They came for me when it was dark—save for candles a man standing just outside the door held in either hand. The crone had put away her bright clothing. Now she wore a loose robe of black, caught in about her middle with a blue sash. Her headcloth, however, was the same. The man with her was bare of body save for a blue cloth about his loins.

One on either side they took me under the arms, pulled me up, and marched me forward, the man with the candles in the lead. So we came into a much larger room. Here was light from torches thrust into iron rings set in the walls. Under those stood a number of people, the women wearing robes of white or blue, the men only pantaloons. And some of that company were as white of skin as I.

The center of the room was bare and marked out there on the floor was that symbol I had seen on the crumpled scrap of paper in Victorine's room—a black heart with a sword wreathed by a yellow serpent. To one side was a hogshead, one end covered with a tautly drawn skin. Sitting astride this crude drum, two long bones in his hands to be plied as sticks, was the third man who had brought me here. He was flanked by another holding a chain on which had been strung a number of bells, on the other side by a woman holding a large gourd.

Beyond the design on the floor was a long table draped with black; pinned to that many of the same bunches of feathers as were on my robe, as well as bones. On the surface of the improvised altar lay two cocks, one white, one black, their feet cruelly bound. The wretched birds were alive and kept up a frenzied crowing.

My guards led me past the heart, being very careful not to set foot on its tracing. We passed beyond the altar to one of the pillars supporting the roof of this great room. As if they were no longer sure that their stupefying hold would continue, my captors lashed me to this upright.

On the floor behind the altar, perhaps not visible to those gathered at the other end of the chamber, was a big basket which shook of itself now and then as if something was imprisoned within.

Our entrance signaled the beginning of the rite. The man seated on the drum began to beat softly in a strange rhythm, accented at intervals by a ring of the bells, a rattling as the woman shook the gourd.

Then followed a chant, low at first, gathering volume. The crone moved to the fore of the altar, raising her arms, wrinkled leather drawn over bone, uttering sharp cries as if to summon someone—or something.

From the shadows at this end of the room where there were no torches advanced another group. Two tall men, wearing only pantaloons, supported between them a third who walked haltingly, his head lolling forward on his chest. His slender body was bare save for a scarlet cloth, and about both his ankles and his limp wrists were chains of gold hung with bells. His head was bound with a bandage and I caught sight of his pale face as they passed me.

D'Lys! Then he was not dead!

His supporters brought him to the altar, raised him to be laid upon it, the struggling, squawking birds at his head and feet. While the tempo of the drum quickened, until its beat shook my body, willing me to some action I did not understand.

A shrill cry broke from the crone, echoed by those in the chamber.

"L'appe vine, le Grand Zombi."

"L'appe vine, pour le gris-gris!"

There was a wild leap out of the shadows, the figure clearing both the altar and the man upon it, to land in the exact center of that symbol on the floor. Her ivory body was almost entirely nude, her hair loose on her shoulders. This Victorine had no kinship with the girl I had known.

Around her waist was a belt of small bones clacking together at her every move, and at her throat the serpent necklace glinted. She began to dance, hardly moving her feet, but so twisting and swaying her body that the obscenity she suggested was clear to me, even though I had never seen such before. The crone scurried to open the basket.

She returned carrying a snake, such as I had never believed could exist. It writhed upward to coil about her shoulders until she staggered under its weight. Slowly she came to Victorine, halting only at the edge of the symbol.

Victorine turned, held out her arms. The snake reared its head, lifted the forepart of its body from the crone, stretching to meet the girl. Then it seemed to flow to her through the air. As it came into her grasp she held its head level with her face, the forked tongue darting at her cheeks. There was a shout from the watchers:

"Ah—yah—Ezili Coeur-Noir!"

The snake moved its head as if it whispered in her ear. I saw her laugh and nod. Grasping it firmly, she jerked its full length to her.

Though it had made the old woman a heavy burden, to Victorine it could have been the lightest cord. She used it like a whip, holding it behind the head, snapping its length out toward the others. They swayed from side to side, mimicking the serpent. Three times she lashed it, then she allowed it to coil about her waist, its head resting on her shoulder.

She finally made a quick dart to the side of the altar, loosened the hold of the snake, making it caress with flicking tongue the face and breast of D'Lys. Finally the reptile flowed from her to the floor, to coil by its basket, its head still swaying to the rhythm of the drum. Victorine whirled and caught up the black cock—

I will not allow myself to remember what she did, I dare not. She could not have been wholly human in those moments, rather possessed by a devil. For now I can accept that evil incarnate *can* walk this world. What most men dismiss as superstition—that I have *seen!*

There was blood on D'Lys' body, not his own. Blood on her mouth and hands—

She faced the worshippers. "Ahhhhh!" she screamed. "Here stands Ezili Coeur-Noir. She is mam'bo!"

"Mam'bo!" they wailed. They had crept closer and their eyes had a glazed stare. They were flushed as if drunk. Here and there one of the women had thrown off her robe.

"Here lies our houn'gan!" Victorine pointed to D'Lys. "He is not dead, he is possessed by Baron Samedi of the Grave. Ahhh—let him rise, rise, rise!" She screamed louder and louder.

"What do we bring to Baron Samedi that our houn'gan may live, may have breath within his nostrils, feel the beat of his heart, be a man again—what do we bring?"

"Ahhhhh—" the others moaned.

"We bring the white goat without horns. Tender flesh for his tearing, for his eating. Ahhh—the goat without horns do we bring!"

She made another of those leaps, this carrying her to me. At the same time someone behind the pillar cut free my hands. There was a flash of light in the air, Victorine now held a knife. With that she made a lightning thrust I could not dodge. But that blow had not been intended to kill, rather my slashed robe fell to the floor.

"Behold the white goat without horns," she cried. "Let it come that its blood be the drink, its flesh the food, and our houn'gan rise again."

She beckoned as if she expected me to walk forward and have my throat cut. I did not move. Her face contorted into a devil's grimace.

"Come!" She backed to the altar beckoning.

Perhaps what saved me was that instinct which makes us all fight death, perhaps part of it was my victory over the earlier hallucinations. Though compulsion urged me forward, I had the strength and will to stand fast.

The beat of the drum, the clash of the bells, the rattling of the gourd made a hellish noise. Within me there was that which continued to fight.

"Come!"

I needed some weapon—there was none to hand. When would she grow impatient and use the knife? I raised my hands to cover my breasts in useless defense.

So I touched the dangling bracelet. What aid it could be—? I ducked my head, drew off the cord, swung it in my hand. So poor a thing, but all I had.

"Come!" Victorine cried for the third time. There were flecks of foam on her lips. Her eyes were not sane.

I did not move. Though the pack could easily pull me down. Behind Victorine I saw the crone draw near.

She screamed some injunction into the girl's ear. Why they did not rush me I did not understand. At any moment I expected them to seize me, drag me to that altar, and use the knife. Yet now I was more clear-headed than I had been for hours, as if fear had burned the last of their poison from my mind.

Sweat dripped from Victorine's chin, ran freely from her temples. Her body swayed from side to side though her feet did not move. She was—the snake! Even her tongue flicked in and out, her head appeared to flatten, her eyes were set in a reptilian stare.

She raised both hands over her head and brought them down. There was instant silence, drum, bells, rattle, chant all ceased. The quiet was so intense I could hear the sputtering of the wall torches.

"You *shall* come!" She did not scream now. "At the bidding of Ezili Coeur-Noir you shall come. For the Loa is strong in me—*she* desires you—"

Swaying, she approached me. I had but one small, near hopeless chance. In her hand the knife was ready; the torchlight seemed to cling to its cruel blade.

Once more Victorine began to chant, though this time the others did not join in, nor did the drum, bells, and rattle sound. I still could not understand why they did not force me to their will. It was as if they must have me approach the altar willingly. And that I determined I would not do.

I dangled the bracelet-weighted thong in my hand—if she would only come closer. I must be alert to her every movement. At that moment I was conscious of nothing save that the woman facing me was as oldly evil as the Lucifer fallen from heaven. One step—and another—

The knife snaked out. Whether she meant to rip living flesh as she had my robe I shall never know. But I swung the bracelet. The circlet struck her upper arm. She cried out, staggered back. What I saw then—no, I cannot swear to it—

Perhaps the setting of the spider had loosened. That can be the only rational explanation. I will not allow myself to believe that—

To Victorine's white flesh that loathsome black thing clung. She screamed again, hideously, dropped the knife to beat at it with her other hand. Then she ran to the altar, still trying, as she went, to scrape off the creature. I could hardly believe it had been driven into her flesh.

The crone screeched also, seized the knife. She turned on me, slavering, her eyes rolled up until all I could see were the whites. Still she seemed to be able to perceive me and came on for the kill.

She never reached me. There was a shot and she crumpled to the floor. Men poured in from the darkened end of the long room. My head whirling, I slipped into a crouch beside the pillar.

I saw Victorine. The black blot was gone from her arm and she had thrown herself on D'Lys, who was stirring feebly. Together they slipped to the other side of the table and rolled off it. And that was the next to the last thing I was to remember.

The last was arms about me, a soft covering lapping me around, and I was being carried while someone repeated my name over and over—

CHAPTER EIGHTEEN

I opened my eyes on only a faint night light. Had I been ill? It was hard to remember. Terrible dreams—Victorine—nightmares which could only have been born of illness—

Someone was bending over me—I fought for a name to match a face.

"Fenton?"

"Miss Tamaris—you know me!" She sounded as if she had been crying.

"Have I been—ill?" Not memories—just fever nightmares, I prayed.

"You've been asleep for nearly two days. Your poor face, and him not knowing what drugs you had been given—"

I pushed myself up on my pillows. "Then the dreams—were true!" Something within me broke and I began to cry as I had never wept before, not even at the news of my father's death.

"Miss, oh, Miss Tamaris, hush you now. It is all right, you are safe—" Fenton sat on the side of the bed, took my hands in hers, crooned over me as if I were a child. "God forgive my tongue, I should not have told you, made you remember. It's all right, you are safe now."

I gripped her hands tight in return, they were my anchorage. "I cannot help crying—"

Thus I wept myself quiet. Then I knew a kind of dull peace. Fenton brought me a cup of broth, later rolls spread with butter and honey, hot milk. I slept again—there were no more dreams.

When I awoke for the second time there was sunlight in the room. And I knew this for the hotel chamber I had left—when? It seemed weeks since I had last rested in this bed, and all my recollections were oddly detached, as if they were now the memories of another person.

I sat up as Fenton entered the room. When she saw me she laid down an armload of freshly laundered linen and came to me.

"Miss Tamaris—how are you?"

"Hungry—"

A smile lighted her plain face. "Give me but a minute or two." She bustled out, to return with a basin of warm water, scented soap, and towels, and proceeded to wash me as if I were five, instead of five times that age. When she touched my cheek I flinched.

"Oh, that bruise. I shall try not to hurt you—"

A scrap of memory again. That blow Bessie had used to silence my call for help.

"Bring me a mirror."

"But, miss, it is fast fading and—"

"Please, Fenton. Let me see."

With pursed lips she brought my hand mirror. In spite of the pain I was only half prepared for what I saw. The skin from near jawline to hair was a huge bruise several shades of color. I looked hideous, so I dropped the mirror quickly.

"I had better wear a veil." I attempted a laugh, more shocked than I wanted her to know.

But that reflected face had brought me sharply into the here and now. All the ugliness I had been a part of was branded on me and I could not escape the memory.

I shrank from asking questions; rather I lay back on my pillows as Fenton left, making myself explore those dark recollections. I had escaped or I would not be here. But what had I escaped? Only death itself.

I had not been rescued from that defilement of mind and body. The feeling of being unclean closed in upon me. I was not the Tamaris Penfold I had always known.

And Alain—what had happened to Alain?

Above all I wanted to ask that of Fenton, yet I dreaded her answer. Still I must face the truth squarely, no matter how bleak—and I was summoning my rags of courage when she returned with a tray.

I was hungry and what she offered was tempting. Because of that hunger I did not at first notice a small bowl on the left-hand side of the tray. Then my eyes were drawn to it.

It was no larger than could fit comfortably into the hollow of my cupped hand. White, possessing a relief design of flowering branches. I had seen its like before—a treasure of a house of many courtyards half the world away.

"Mutton-fat jade," I whispered.

Some Chinese artist had created this exquisite perfection. Now it held a cluster of white violets, their own green leaves making a frame to highlight their frail beauty. Tears smarted in my eyes, a choking lump arose in my throat.

"Fenton!"

When she came I could not master the shaking of my hands.

"What is it, miss?"

I fought to keep my voice natural. "The violets—the bowl—"

She smiled. "The master sent those. He said to give them to you."

"Please, Fenton, take them away!"

She regarded me anxiously. Let her believe my mind was disturbed, anything—only let her get them out of my sight!

"Please—" I no longer cared what Fenton might think. I only wanted it gone.

"Of course, miss." She whisked it away.

My appetite had vanished. I crumbled a roll, tried a forkful of creamed chicken, drank a sip of coffee. The food had no flavor now and to choke it down was painful.

"Fenton—I must get up."

"But, miss, the doctor said—and you've hardly eaten anything."

"I find I am not hungry after all. And I must get up—now!"

Unfortunately I discovered I did need her help. I was

very weak and she had to draw on my stockings, fasten my shoes, aid me with my clothes.

"The dark green dress if you please, Fenton."

"But you can't be going out, miss! Here is your wrapper—"

I shook my head with determination. "No, the dress, please."

Shaking her head, she brought it, hooked the bodice, fastened the skirt. I was trying to think of what must be done and how. The money which the crone had taken from me—how I needed that! What else did I have?

"Fenton, bring my jewel case—"

I wanted the packet of eastern bank notes I still had kept and now I counted those. But I had no idea what a ticket for a transcontinental train trip cost—did I have enough? If not—to whom might I appeal for a loan?

I had only five contacts within the city. And two of those I would not approach. There remained three—and the last was the closest. Holding the notes in my hand I looked to Fenton, hovering over me.

"Is Mrs. Deaves here at present?"

"If she hasn't gone out with the master. They've been in and out so much—"

"Ask her to come here."

Fenton went reluctantly. But Mrs. Deaves came with a promptitude which suggested interest in my affairs, an overwhelming interest. She studied me closely, I no longer cared.

"I am so glad you are feeling better—"

I raised one hand to brush aside the need for polite speech between us. All but my purpose was unnecessary.

"I must ask for a loan of money." That was blunt enough but I felt that time was against me. "Though I have these notes, I have no other resources at hand. And I fear that this is not enough to pay for my fare east."

She was startled, plainly taken aback, as if those words were the last she expected to hear. They should give her pleasure, she had never wanted me here.

"You plan to return east—when?" Now she was as terse as I had been.

"As soon as possible. I shall go by coach, of course, but there is the matter of fare and food."

"You have discussed this with Alain?" She watched me narrowly.

"There is no need for discussion now. My reason for being here no longer exists. And I have not found my visit to San Francisco so pleasant that I desire to prolong it. As for Mr. Sauvage, I shall leave him a letter. I think you will agree with me that this is the best course?"

She licked her lips. "You have asked no questions—concerning Victorine, what has happened—"

"What has happened I shall endeavor to forget as speedily as possible. As for Victorine—I assume her brother has taken the proper steps to control her activities."

Mrs. Deaves shook her head. "She is gone—with her husband—that creature *was* her husband. Alain put them aboard the *Tangus* yesterday—they will be taken to the West Indies. He could not have them charged by the law —the scandal would have been too great. And Victorine was not truly his sister, no Sauvage. He discovered that from someone who knew the facts of her birth. She is the daughter of his stepmother's lover. Learning that, he had no reason to keep her from the man she had chosen."

Mrs. Beall, or Mrs. Pleasant? Which had told Alain the truth? And if Mrs. Beall, why had Alain not recognized her—unless his contact with his stepmother had been very slight and the woman had later disguised herself well. I might never know, but the matter was none of my concern.

"Mr. Sauvage himself took no hurt?" I asked the one question which would give me a small peace of mind. However, I kept my voice steady and cool, as if our relationship had never been more than that of employer and employee. Had it been really? It is far too easy for a woman without experience to deceive herself in such matters.

"He suffered some bruises, a slight cut on the arm. Nothing to signify."

"Very fortunate. But is it possible for you to honor my request?" I could not bear to discuss Alain with her.

"I can. If you are determined to go, Teresa can accompany you across the bay tonight. There is a train leaving for the east tomorrow morning. I shall have the money for you."

"As a loan. I have funds in the east from which I can repay you."

I believed I knew what lay behind the offer of Teresa's company—Mrs. Deaves wanted to make very sure I *was* going. She need have no fear. I expected her to leave forthwith, but instead she paused by the door to study me curiously.

"You are sure this is what you wish, to go so and at once?"

I was wearied to the point I could hardly endure her presence. But I managed to keep my control.

"Entirely sure. I am grateful for your help. Now, if you do not mind, I am tired and must rest if I am to leave this evening."

"Of course." But even as she reached for the doorknob she still watched me with an avid curiosity, as if she were unable to believe that I would be soon gone out of her life. If she would have said anything more, she thought better of it.

I was alarmed at my own weakness. Though I must harbor my strength, there were two things I had to do before I could rest. And, as Fenton came back, I set about those.

"Fenton, I am leaving tonight. Since I shall be unable to carry much luggage, please pack the small carryall with my toilet things, some clean linen, such articles as I will need in a week's travel by train. Afterwards, if you will be so kind, pack the rest of my clothing and see that the trunks are sent to an address I shall give you. You will not pack those gowns made here—"

Now she wore that old mulish look which I remembered from the first days of our meeting. But her displeasure could be no bar to me.

"Before you begin, please bring me my writing desk. And—this is most important, Fenton—you will, on no account, speak to *anyone* concerning my plans. Will you give me your solemn promise not to do that?"

I held her gaze with mine, willed her to give me that assurance. I believed that I could trust her; once she had given such a promise she would keep it.

Her long, sallow face flushed and she twisted her hands together.

"Please, Miss Tamaris—please don't ask me! The master, he'll—"

I sighed. "Very well, Fenton. I will tell you why I am doing this so you can answer if asked. I have had things happen to me which have changed my life so deeply that I do not even know myself any longer. I must get away from everyone who reminds me of the past. I know this to be true. Do you understand?"

She studied me with a regard as searching as Mrs. Deaves' had been. Her face was still unhappy, but, as if against her will, she nodded.

"Mr. Sauvage will not blame you for my leaving. I will write a letter to be given to him after I am gone. This shall explain to him exactly how I feel and why I must go home."

"If you say so, Miss Tamaris. But—can't I go with you? You ain't well enough to make the trip alone. Look at you—you're so weak you can't even walk across this room!"

"I feel much better than I look, Fenton. And once I am away from here I will feel even better."

With the desk on my knees, inkwell unstopped, pen and paper ready, I discovered what I lacked were the proper words. I could not entrust to paper, even for one person to read and destroy, the innermost feelings which I held now. At last I began, without salutation, for my heart said "Alain" and I had no right to that:

You will understand my feelings. I must leave the scene of events which have caused me such pain. And in going I cannot leave any better farewell than this, for I have discovered I cannot bear to look at anyone who witnessed my degradation. Pity and scorn are equally painful. Once I am away perhaps I can in time forget.

It was stiff, but I could find no other words. I put the sheet into an envelope and sealed it. Then I resolutely composed myself for the rest I knew I must have.

Though I closed my eyes I could hear Fenton moving quietly, carrying out my orders for packing. Then I must have dozed for I awoke suddenly with her hand on my shoulder, before me a table set with a substantial meal.

"You didn't eat before," she said as if she expected me to spurn the food, "but you must now, Miss Tamaris. If you don't you won't have strength to get to the train."

As I ate she spoke again: "Mrs. Deaves—she says that Teresa will go across the bay with you. Why can't I do that much?"

"Because I am depending on you, Fenton, for two important tasks—to deliver my letter and take care of my luggage."

"Oh, Miss Tamaris—I do want to go with you, all the way! You can't manage by yourself, I know it!"

I shook my head. "Fenton, in the East I have never lived the kind of life in which I required a maid. You have been very good to me, and I deeply appreciate all you have done. I have a small token for you, it was a gift to me from my father." I brought out a remembrance I had taken from my jewel box—a cross carved from ivory with a vine entwined in high relief around it.

"Oh—miss—" There were tears in her eyes.

I pressed the cross into her hand and then I added more briskly than I felt, "Have you been able to find me a veil?"

She slipped the cross into her apron pocket and lifted from the table my traveling hat with a thick veil pinned efficiently about it to give the fullest concealment to my face. That it also gave the impression of one in half-mourning was appropriate—was I not in mourning for the person I once was and could never be again?

My loose coat was also black, and under it, snapped to my belt, was the purse holding the funds Mrs. Deaves had sent. This hour was one in which few were to be encountered in the halls, since those staying here would be dressing for dinner. Fenton picked up my bag, jealously holding onto it. While Teresa, bonneted and shawled, waited by the outer door of the suite. We took a back way down the servants' stairs, and came to the rear door where a hack waited.

I pressed Fenton's hand as she helped me in, but was too uncertain of voice to bid her goodbye. Her kindness had cushioned a bad time for me. Yet at that moment I never wanted to look at her face again. For she, too, was one of those who must *know*.

From the deck of the ferry I could see the setting sun making a brilliant path across the bay. The city which had been to me such a place of threatening fog and evil shadows, was, in my final glimpse of it now, golden. But that promise was only fantasy.

Teresa urged me into the cabin, but I could not bear to leave the open air. The wind and the sea calmed my nerves, assured me that I could again become the mistress of myself. I asked the maid to leave me on one of the deck benches and she went willingly enough as I turned my back upon the false promise of the city. Now I must set the past firmly behind me.

Some mysteries I might never solve, but in this life that is often true. Perhaps in years to come, I would wonder about those—how Alain had been able to meet Mr. Whicker and so follow to Bessie's foul hole, and again, how he and those with him had tracked me to that makeshift temple of Victorine's vile worship. Or had his second discovery of me been chance only when he was in pursuit of the girl? And how, in turn, had she escaped Mrs. Pleasant to be reunited with D'Lys?

Not that any of this mattered. Mrs. Beall—Mrs. Pleasant—Victorine—they had played their several games. And I was somehow sure that Mrs. Pleasant had tried to set her seal on me also. What if I had accepted that bold offer she had made me?

I would never have been free again, either from her or my own conscience. I had not written her any farewell note, perhaps because I had a submerged fear that she, above all, might have been the one to circumvent my escape.

A rising wind tugged at my veil, but that was too well pinned to be so loosened. Victorine was at sea also, on her way to those islands where cruel and bloody slavery had nurtured devil worship. But once in truth she must have been as pure and untouched as she looked. Was it only through the influence of D'Lys she had become the priestess of the dark sect? Or had the taint lain within her from birth, needing only the right touch to awaken it?

At least D'Lys lived and I was no murderess. Though I well knew that were I forced to face him again I would once more use any weapon in my own defense.

So within me, too, there was violence.

I shivered. How little we know of ourselves until we are put to some testing. Who was I now—?

Dimly I was aware that someone had come close to where I huddled on the bench. I turned my head aside, though I knew my battered face could not be seen through the veil. I did not want to leave my seat bathed by the dying sun, to go out of the clean breath of the sea.

"Tamaris—"

I bit hard upon my lower lip, refusing to accept that I had heard my name called by *that* voice.

"Tamaris! Don't you turn from me now!" He closed the distance between us with a single stride. His hand gripped my wrist in a hold I could not break without a struggle.

"Let me go! For the love of heaven let me go!"

"Not until we have talked. Did you think to escape me so easily?"

I kept my face turned from him. His body was between me and the setting sun.

"How did you know where I was? Fenton?"

"Fenton kept her allegiance to you. I did not have your letter until you had gone." None of the anger left his voice, but he was controlling himself so rigidly that I could feel that tension. "As to how I knew—thank Amélie!"

"Amélie!" He had startled me out of my self-absorption. "What has she to do with me?"

"You saved her life when that hellcat would have left her to die. Yes, Amélie has a part in your story, too. Now you are going to listen!"

Without invitation he sat down. I think if I had tried to move away he would have used his superior strength to hold me. Still I would not look at him, but I could not close my ears to his voice.

"You owe Amélie—*we* owe her—a great deal, Tamaris. She is grateful to you, not only for saving her life, but for taking the spider bracelet—"

"But—"

"That nasty piece of work was Victorine's hold over her. She had persuaded that poor superstitious girl that the creature on the band would come to life and bite her if she did not obey Victorine's every whim. And if she were to lose or destroy it she would die immediately. But when you took it away Amélie firmly believes you took upon yourself its curse. In the end you returned it to Victorine, so she who invoked it had to bear it. Amélie was indeed in slavery, a blacker, more perverted slavery of the mind and spirit than any slavery of the body."

"But Amélie appeared so devoted," I protested.

"That was her only salvation, as Victorine often told her. Complete and willing service or devilish revenge."

How wrong that I had believed Amélie the darker spirit, when in truth the roles had been reversed.

"It was Amélie," Alain continued, "who supplied us with a list of the haunts of D'Lys, told us of the derelict ranch he had turned into his temple. Though he had traveled with us on the same train from the East, keeping in touch with Victorine through Amélie, he had sent his people ahead. They were islanders steeped in voodoo, who believed that D'Lys was the incarnation of one of their dreaded gods—Baron Samedi who rules the dead.

"You see, Victorine and D'Lys had a plan; they were not preparing any elopement." Alain laughed harshly. "Because of their plan she played her part of *jeune fille* well enough to deceive us all. I could accept that she was

a young girl, her head turned by a convincing rascal.
Even until I saw her in the temple I did not credit all
Amélie told me of her when I returned to San Francisco.
No, Victorine was not to elope with an undesirable suitor.
She had bigger game in mind—me!"

"But how—"

"Again by working through the ways of voodoo, in the
power of which they firmly believe. You saw one—the
gris-gris Victorine made Amélie leave on my desk."

"But you were not one of their followers. How could
they expect to influence you?"

"They believe in their powers, Tamaris. And it is an
odd thing that complete faith in either good or evil can
produce strange results. They began to work on me in the
traditional manner with the gris-gris, so directing their
power, as they thought, against me. Tell me, Tamaris, did
you discover anything of a like nature among your own
belongings? Amélie was evasive but I believe she planted
such."

"A tiny bag sewn into the hem of my shawl, but I destroyed it. And—perhaps the wax thing—" I described
the crude image I had found in the worktable.

"Yes. Those were of their doing. Later they would
have tried drugs."

I shivered as memory reared again.

"Tamaris." His arms tightened about me until I struggled violently. I could not bear his touch. "Tamaris, what
is it?"

"Do not hold me so, I beg of you! Do not!"

"Certainly." He released me instantly. When he continued he spoke matter-of-factly as if he discussed a piece
of business.

"They would have turned to drugs. It was their plan
to weaken my will, perhaps my body and mind, that
Victorine might come into control of the family affairs.
According to Amélie, these devilish substances they employ can make a person obey any order given, while he is
under the influence of such poison. In addition the poor
wretch comes to crave more and more until he is fully
enslaved. Luckily business demands took me away at the

time of your arrival. They were not yet ready to move in because they were not yet immune to counterattack.

"For, once they arrived in San Francisco, they discovered a rival in their own field, a person so well established and commanding such a wide range of power, as to make their situation dangerous. They were put on the defensive before they could make their initial move—"

"You mean Mrs. Pleasant. It is true, then, she uses voodoo?" I was pulled out of my own dark misery by his story, thinking more of what he had to say than what had happened to me, before I knew what was happening.

CHAPTER NINETEEN

"Yes, Mammy Pleasant. But you speak as if you know her—"

I caught the inquiring note in that statement, which was more of a question.

"Long ago, before the war. My father was an abolitionist, he hated slavery. The *India Queen* sometimes smuggled slaves to freedom. She was then Mrs. Smith and she had to do with the shipping of such fugitives. On the first day I was in San Francisco she saw me and sent a note saying I could call on her if I ever were in trouble."

He nodded. "Yes. I know now that she and her people were already aware of D'Lys and what he planned. Thus she must have wanted contact with you to further her surveillance on Victorine. Mammy Pleasant is a woman of power, claims herself to be a voodoo queen. As such she had no intention of surrendering any influence to D'Lys. In the voodoo worship, I am told, the queen is supreme, any priest subservient—which would not suit D'Lys. But with Victorine as her rival that was another matter."

Alain fitted the puzzle together piece by piece. For all her talk of a debt to my father (which could be true, for I did not doubt she could be entirely honest when it suited her purpose) Mrs. Pleasant had excellent reasons to wish to get Victorine under her control. And, had I listened to her, then, I, too, would have been one of her pawns.

"We raided the Rooster just after they had taken you away, hunting D'Lys. Célie told the truth when Captain Lees got at her. He could have crushed her, as she well knew. But D'Lys' men must have been in hiding, saw him dumped, apparently dead, in the street. Also, they got to Victorine and released her when Mrs. Pleasant was called away to the Lanthens'."

"I thought I had killed him—D'Lys," I said dully. The old horror was drawing about me once more, like a blood-sodden cloak.

"I would have, had I laid hands on him!" There was a grim note in Alain's voice which enforced belief. "Unfortunately, Bessie has two places on the Coast. We had to split forces, Lees and his men heading for the largest. I was on my way to the other when I met Whicker, who told me what he had seen. He and Covens had tried to rescue you and had been beaten off by Bessie's bullies. In fact, my arrival, with two of Lees' men, was all that prevented murder. Whicker went to round up more of the crew, I found that window. Then—after I dropped you out, Bessie's men rushed me. When I got free you were gone."

"They were waiting—D'Lys' people—somehow they drugged me—"

"Their damn drugs! Earlier they had handled one of our men the same way. However, Amélie told us about the ranch, except she was not sure where it was. We wasted more than half a day hunting it. Almost too much time. When we got in and saw—" His grip on my arm tightened.

"You sent them away—Victorine and D'Lys."

That set look of his Indian ancestry was on his face, and I knew it was a cover for blazing fury which only his strength of control held in check.

"They are gone. I wish I might have made them suffer for what they did and tried to do. But there was little we could prove against them in any court; intentions are not acts. Had we tried them—there would have followed ruin for innocent people. Do you think I would have allowed *you*, Tamaris, to testify before the curious of what was done to you?"

I cringed, both physically and mentally, at the picture his words summoned up. Alain must have felt my movement, slight as it was, for he laid his hand gently over the two of mine clasped so tightly together.

"No, they could not be allowed to drag others down. When I faced Victorine she was like one possessed by the devil. I can almost believe those old tales of demons who take on the likenesses of fair women."

"But she cannot do you any harm now?" I ventured.

"No, thanks to two courageous women."

"Mrs. Beall?" I guessed.

"How did you learn of her?" Alain demanded quickly.

"Just by chance. I shall never repeat what I did hear."

"She will be grateful for your silence. She has paid in suffering many times over for the mistakes she made in her youth. When she married my father she was very young, and she was coerced into that, I have just learned. The marriage was arranged by her family, as is customary in France, though she was in love with another. She hated this country, and, as I think back now on some of my own memories, she feared my father.

"He was not a genial man, and much immersed in his business projects. Also he considered her frivolous, and tried to make her over into the pattern of my mother, who was a very different type of woman. The result was, as might be expected, disastrous. But how much blame had been wrongly apportioned I learned only when Mrs. Beall came to me, to enable me to cut any claim Victorine might have on me. Her courage was very great, for I think she believed I might be as censorious as my father, and she would be exploited for her past."

I was glad for the distraught woman I had seen with Mrs. Pleasant. And gladder still that Alain was as he was. So the story was now all told. But why had he followed me to tell it? He could as well have written a letter—

The ferry whistled, we were docking. This was my time to say goodbye with such a firmness as to discourage any further communication between us. I arose, pulling my coat closer about me. The sun was now down, there was a cold wind rising to match the chill about my heart. Would I ever be warm again? Sorrow passes with time, but there are things even harder to erase from one's mind and emotions.

"Teresa will be waiting. You have been very kind—" I tried to find conventional words (words which would convince him of my detachment by their very insipid rightness) to prove he owed me nothing.

"Where are you planning to go?" He stood between me and escape like a sentry forbidding me my freedom.

"Back east."

"To Ashley Manor?"

"Perhaps."

Alain shook his head. "I think not. You cannot fit yourself again into the pattern of the perfect lady instructress, Tamaris."

The blow was so sudden, so cruel, that for a moment I could not believe I had heard him say that. I think then that I cried out, as might an animal when death struck.

"What is it?" Again he caught my arm, held me fast. Then he glanced at the passengers pushing past us, preparing to disembark. "We can't stay here. There is much more—come!"

I had not the strength to withstand him; he bore me along before I could protest. Shortly I found myself in a cab, watching him speak to Teresa on the wharf. She turned, went back on board the ferry before I could call out to her, leaving me alone with Alain. He tossed my carryall up to the driver, and climbed in to share my seat.

"You must let me go! I cannot stand—" The dull pain in my head was worse, and once more I experienced that vertigo.

"Be quiet. I am taking you to friends where you will be very welcome. I wired them before the ferry left San Francisco."

His touch, his voice, were so gentle. Yet only moments

ago he had flung in my face the fact of my degradation, that I was no longer fit to teach the young. I was bewildered, half sick. Still I did not have the strength to quarrel with him, any more than I had been able to withstand the voodoo drug.

"You will like the Collmers, they are old-timers. Made the overland journey in fifty-four. He had a small lucky strike in the gold fields and was shrewd enough to use it to build Collmer House, a small quiet family hotel."

I did not reply, reserving all my failing energy for the final struggle of wills I could sense was shaping now between us. He said nothing more, nor did he look at me. His face was set and severe—his "Indian" face. At length the hack pulled up before a three-story building and he handed me down.

We were welcomed at the door by the Collmers themselves, white-haired, elderly, and manifestly more gentlefolk than many I had seen in the glittering frame of the city across the bay. When they spoke I recognized the New England inflection in their voices. Mrs. Collmer escorted me at once to a small suite of two rooms, a sitting room with a bedchamber beyond.

I looked about me and sighed with relief. Here was no red velvet, no marble and gilt. The curtains were cream-white, the furniture covered with an old-fashioned, eye-restful chintz. It was as if I had come out of a nightmare into cool, clean, quiet, and peace.

My hostess said that dinner would be served here in private, for which I was devoutly thankful. But when she had gone and I unpinned that cloaking veil, removed my coat and hat, I made myself go directly to the mirror on the wall and stand there, studying my reflection. So I firmly impressed upon my mind again what lay behind me, that I might not weaken in my resolve to leave all the immediate past behind.

At the sound of a closing door I turned swiftly. Alain stood there and I deliberately turned my battered and discolored face to the full light. The bruises would fade, yes; however, there were other hidden marks I felt would never be erased by the passage of time.

"Now we have time and privacy." He came directly to the point as if it were a matter of business, an outspokenness I welcomed. "I must know, Tamaris, the reason for this foolishness, why you want to leave—and why you feel the way you do about me. Oh, yes, Fenton has clear eyes, she reported your reaction concerning this to me—"

From his coat pocket he brought out the white jade bowl. Now he held it out, his hand cupped as if he cherished a treasure, which indeed he did.

"Why make me," I asked, "put into words what no gentleman should want to hear?"

"There is no time now for the evasions of courtesy. I want the truth! I learned long ago that only a relationship founded on truth can last. Give me that truth now, Tamaris. I know that you felt you could not face this, that it upset you so much that you immediately set about this folly of running away when you are hardly able to stand on your feet. You must tell me why."

I forced myself to look directly at him, though I shrank from the ordeal of meeting his eyes.

"You sent me a gift which should only go to one—who—who is"—I searched frantically for the right word—"untouched."

A dark flood rose from his jaw to his cheeks. There was such a merciless look in his eyes that I thought death must look like this.

"Then D'Lys—he did force you—" Alain seemed to be having the same difficulty with words as I had had.

"No! But he—all of them—made me a part of their evil. They have made me feel unclean. I can never return to what I was, I must always remember. You already understand—why are you making me say this? It is cruel! Only a short time ago you yourself taunted me with the fact that I cannot return to Ashley Manor, that decent people will not want my company now—"

"Taunted!" He closed the space between us with a single stride. "You are out of your mind, girl! You have nothing to be ashamed of—and courage any man would be proud to own! I said that two women had had the courage to free me of the net Victorine tried to weave. One was Mrs. Beall—the other was you, Tamaris!"

I could not escape him, his strength held me prisoner. Just as his lips were first gentle on my bruised cheek, and then demanding, hotly demanding on my own. The will which had sustained me melted—was gone—

"Tamaris!" Alain's voice sounded sharp with fear as the room whirled around me. Then I was on a settee with his arms still supporting me.

"I am so tired—" But I found a second later the strength as well as the need to ask, "Did you mean what you said?"

"I shall never tell you anything but the truth, Tamaris."

He said that as if repeating a vow. Once more I felt as I had for those very fleeting moments when I had first awakened, that all the burdens of life had been lifted from me, that I was light and free. Light and free and happy— with a happiness which swept in and in, to fill empty places I had not known existed.

We were married the next day, with the Collmers attending us. I did not return to San Francisco, but rather remained quietly at Collmer House while Alain went back and forth, settling his affairs. For he now decided on a long-considered plan, to transfer the headquarters of his business to the East for some years.

Fenton came to me and with her Amélie, whom he had promised to provide for. The girl had no desire to return either to the islands of her birth or to France. As she was so skilled a dressmaker, Alain set her up in her own business.

But that I return to a city so full of evil memories for me he sternly forbade. Nor did I hear again from Mrs. Pleasant, that enigmatic "power." Perhaps she thought of me as one to be written off on the "loss" side of her ledger, or perhaps she had always been strictly honest in her desire to help me. I shall never know, nor do I want to ask.

At the end of the month we were again on a train, this time eastward bound. And Alain found a house of cool and gentle peace for us in the country along the Hudson.

There is no red velvet, no gilt, no marble. Most of Alain's fashionable acquaintances would deem it sadly old-fashioned. I love it.

Now I watch through the window for the return of Alain—and happiness. Perhaps our love will not always be the same, this first wild rapture will be tamed into a steady content. But there will always be Alain. And I want no more.

A HISTORIC
NOTE ON
"MAMMY" PLEASANT

Mary Ellen Pleasant was one of those individuals whose lives are so filled with the unbelievable that no novelist would dare to create them. Born in slavery of a quadroon mother who was also an acknowledged voodoo priestess, she determined early not only to release herself from bondage, but also to obtain power over the race owning hers.

In childhood she was purchased and sent north, her race concealed, to be given a good education. On the death of her master, still without realization of her servitude by those now her guardians, she was taken to New England and "bound out" to one of those intrepid women who, as the wives of whalers, kept businesses of their own during the long absences of their seagoing husbands.

Both in the store and the household Mary Ellen proved herself indispensable and earned the goodwill and affection of her mistress's daughter, the wife of a sea captain. On the death of her mistress she went to the daughter's household, where she was received not as a servant, but as a good friend. It was there that she became active in the "underground railway" of the abolitionist movement.

Rising high in their councils, she met and married James Smith, a planter from what is now West Virginia.

Abhorring slavery, Smith had freed his own people and was very active in aiding others to escape. Upon Smith's death Mary Ellen devoted nearly all the estate he had left her to further this cause. It was during this period that she also married secretly John Pleasant, the octoroon overseer her husband had greatly trusted. But the marriage did not endure long and John Pleasant went to California in the days of the Gold Rush.

Mary Ellen remained in the East. Using various disguises, she ranged through the South, exhorting slaves to escape, providing them with the means. She was an inspired cook and, her racial mixture being unknown, she went from one wealthy employer to the next. In New Orleans, seeking a new way of concealing her purposes and overawing those with whom she dealt (so she might not fear betrayal), she turned to voodoo, learning some of the techniques of the great "queen," Marie Laveau.

Suspicion arose, however, and Mary Ellen was forced to leave New Orleans in haste, choosing a vessel bound around the Horn for California. During the voyage this ship took on more passengers in Chile, among them Thomas Bell. With her gift for recognizing the potential of those she could use, Mary Ellen made Bell her lover and by the time they reached San Francisco he was well under her influence.

As an expert cook, Mary Ellen found her ability brought her an offer of five hundred dollars a month to manage one of the famed boardinghouses which had been early established by the homeless but wealthy and lucky gold seekers. To Bell she passed along not only funds for speculation, but stock tips, becoming his silent partner, greatly to their mutual benefit.

For the blacks in California she was not only a "voodoo queen" of unlimited power, but a benefactress. She used a loophole in the local law to prevent some being unwillingly returned to the South and hired those who were free, setting them up in business. In a short time she had a laundry, a saloon, livery stables, all staffed by those who had good reason to be grateful to her.

When she heard of the activities of John Brown in the

East, Mary Ellen returned, carrying over ten thousand dollars to further his cause. Arriving too late to aid Brown, she remained. The actions of the next year or so are deeply veiled in mystery. There are stories that Mary Ellen, disguised as a man, journeyed through the South trying to spark a slave uprising. Whatever her efforts, they came to nothing, and she went back to California.

During the Civil War she contributed heavily to the Union cause. But in secret she began to lay the foundations for her own web of power which, in time, was to reach clear to the governor's office.

From houses of ill fame she carefully selected new arrivals who, she believed, had the appearance and manner of respectable girls. These, all of the white race, she had educated and trained in the manners of society. Some made "good" marriages engineered by her. Others became the mistresses of influential men. In addition she hired newly freed slaves, and, through an informal employment service, placed them in hotels, restaurants, private homes, as servants, to be her eyes and ears.

Her stock assets continued to grow. Bell became one of the highly respected men of business without the general knowledge that there was behind him one of the most remarkable women of her generation.

Outwardly Mary Ellen remained an upper servant, housekeeper for a time to a millionaire. She dressed in an old-fashioned style, made no show of either her power or wealth.

If she used blackmail and bribery to gain her ends, as was hinted, it was done so astutely there was no proof. To many her known kindnesses and charities ranked her close to a legendary saint. But rumor continued to whisper darker things of her.

At last she invested a huge part of her fortune in the building of the famous "mystery house" with its many secret passages, overwhelming luxury, and imported furnishings. This became the home of Thomas Bell and in it he was to die an unexplained and suspicious death. Though Mary Ellen had fitted up a suite therein for herself, she apparently never occupied it. Bell's wife, one of Mary Ellen's protégées, was the only mistress under its roof.

No one knows what became of Mary Ellen's great wealth. After she made the fatal mistake of trying to force her way, through blackmail, into San Francisco society, her power, even over those beholden to her, began to decline. Times were changing and San Francisco society wanted to forget the gaudy patches in its past.

She died in surroundings of poverty, an enigma still, the tangled intrigue behind her acts never explained or more than guessed at. But in the sixties, seventies, and eighties of the past century she ruled much of San Francisco from the shadows.

FAWCETT CREST
BESTSELLERS

THE JARGOON PARD

by Andre Norton   Q2911 $1.50

THE SHAPE-CHANGER

I lifted my head. My position seemed awkward. I could see only at an angle. But—I was on my hands and knees—no! I was—on four padded paws, wearing a body covered in light golden fur. I opened my mouth to cry out, but what issued from my jaws was a heavy half-grunt, half-growl sound. . . . . .

He was called Kethan and the secret of his birth had been hidden—until now.

He had been chosen to lead the great house of Car Do Prawn in the ancient land of Arvon. But his cousin Maughus was jealous and hated him, and Ursilla, his mother's evil Wise Woman, had already begun to tamper with his destiny.

Then one day Kethan was given a gift—a belt of incredible beauty and possessing great powers. From this moment on, Kethan's future was in other hands—and his body in a strange new shape. . . .

Fawcett World Library